The Rotten Core

A Jake Pettman Thriller by

Wes Markin

Contents

About the Author	v
By Wes Markin	vii
Praise for Wes Markin	ix
EARLY 1800s	1
Chapter 1	29
Chapter 2	40
Chapter 3	55
Chapter 4	67
Chapter 5	82
Chapter 6	94
Chapter 7	110
Chapter 8	125
Chapter 9	139
Chapter 10	155
Chapter 11	171
Chapter 12	181
Chapter 13	193
Chapter 14	201
Chapter 15	211
Chapter 16	219
Chapter 17	226
Chapter 18	233
Chapter 19	239
Chapter 20	252
AFTER ...	258
YOUR FREE DCI YORKE QUICK READ	267
CONTINUE JAKE PETTMAN'S JOURNEY WITH ROCK AND A HARD PLACE.	269

Also by Wes Markin	271
JOIN DCI EMMA GARDNER AS SHE RELOCATES TO KNARESBOROUGH, HARROGATE IN THE NORTH YORKSHIRE MURDERS ...	273
Acknowledgments	275
Stay in touch	277
Review	278

About the Author

Wes Markin is the bestselling author of the DCI Yorke crime novels set in Salisbury. His latest series, The Yorkshire Murders, stars the compassionate and relentless DCI Emma Gardner. He is also the author of the Jake Pettman thrillers set in New England. Wes lives in Harrogate with his wife and two children, close to the crime scenes in The Yorkshire Murders.

You can find out more at:
www.wesmarkinauthor.com
facebook.com/wesmarkinauthor

By Wes Markin

DCI Yorke Thrillers

One Last Prayer

The Repenting Serpent

The Silence of Severance

Rise of the Rays

Dance with the Reaper

Christmas with the Conduit

Better the Devil

A Lesson in Crime

Jake Pettman Thrillers

The Killing Pit

Fire in Bone

Blue Falls

The Rotten Core

Rock and a Hard Place

The Yorkshire Murders

The Viaduct Killings

The Lonely Lake Killings

The Cave Killings

* * *

Details of how to claim your **FREE** DCI Michael Yorke quick read, **A lesson in Crime**, can be found at the end of this book.

Praise for Wes Markin

"An explosive and visceral debut with the most terrifying of killers. Wes Markin is a new name to watch out for in crime fiction, and I can't wait to see more of DCI Yorke." – **Stephen Booth, Bestselling Crime Author**

"A pool of blood, an abduction, swirling blizzards, a haunting mystery, yes, Wes Markin's One Last Prayer has all the makings of an absorbing thriller. I recommend that you give it a go." – **Alan Gibbons, Bestselling Author**

"Cracking start to an exciting new series. Twist and turns, thrills and kills. I loved it." – **Ross Greenwood, Bestselling Author**

"Markin stuns with his latest offering... Mind-bendingly dark and deep, you know it's not for the faint hearted from page one. Intricate plotting, devious twists and excellent characterisation take this tale to a whole new level. Any

serious crime fan will love it!" – **Owen Mullen, Best-selling Author**

This story is a work of fiction. All names, characters, organizations, places, events and incidents are products of the author's imagination or are used fictiously. Any resemblance to any persons, alive or dead, events or locals is entirely coincidental.

Text copyright © 2022 Wes Markin

First published 2022

ISBN: 9798788418889

Imprint: Dark Heart Publishing

Edited by Brian Paone

Cover design by Cherie Foxley

All rights reserved.

No part of this book should be reproduced in any way without the express permission of the author.

For Wayne and Cherish

EARLY 1800s

THE MOON HAD been receding of late, and this night was darker than the last. Hamlin Smith welcomed this; it made foraging all the easier. He stood with his back to the mine where his grandfather had sweated away his years, health, and, eventually, life and gazed out over his broken world—Brady Crossing.

Brady *fucking* Crossing.

Hamlin coughed. In his saliva, he tasted the filth of the mine where he had just begun his tenure at the ripe old age of fourteen. He spat on the floor, glad of the darkness that would prevent him from seeing the shit already invading his body.

He heard howling and smiled. Wolves, wild dogs, and the like ran free. He *too* would one day run free—just as soon as he had enough money to do so. No, sir. Hamlin Abraham Smith was not working himself to death in an old mine. That was as certain as the sounds of freedom high in the hills behind him—sounds that were alien to him now but would one day be the actual sounds of his existence.

Foraging had been good to him these past months.

What had begun as simple pickpocketing on Main Street had progressed to cautious thievery in the general stores in all three of Mossbark County's towns. The prices he then charged for his pilfered goods to some of the older, more disenchanted miners ensured a lack of questions and, as a result, a certain amount of complicity.

As his confidence had grown, so had his brazenness, and he would slip from his home late at night and prowl the sleepier roads in the three towns. Many of the single younger miners would be out, drinking away the evening, and although men of this age had little, he could often find something in their dusty cupboards—anything from tinned goods to a smart shirt and, if the going was really good, a family heirloom. He'd once lifted a silver wedding ring! A miner had quickly snagged it, who'd been desperate to put a band on his loved one's finger for close to two years. Of course, Hamlin *never* stole from his regulars. Hamlin was a clever boy, even if this was by his own admission, and he wasn't about to shit on his own doorstep.

He started away from the mine and down the road. He forced his mind from the mountain of coins building beneath a floorboard under his bed, because that would put a spring in his step, and the name of the game right now was stealth.

He heard a grating cough ahead, not unlike the one which had emptied his own lungs minutes before, and he darted into the shadows of Lewin's storefront. The store was detached from the one beside it, so he could slip into the darkness between them while still allowing himself a view of the road.

Despite the lack of moonlight, Hamlin immediately recognized the man from his silhouette, and his breath caught in his throat.

The Rotten Core

Miles Libby skulked past, dragging his damaged right foot behind him.

Hamlin gulped, not over his recollection of the story in which Miles's foot had been crushed beneath a derailed mining cart before he'd refused amputation, despite the overwhelming chances of death. Yes, that did speak of a rather unhinged man, but that wasn't the reason he gulped now. He gulped because of the rumor attached to him.

Apparently, many moons ago, a young woman had taken an interest in the then younger, lonely man and showed up on his doorstep with a homecooked offering. When he didn't greet her, she had wandered in to see if he was okay. She had discovered him naked, with an open wound on his upper arm. After watching him drop a thin piece of his own flesh into a cage full of ravenous rats, she had fled the scene and—so the rumor goes—fled the county, fearing for her life.

The rumor had been further fueled when the men had shed their shirts on the more grueling days in the mine. Miles would *always* leave his shirt on.

"The scars are there, Smithy," Alvin, one of the oldest miners, would whisper to him. *"The scars from the flesh he peels off for his vermin."*

Hamlin shuddered.

In profile, Hamlin saw the hunch in Miles's back and his long head hanging forward slightly. That, and the scratching sound that came from his foot skimming the ground, really did paint a decrepit picture.

Was this really a man to be feared?

Really?

Hamlin smiled.

And that was when he had the idea to rob Miles Libby's home.

* * *

NOW

PASTOR FREDERICK DEERING gazed across his congregation of a hundred strong—although still not strong enough. He ran his hand through thick hair, which was still holding out despite his fifty-five years, slammed his finger onto his pulpit, leaned in toward the microphone, then raised an eyebrow as he spoke for those he loved and who loved him in return. "And now we finish this session, Brady Crossing of Mossbark County, as we always finish, at our *core* value."

Everyone clapped. Some of the rowdier clientele hollered.

"The core value is close to my heart." He paused, took a deep breath, and raised his voice. "In fact, it's in my heart! I pray it's in your hearts too!"

Another clap. Another holler.

He held his hands in the air and made a show of interlocking his fingers. "Community adhesion."

This time, as well as claps and hollers, feet stamped too.

"Together," the pastor said. "Let us hear it, together!"

The congregation chanted, "The Mossbark Bible Fellowship glues communities together through worship. To share our values, to grow our families, to break the needs of money, of power, of the flesh."

Frederick stood back, smiled, and bowed to his flock.

* * *

EARLY 1800s

The Rotten Core

MILES LIBBY HAD built a home which mirrored the way he led his life when in the company of others—in the shadows at the edges. This made his home an easy target for Hamlin.

When the fourteen-year-old boy had been confident that Miles was continuing his loping skulk in the opposite direction from his home, he left his place by the storefront and rejoined the road. After bypassing several of the more conventional wooden homes and newer stone homes he was more familiar with stealing from, he traversed a narrow pathway that reached a small wooden structure which Miles had built. And just like its creator, the dwelling was peculiar, for it had been built around the base of a tree.

It took Hamlin's breath away because he'd only ever gazed on the weird home once. Most people, himself included, tended to steer clear of this home and the narrow pathway that led to it.

He surveyed the twisted branches which both wound over and *into* the roof, forming part of its structure, wondering how such a place could even begin as an idea, never mind be brought into actual being.

A horse, which was tethered to a post beside the structure, neighed. Despite the adrenaline building within the boy, he gave the beast a nod and a wink. He was fond of animals, and he found horses to have an agreeable demeanor.

Knowing the place was unoccupied, Hamlin tried the door first and wasn't really surprised to find it open. A man in possession of such a grotesque history had no reason for security. After all, who in their right mind would go into this monster's property? Despite his adrenaline, Hamlin smiled. *Me.* A man desperate to leave Brady Crossing of Mossbark County must be capable of anything.

When he entered the property, he was overwhelmed with awe; the trunk and lower branches formed the bulk of the far wall, making the tree a living residence of the property—and disappointment; the room was almost completely barren. Besides a mound of straw in the corner, which Hamlin assumed was where Miles slept, and a few tins of food, some of which were open and swollen with flies, Hamlin could pillage very little, if anything, here.

Something next to the tree drew Hamlin's attention, and his blood ran cold—a rectangular structure, about the size of a coffin, with a blanket draped over the top of it. And from within, the sound of *shuffling*.

Rats?

Hamlin took a deep breath and glanced behind him at the open door. There was little point in him remaining here any longer. Nothing here could grow his burgeoning wealth. *Yet ...* He turned back to the coffin-shaped structure. *Yet ...*

He took slow, tentative steps toward it, guided now by curiosity rather than greed. He thought of the tall man dragging his foot and his excessive clothing in the fiercest of summer days. Was the rumor true? Had that young lady with her casserole really seen him feeding parts of himself to rats?

Despite the shuffling and the cover over the mysterious structure, a large part of Hamlin still struggled to believe it. He was a rational boy and had made it his mission to develop both shrewdness and cynicism to escape the hell of his life.

He reached the structure, removed the cover, and looked into the wide cage. At first, it looked to be one pulsating organism, but then his eyes separated the many writhing, twisting furry bodies from the whole.

The Rotten Core

There were too many to count.

Disturbed, the rats threw themselves at the side of the cage. Most toppled backward, their tiny feet clawing at thin air, their long spiny tails whipping from side to side. Some rats clutched the side of the cage with razor-edged claws, making Hamlin shudder. He stumbled backward and struck something which felt like a wall, except he knew it wasn't, because he had ventured too far into the dwelling for it to be that.

Then he was shoved in the back and fell forward. Inches from the cage, he stared into the black eyes of a rat which was pushing its snout desperately through a gap between the bars. It snapped its jagged teeth at the air. "No!" Hamlin rolled onto his back and looked up at the tall, bent figure of Miles Libby. "Sorry!" Hamlin said. "I'm *so* sorry for coming here."

Miles took a deep breath through his nose. He didn't say anything. This was unsurprising. Hamlin, or anyone else if you asked them, would not be able to recall a time he'd ever done so.

Behind him came the steady thump of the rats colliding with the cage wall, punctuated by snarls and hisses.

"I was out walking. I went down the path. I saw your house, I didn't think. It looked interesting ... the tree ... it looked so *different*."

Miles dropped his head to his shoulder, examining him. Sizing him up for his rats? *Please God, no ...*

"I smelled you," Miles said.

Hamlin's eyes widened, as he realized that for all this time, him and the other miners had been blessed by this monster's silence. Miles's voice was deep, grating, almost otherworldly, and had seemed to work its way through

Hamlin's entire body and soul before settling like hot lava in his stomach.

"I smelled you watching me from beside the shop." Miles knelt.

More rats crashed into the side of the prison bars behind him.

Hamlin shook his head and started to cry. He wet himself.

Miles eyed Hamlin's crotch, shaking his head, undoubtably noticing Hamlin's accident. "I smell what you did." He looked back up at Hamlin's face and leaned forward. "And now I smell *what* you are."

NOW

WITH SOME, PASTOR Frederick Deering laughed and joked, with others, he reassured and sympathized. Saying farewell to each member of his flock after the service always put him in his element. Being emotionally sensitive to his fellow man was, and would always be, one of his strongest attributes, as was his ability to make people feel warm and safe with his physical presence.

He often recalled fondly in conversation with parishioners—and was also known to open a service or two with it as well—that teachers had sometimes reprimanded him at school for invading the personal space of his fellow students. *"Well, I tell you!"* he'd always finish the story, *"if wanting to be close enough to feel the warmth of others and for them to feel yours is a sin, then I don't know what else I can say?"* The question was quite leading, as it would always call for a compliment from whoever was listening

The Rotten Core

about how this was part of what made him so personable and just about the best and most loving pastor they'd ever had the good grace to pray with.

Now, standing at the door to his modest church, overlooking a small flowerbed circled by young trees which had been planted to mark the passing of several members of the congregation, he shook his ninety-fifth hand. He *always* counted. One hundred and two parishioners in the Brady Crossing church of the Mossbark Bible Fellowship. More attended the other two churches in Lewis and Sharp Point, of course, but this had the biggest congregation by far. Not that it was enough. For Frederick, it was nowhere near.

So, he always counted—partly from hope that he may notice an increase, partly from fear that he may notice a reduction.

As he neared the end of his flock, he recognized he was one member short today, but he had expected this, so he could weather this disappointment.

A pale man stood before him, proffering a trembling hand.

"Come here, Parker." Rather than take Parker's hand, Frederick put his arms around the elderly man and drew him in tight. He whispered into his ear, "Evelyn?"

"She's resting, Pastor. As comfortable as can be."

Frederick stepped backward and held Parker at arm's length. He offered him a sympathetic smile. "I will be over this week, Parker, to spend some time with her. If I have your blessing?"

"Yes, Pastor, of course. Nothing would make her happier."

"Good," Frederick said, rubbing the elderly man's shoulder. He noticed Parker's eyes flit over to the fledgling trees. There was a sigh—an acknowledgment, perhaps, that it would soon be time for them to plant again.

As Parker slipped away, Frederick lowered himself to two seven-year-old children. He shook each of their hands in turn. No member of his parish left his church without a handshake, no matter their age or condition. "So, my two favorite twins, James and Anna, how are we this fine day?" He smiled, knowing he could get away with calling them his favorites, because he didn't know any other twins.

"We're going to a picnic," Anna said.

"And we have Dr Pepper!" James said.

Frederick smiled up at their youthful parents, Laurie and Charlie, who always attended church in business wear, due to their position on the Mossbark County Council.

"A small amount of Dr Pepper," Laurie said, reinforcing this by showing her thumb and forefinger pinched together.

"And lots of fruit," Charlie said, ruffling his son's hair.

After Frederick shook his hundred-and-first hand, he didn't, for the first time today, draw too close. The woman before him, Nora Ouellette, shared both his age and passion for religion and clearly adored him. The problem was, somewhere along the line, that adoration had morphed into infatuation. Combined with the fact that she was widowed, and therefore, *available,* made her more of a burden than a confidence booster.

"Thank you, Nora, for that lasagne you dropped off the other night. I don't believe I have ever tasted one so good."

"You're welcome, Pastor."

He noticed she was drawing closer to him now. It made him feel uncomfortable, and he wondered, not for the first time, if anyone felt like he currently did when he drew close. He certainly hoped not.

"I have a stew that Eric used to be partial to. Would you

like to come over this evening or, if you're too busy, as I know you always are, sometime this week?"

"It's been a taxing time at the moment, Nora." Frederick shook his head from side to side. "Such a taxing time. And it doesn't stand to get any better over the next weeks. I wish I could accept, but I know I may be making empty promises."

"I understand," Nora said with a smile.

He could tell immediately that the hint wasn't taken, in the same way it wasn't taken last time, and the time before that.

"It must be busy work," she said, "fostering community relations—"

"Gluing communities together," Frederick interrupted with a smile.

"Yes ... gluing communities together. It must really take it out of you. I will drop the stew on your doorstep later, like I did last week."

Frederick put both hands to his heart. "You spoil me, Nora. Thank you."

She blushed. "There was one other thing, Pastor—"

Frederick's loud ringtone cut her off. He grinned. "I'm sorry, the volume is all the way up." He pointed at his ears. "These are not what they once were."

"Tell me about it, Pastor."

He retrieved his cellphone and checked the screen. "Sorry, Nora, I really must take this." He shook her hand again. "I cannot wait for the stew."

"Of course, Pastor." She smiled, blushed again, and turned and exited.

Frederick stepped into his church with the phone pressed to his ear. "Yes?"

Heavy breathing. No reply.

"Yes?" Frederick repeated.
"It's time, Frederick."

***

EARLY 1800s

EMMA SMITH didn't want to believe what Amelia Sachs was saying. She turned from her visitor and ran into the house to check Hamlin's bedroom. When she confirmed her son's absence, she bit her bottom lip so hard that she tasted blood.

She returned to the front door and looked up at her husband Devin's graying face. "He isn't there."

"I'm so sorry," Amelia Sachs said from beside their front door. She gripped tightly to her horse reins as the beast paced back and forth, clearly on edge having been dragged out in the middle of the night. "I saw it all from my window. He never came back down the path."

"You certain?" Devin asked.

"Yes ... I'm sorry. As soon as Miles came back, I rushed here—"

"What the *fuck* is Hamlin doing at that crazy bastard's place?" Devin turned and headed into his house.

"I really don't know," Amelia said.

Wanting to be ready to help her son, Emma suppressed tears, but judging by the concern on Amelia's face, Emma must have looked a desperate state.

"I'm sure it will be okay, dear," Amelia said. "There must be a very good reason your son—"

"Are the rumors true?" Emma asked. "Is he dangerous?"

"Strange? Definitely. But there is no evidence he is dangerous."

"If he is," Devin said, coming up alongside his wife while loading the muzzle of his long rifle, "then he won't be dangerous for much longer." He approached his own horse tied to the fence.

"I'm coming too," Emma said.

"You're not dressed right." Devin nodded at her long white nightgown. He wasn't either really, but he was wearing long, cotton underwear, and so his dignity was under wraps.

"I only need a moment," Emma said.

Her husband turned his horse and slapped one of its flanks. The rifle bounced off Devin's back as he bolted off.

"Dammit!" Emma said and eyed Amelia, but her visitor looked away. "Please ..."

Amelia sighed and looked back. "Put on some clothes, and I'll take you."

* * *

Opposite Amelia's house, Devin stopped just before the turn off to Miles's place. He tied his restless horse to a hitching post and, readying his long rifle, turned quickly onto the path. He saw a shape ahead and heard the thumping of hooves.

The thumping grew louder.

Devin considered raising his weapon and gunning down the approaching horse rider but was struck by doubt. What if his son, Hamlin, had stolen the horse to flee the madman?

He pressed himself against the fence so he didn't fall beneath the approaching horse's hooves and watched the dark legs of a Buckskin draw close. He looked up and recognized the bent, lame sonofabitch who never spoke or looked at anyone but simply shared the little air they were permitted underground in the mine.

Miles looked intent on getting forward and had yet to notice Devin.

Devin saw a sack tied to the back of Miles's horse. It appeared to be moving, as if someone was struggling to be free. It could be the vibration through the horse's flanks, but Devin chose to hope instead that his son was alive in one of those bags. With that as a possibility, using his long rifle was not an option.

"Come back with my son!" Devin shouted at the top of his lungs but suspected Miles hadn't heard him over the thumping of hooves. He ran to the main road and tried again. He watched the deformed man, his horse, and, potentially, his first and only born disappear down the street.

* * *

NOW

PASTOR FREDERICK DEERING reached for the dwelling's handle, but the door swung inward before contact was made.

A large, hulking man stepped from the wooden structure into the pool of light, breaking through the thick canopy.

Frederick couldn't ever recall seeing Merithew without frowning, and it seemed today would offer no exception.

"You took your time," Merithew said.

"Is it done?" Frederick asked.

Merithew showed large, bloody palms. "Yes."

Frederick nodded. "You seem to have a talent for it."

"It is something we've always done. Not just me."

"Good to know. Are my colleagues inside?"

"Yes, they are. Are you not their leader? Would it not be better for you to arrive here first?"

"They're capable; there is no need to worry."

"Still, maybe you should increase your urgency."

"For what reason?"

Merithew sighed and spied the trees, the large empty fields, and the scattering of black huts. "Suffering, Frederick. In your line of work, surely it is something you'd like to keep to a minimum?" He walked away.

There goes one of the few men, Frederick thought, *who will never offer a hand to me, despite everything I have done here.*

He turned into the hut, and his two colleagues came to him from each side of the door, as if they'd been standing in ambush. He regarded the gaunt, pale man on his right flank, whose top lip was always at the mercy of a twitching nerve. Frederick nodded his greeting. "Pastor Alton Banks."

He faced the squat man on his other side, whose plump red cheeks and nose betrayed his love for wine and late nights. "Pastor Norman Flagg."

Frederick turned his attention toward a whimper.

Sophia Stevens was lying in the bed in the center of the room. Her knees were high and bent, while her legs were still parted. Bloody towels were strewn over the bed.

Frederick walked up alongside the bed and cast a sympathetic look down at Sophia. He stroked damp hair from her pale forehead.

"Is she okay?" Sophia asked. "Can I see her?"

"She's fine," Frederick replied, answering the first question but not the second.

"It was so quick … which is good, I guess … but I barely had time to see her … to touch her. I heard her cry and reached out. I wanted to feel her skin ... but then she was taken." The stream of words came in a varied mess of volume, pitch, and tempo, punctuated by gasps of breath.

He suspected the herbs Merithew had given her proved strong, and she was still keenly feeling their effects. He stroked her hair again. "You don't need to worry, Sophia."

"She looked beautiful ... but it was so quick! Is she beautiful?"

"Yes, she is. As I said, nothing to worry about."

A fearful look passed over her exhausted, pale face. Her rationale mind, no doubt, Frederick thought, hacking through the medicinal vines which had been, until now, protecting her from clarity. "Who are you?" She recoiled her head from Frederick's fingers.

He left his hand there, hovering. "I'm Pastor Frederick Deering."

"A pastor?"

"Yes. I lead the Mossbark Bible Fellowship. My colleagues behind me, Pastor Norman Flagg and Pastor Alton Banks, lead two of our churches."

The rigidity in her expression subsided, her lips parted, and she drew a deep breath. "You're here to help me?"

Frederick's hand was still close to her; the heat from her face warmed his fingertips. He nodded. "Yes." He turned his head to nod at each colleague before refocusing on her. "I told you that you don't need to worry about anything."

He heard both his pastors approach the bed and watched her eyes widen when Norman, as planned, seized hold of her ankles and pulled her legs straight. "Nothing at all."

She gasped when Alton leaned forward and pinned her arms to the bed.

Frederick pinched her nose closed, forced his palm over

her mouth, and leaned in, using his body weight to press her head into the pillow. He'd warned his colleagues that she would fight. It wouldn't matter how weak she was following childbirth; she would find strength for preservation. It was the nature of all beasts.

Secured by three men, she stood little chance, but the thrashing and arching was commendable, and Frederick felt sweat form on his forehead, and he heard Norman's grunts as he wrestled with her legs. It surprised Frederick how long this was taking. Seeing her daughter, even for the briefest of moments, must have inspired her toward the extraordinary.

Then came another surprise—Alton's tears.

Frederick glared at the crying man. He tried for eye contact, but the despairing pastor shook his head as the tears rolled down his cheeks. "*Alton!*" Frederick hissed.

It didn't work; his colleague continued to lose control, then he did the thing Frederick feared the most. He released his grip on Sophia's wrists and stepped backward.

Frederick refocused on Sophia, pressing as hard as he could onto her face. Her arms flailed, and he realized he was fortunate, because she was clawing at the jacket of his suit and may not have much time left to find the exposed flesh she longed to scrape at.

"I'm sorry ... I'm sorry ..." Alton muttered from the corner of the room.

You will be, Frederick thought. *Very sorry—*

Sophia's fingernails sank into his neck just below his right chin.

He gritted his teeth against the agony. Surely, she must be close now? Surely?

She dragged her fingers, filling the underneath of her fingernails with his flesh, and he dreaded to think what a state he would look after this.

He squeezed his eyes shut, forced back the pain in his neck, and pressed as hard as he could one last time.

Her hands dropped away.

He continued pressure for a few moments longer, ensuring everything was final, before he backed away from the bed, sweating and catching his breath. He eyed Alton in the corner, hunched over, hugging his knees, repeating, "I'm sorry ..."

* * *

Early 1800s

AMELIA GAVE HER horse to Emma so she and her husband, riding abreast of one another, could chase the peculiar man who may have taken their son.

Hooves clapped and thundered against the stone. Despite it being a strange thing to experience in so terrifying a moment, Emma felt relief that she'd had her husband's horse reshod the previous day; they'd neglected the mare for too long, and, of late, it had become unsteady on its feet.

Tonight though, her husband's horse, and Amelia's, moved like the wind. Even though it was a rather warm evening, the rush of air chilled Emma—especially her face, which was damp with tears.

At the end of Main Street, they reached a dirt track that split in two directions, they stopped.

"Fuck ... fuck," Devin said repeatedly.

She felt a tight, cold compression in her chest. They'd lost Miles Libby. Her hand abandoned the reins for her mouth to stifle a gasp. She faced her husband and forced her hand away from her mouth. "Devin, maybe Hamlin's at Miles's house still? Maybe he's hurt? Maybe he needs us?"

"*No*," Devin said, not looking at her. He was scouring the landscape with squinted eyes—a difficult task, no doubt, with such limited light. "He has our boy. He's put him in a goddamned sack."

This time, Emma was too late to stifle her gasp, but when it broke free, it emerged as little more than a whimper.

"*There!*" Devin pointed at the hillside at the far end of the field. "See?"

She looked. "It's too dark—"

"No, there's movement. He's riding up the hill. Stay here and get help." He kicked the flanks of his horse and bolted down the dark track toward the field.

Emma turned and looked down Main Street. For sure, Amelia would already be raising some kind of alarm, although she would have no idea that the monster was taking her son up the hill at the center of the towns. Devin had made a sensible call. She should head back now and tell everyone where Miles was going, except ...

She looked back in the direction where Devin had rode. He'd already disappeared into the darkness. Her boy was vulnerable, and, in such a situation, he would need his mother. She kicked the flanks of Amelia's horse and drove the beast toward the hill.

* * *

She didn't see her husband or her son's kidnapper on that journey up the hill. Desperately, she drove on, praying she would locate them. After reaching the crest of the hill, she started through the forest, which forced her to slow

Amelia's horse. The canopy was thick this time of year, and it was darker within the woodland than it had been out of it. She forced back tears, because she wanted to keep her hearing tuned to the land around her. Eventually, the suppression of her emotion paid off, and she heard her husband's shouts ahead.

She followed her husband's cries to a small break in the woodland. She could already see the moonlight, although limited, had found some entrance into the glade. She slipped from her horse, tethered it to a tree, inched forward, and peered out.

Miles Libby was on his knees. Devin leaned over him with the muzzle of the rifle inches from Miles's forehead while shouting, "Open the sack, you fucking animal!"

Miles didn't reply.

"Then I'll do what I have to and open it myself."

Emma noticed a horse only a yard or so behind Miles. A sack hung from the back of the buckskin. Even from this distance and in this light, she could tell it was covered in blood.

It was also writhing.

She cried out at the top of her lungs, *"Hamlin!"* She burst into the glade from behind the tree and tripped over a stray branch but kept her feet from stumbling. She caught her husband's wide eyes.

"Emma! I told you to stay!"

"Hamlin," she said again, lurching forward, and clutched the bloody sack.

"No!" Miles shouted, looking back. His voice sounded inhuman.

Emma reared away from the sack, gasping and clutching her chest—not because of Miles's warning but because of what she'd *felt* on that hot, sticky material.

Lumps. Large, wriggling lumps. "What's in there? Tell me!"

The sack pulsated; the lumps swelled and slid up and down the material.

"He's a thief." Miles's voice sounded distant, as if it was echoing from another, far darker world.

"Liar," Emma hissed. "You hellish liar! What have you done with my boy?"

"A thief," Miles said. "Everyone knows."

Miles turned his head to look up at Devin. "You know that, don't you, Daddy?"

Devin pulled the trigger. The rifle flashed, a loud crack throttled the quiet of the forest, and the top half of Miles's head lifted clean away.

Emma felt the monster's hot blood in her eyes, and she rubbed at them, but this made her vision worse, because her hands were already covered in blood from the sack. She chose, instead, to rub at her eyes with her sleeve and eventually managed to see. She saw Devin standing over Miles's corpse and reloading the muzzle of his long rifle.

"Hamlin!" She lurched for the sack again. She tugged hard, and it came free of the saddle and thumped to the ground.

The sack pulsated so hard that she wondered if it might actually start to flee from her. Whatever was in there was not human ... or, at least, whatever was in there *with* Hamlin wasn't.

She fell to her knees and started to unfasten the knotted rope that closed off the sack.

"No, Emma, *wait*!"

But she didn't wait, and her nimble, desperate hands worked quickly. When she opened it and the hairy creatures started to spill out, she scrambled away like a crab, but the rats were fast and came in her direction. She screamed, expecting the beasts, with their blood-matted fur, to start feeding on her, but the stream of rats parted when they reached her legs and scurried beside her and away, clearly satiated by whatever they'd been in the sack with.

"No, Hamlin ... *no!*"

One of the little monsters stopped at her feet and regarded her. Its hindquarters bunched up, its whole body tensed over, and it quivered.

She tried to kick out at it but missed.

It leaped at her and buried its sharp incisors into her knee.

She screamed at the gorging beast that was spasming with enjoyment. With her back arched, she grabbed the furry beast and tore it from her knee. She watched a piece of skin stretch between the rat and her leg; when it finally snapped, she threw the rodent as far as she could.

She heard Devin cry out behind her. She turned in time to see one of the vicious bastards crawling up his leg.

After dropping his rifle, he tried to bat the creature away, but it was strong. He wailed as the rat bit deep through his long johns and into his groin. Blood billowed over the white cotton. He hit the rat until it lost its grip and simply swung from Devin, clinging on tightly with its teeth. "Help me!"

On all fours, Emma scurried close enough to Devin to yank the rat off him. She heard her husband's flesh tear. Holding the writhing animal by the scruff of its neck, she rose, painfully, and charged until she reached a tree. She slammed the beast as hard as possible against the bark. It continued to fight. She slammed it again ... and again.

Eventually, she discarded the twitching, smashed rodent and faced Devin.

Devin was rocking from side to side on the floor, pale and gasping. "I'm bleeding a lot." He wasn't wrong. Blood drenched his groin and the top of his legs.

Fighting against the stiffness and agony in her damaged kneecap, she limped to the sack. A flicker of movement bulged the material but not to the same extent as before. She grabbed the bottom of the sack, yanked, and shook out the contents.

What was left of her son spilled onto the floor.

Two rats were still feeding on him, so she swooped. The first, which was burrowing into her boy's skull through his cheek, came away easily. She threw it as hard as she could. The second rat took a lot more effort, and when she finally pried it loose, it had a piece of her son's eyeball between its teeth. She launched this beast after the other. She fell to her knees, took hold of her dead son, and brought him close to her chest. Most of his face was gone, so she let his head slump downward to could kiss the damp, matted hair on his crown. "Hamlin, my boy ... I'm sorry."

She ran her hands over his still body as she embraced him. She felt torn clothes, hot, ripped flesh, and exposed bone. She laid him down and, unable to look at his remains again, turned away as she stood.

Icy, numb, and shivering, she shambled to her husband, who was sucking at the air with great difficulty. She grabbed his rifle.

"I need help." His voice was weak, and his face was almost white.

"Was it true what he said? Was our son a thief?"

"Emma ... please ... I'm dying —"

"Answer the question then, Devin."

He grunted, winced, and squeezed out a response. "I

only found out a couple of days back ... someone in the mine ... told me."

She narrowed her eyes. "And what did you do about it?"

"I *was* going to speak to him."

"But you didn't?"

"I didn't see him ... He worked different shifts."

"Last night, you were out drinking. He was home."

"Yes ... yes ... I know ... I'm sorry ... Help me *now*, Emma."

"You're his father. You should have made time for him."

"Please, Emma, I will die—"

"He relied on you for guidance. You should have showed him the way."

"I tried—"

She shot him in the chest. "No, you didn't. You never did."

* * *

NOW

PASTOR FREDERICK DEERING sat at the edge of the bed where Sophia Stevens had been put to rest. His head was in his hands, and he'd instructed the other pastors in the dwelling to remain silent while he thought. His problem was easy enough to identify; the solution to it anything but.

He looked up and glared at the problem. Pastor Alton Banks stumbled backward under the force of the stare, then steadied himself against a five-foot plastic display case—a macabre presentation which always turned Frederick's stomach and should really be removed.

He felt Norman's hand on his shoulder. "Are you okay, Frederick?"

He looked up at the red-cheeked, overweight pastor. "I'd like you to leave, Norman."

"Yes. Would you like me to wait outside?"

"No, I would like you to head to Lewis. I'd like you to spend the afternoon visiting members of your congregation." He turned his gaze from Alton to Norman. "It's one of the things we do *after*." He gestured to the body in the bed behind him with a flick of his head. "It's how we regain balance."

"But of course, Frederick. You know you don't have to explain that."

"Yes, I'm sorry, Norman, but ..." He spied Alton against the ghastly display case. "You must forgive me for my slight wobble in confidence."

"Yes," Norman said.

"Lewis calls now, Norman. But you, *Alton,* you shall stay with me a while."

Paling, Alton nodded.

After Norman had left, Frederick rose from the bed.

Alton shrank away as he approached.

Despite what his headteacher had told him at school, Frederick genuinely believed his invasion of personal space was always welcomed and greeted with the same warmth that he, himself, was careful to exude. Alton's alien response to his presence was something he had never experienced.

"Stop cowering, man." Frederick touched the scratch on his neck, then studied the blood on his fingertips.

"Sorry," Alton said, although he continued to stoop and tremble.

"I chose you, Alton, because of your strength."

"Forgive me, Frederick. I don't know why it has left me."

"Has it, Alton? Has it *left* you?"

Alton eyed Frederick for a moment, clearly summoning the courage to lie, but following his failure to do so, simply nodded.

"Look into the case behind you," Frederick said.

Alton turned.

"Don't those bones of a long dead boy remind you of why we do this?"

Again, Alton nodded.

Frederick also ran his gaze down the yellowing skeleton presented in the plastic case.

"Do you *forget* everything? Everything we wanted? Everything we built?"

"No ... I'm just not sleeping well ... I was—"

"Face me."

Alton turned.

"No more excuses, Alton. We are close, me and you, always have been and, regardless of today, always will be."

"Yes."

"So, I owe you the opportunity I'm about to present to you."

Alton was still trembling.

"I will ask you only once, Alton, and then we move on, one way or another. Do you want to leave the fellowship?"

Alton chewed his bottom lip; his eyes darted left and right.

He put a hand on Alton's shoulder. "Tell me, old friend. Tell me truthfully what you want, and I'm there for you. Have you changed your mind? Would you like to opt off the path we have begun to walk?"

Another chew of the lip, another dart of the eyes, followed by a trembling nod. "Yes ... I'm sorry, Frederick ... but yes."

Frederick embraced Alton. He pulled his head onto his

right shoulder and stroked his hair. "Thank you for being truthful with me, Alton. For that, you can leave with my blessing."

"Thank you, Frederick. Thank you so much."

As Frederick stroked his ex-pastor's hair, he looked at the skeleton, thinking, *Is it really true how you died? Well, know this, Hamlin, the way you were taken that day was hideous, but it will not be in vain. You set in motion events which have led to this day, this time—a time of great change.* He kissed Alton's head. *But a few more sacrifices need to be made first.*

* * *

Mid 1800s

Althea reached into the open five-foot display case and caressed the remaining finger bones on the young boy's left hand. She ran her fingertips up the cold arm before stroking the cheek bone. Althea recalled the final moments of Emma Smith and this boy, the boy Emma had *so* adored—Hamlin. A moment of great pain, but a *necessary* moment. A moment that had brought about change and an era of tranquility.

Althea stepped away from the bones of their birth and wiped away a single tear. She allowed herself only one. A single tear, once a year, at the exact moment, to the minute, that Hamlin Smith's body had been discovered in that glade.

And now that a tear had been shed, Althea closed the case on her son from another life and looked with both wonder and contentedness at the backs of her own knotty hands and reached for her walking stick. The years may not have been kind to her physically, but they had been generous to her emotionally and spiritually, and so a single tear and a moment's reflection over a time, rotten and dark, was all she would grant herself.

She turned her back to the case, and as she hobbled to the front door of the dwelling, she eyed the cage on the floor. She had satiated her pets before paying respects to Emma Smith and her son, so they were tranquil as they moved about each other, stroking each other with their long tails and paws.

Then she stepped from her dwelling.

Outside, Althea's people gathered. A dozen people stood proud and never looked to their leader from their knees, like many other leaders in the rotten and dark world demanded. In the distance, she heard the laughter of small children as they played.

Dorinda stepped forward and put her hand on Althea's arm. "We stood in silence for one minute as requested."

Althea stepped backward and cleared her throat. She was old now, so she knew she would struggle to raise her voice for her growing number of people, but she tried anyway. "Thank you all for that single minute. But the single minute has passed, and the single tear has been shed, but that is where we stop. If we continue too far down the path of sentiment, then we are in danger of becoming like the dark and rotten world we have left behind. One full of religion, control, and pain. In our land, there is only one thing to believe in." She pressed her fist to her heart, and her people did the same.

Together, they chanted, "Us. The heart. The Nucleus."

1

SO FAR, THE journey with Logan, the overweight, sweat-stained, misogynistic truck driver, had not reached Jake Pettman's expectations. This was a good thing, because Jake had expected the man to provide a constant stream of foul-mouthed rants, punctuated by nationalistic cries for purity in white America, and calls for more subservience in the female of the species who were getting way too big for their boots.

Jake was a big believer in avoiding stereotypes, but, in this instance, he believed he could be forgiven his expectations. The driver's behavior at the truck stop sixty miles back had been atrocious:

* * *

The loudmouth had leered at the poor waitress and remarked on her outfit. "No matter how gloomy the day, a woman who wears so little can always bring more sunshine into it!"

"It's not a gloomy day," she said. "At least it wasn't until you came in."

He wolfed down a plate of fried bacon, then asked the chef, who was on a coffee break and completing a crossword, if he was Chinese or Japanese.

"Malaysian," he replied without looking up from his crossword.

Whether or not the offensive prick had been intending to provoke the chef was unclear, but he was clearly unhappy to have someone shrug him off, even if he was the one doing the offending. "That's okay, then. Don't know a great deal about that tribe, but my grandaddy was killed by the Japanese."

"Jesus," Jake muttered and took another mouthful of coffee, which tasted exactly how he liked it, while many others didn't: burned.

A moment of silence passed, in which Jake continued to read his newspaper while hoping everyone in the truck stop's worst enemy had departed for pastures new, before the man strolled over and sat opposite him in the booth. "Did you have something to say on the matter?"

"What matter?" Jake decided to do what the chef had done and keep his face glued in the paper.

"The matter of my conversation with the man over there?"

"How can I have anything to say about a conversation I wasn't involved in?"

"Well, I heard you, so I can assume you heard me."

Jake looked up at him. He craved trouble with this irritating individual, but, at the same time, he knew it was a very poor life choice to make when hiding from people who wanted him dead. He noticed the man wore gloves, which was odd considering the heat. "I was reading the paper."

"About what?"

Jake glanced at the paper, then up at him. "A fall in energy prices?"

"That's good news. You didn't sound like you were reading good news."

"Look, sorry, what's your name?"

"Logan."

Jake raised an eyebrow. "Like Wolverine?"

Logan grinned.

"Well, you certainly have the size."

Logan snorted. "It's not muscle."

You don't need to tell me. "Look, Logan, I'm sure you don't want trouble. I clearly don't want any, so—"

"You British?"

Jake nodded. *Isn't that obvious, Logan?*

"Where are you headed, British man?"

"It's a good question," Jake said and filled his mouth with coffee. "One I don't really have an answer for."

Logan squinted. "You're a strange one. And you say you don't want trouble, but trouble has found you. That nose looks freshly broken!"

"And you're very good looking yourself too, Logan."

Logan laughed. "You're funny."

"I wasn't trying to be, but thank you for the compliment."

Logan laughed again. "Well, don't go falling in love with me."

"I can safely assure you, Logan, there is very little chance of that."

"How did you end up here?"

"I hitched a ride. This was as far north as the driver got before he turned back."

"So, you're waiting here to hitch a ride?"

"About the size of it, Logan."

Logan slammed his fist on the table. "That settles it. I am heading farther north. You need to get lost, and I need some company."

"I don't think that's a good idea."

"It'll be your way of apologizing for involving yourself in my conversation."

Jake looked down and sighed. *What the hell ... What right had a desperate man to turn down help of any kind?* "Okay, on one condition."

"Go on."

"You won't like the condition. So, you might as well call it a day now."

"Try me."

"Okay, here it is." Jake took another swig of coffee. "Apologize to the waitress for your comment on her outfit."

"Why? She didn't mind."

"She did. Very much."

"She was flirting—"

"She wasn't. So, apologize to her, then apologize to the chef for referring to Malaysians as his tribe."

He rolled his eyes. "Come on! What's wrong with that?"

"I'll tell you what, just do it, and then I'll explain on the journey."

"Fine. But you better not turn into the quiet type on me. I've already driven eight hours without hearing another man's voice."

* * *

Several hours into the journey, Jake realized he could happily get away with being the quiet type. This was because Logan spoke incessantly—more than enough to reveal a rather complex individual, whose aggressive, narrow-minded behaviors were clearly a mask for a lot of pain and insecurity. Jake welcomed the story of a childhood destroyed by parental alcohol abuse and the death of two siblings in a house fire, which had also left him rather badly burned. "Seventy percent of my body has second-degree burns."

"Shit, I'm sorry," Jake said, spying Logan's hands gripping the wheel.

"Don't be. I'm fucking lucky that my handsome face was part of the thirty percent."

Jake smiled.

His adulthood was also a tale of woe, and he'd had a brush with drug addiction, which left his young wife dead from an overdose. "I'm not making an excuse for being a prick. I'd be a prick even if I'd had a happy life."

"We all have our moments."

"What's your story?"

"Nothing to tell, really." He stared ahead at the road. He hated being in a car, but he was rather surprised how much better he felt high up in this rig. He recalled some recent hair-raising experiences on the roads of Blue Falls and shuddered.

"That's bullshit. Looking at your face, I warrant you got more scars on your body than I have."

Jake continued to stare ahead. "The reason I'm in the middle of nowhere is because my past is dead. It must stay that way. I'm not about to breathe life into it now. Don't be offended, Logan, even if you were the world's best shrink, I wouldn't give this story the time of day."

"At least tell me your name."

Apart from in the motel logbooks, this would be the first

time he'd been backed into a position of making up a name. He said the first name that came into his head—his son's. "Frank." Then he stumbled on the surname of his closest friend. "Yorke."

"Well, Frank Yorke, thank you for the company."

"You're welcome. Now tell me where we're going."

Logan howled like a wolf and glanced at Jake. "I thought you'd never ask!"

"I'm already wishing I hadn't."

"Oh, you'll be thankful, alright." Logan winked at him.

And to think I was starting to warm up to you, Logan. "Eyes on the road, please."

"Ah yes, you're British, forgot you do things by the book there."

Jake smiled. "Well, if the book is about self-preservation, yes, we tend to."

"Come again?"

"Never mind. Anyway, weren't you about to promise me nirvana?"

"Nirvana? That's a band, isn't it?"

"Again, never mind."

"And that was the name of their album? I've got it if you want a listen—"

"For fuck's sake, Logan, where are we going?"

"Ah, yeah, that. Well, picture this." He removed a hand from the wheel, much to the dissatisfaction of Jake, and weaved it through the air to try to give weight to what he was about to say. "A place where the women are easy."

Jake shook his head and groaned.

"And a place where even I can get laid. My route has taken me via Brady Crossing three times in the last two years, and each time, I have struck gold."

"Gold?"

"Yes, someone of the fairer sex. In fact, I can guarantee that even you, Frank, with your misshapen nose, will stand a chance." He howled again.

"Thank you for the compliment, but I'm not interested. I just want to keep heading this way as far as possible and get as lost as I can for the time being, just until I can get my head together."

"You're not ..." He took his eyes of the road again to look at Jake. "Are you?"

"Not what? Gay?"

"Uh-huh."

"Don't worry, Logan." Jake rolled his eyes. "I haven't sullied your rig with my presence. Now, eyes back on the road."

"Why the lack of interest, then?"

"Because I'm not a caveman, and I'm not here to run wild and populate the land."

"Huh?"

"Never mind. Listen, you do what you got to do. I'm grateful for the lift. I've got some money; the fuel is on me. Once we're there, drop me off at a motel in this Brady Crossing, and I'll figure out my path from there."

"Well, if you're sure? I'll be staying over two nights, and I could always do with a wingman."

"I'm sure. Remember, I'm just getting lost for a time."

"Well, Brady Crossing of Mossbark is certainly the place to get lost. Middle of nowhere it is. And an extremely small gene pool, if you know what I mean?"

"Hence the reason they like the outside influences, eh?"

"Damned right."

Jake stared out the window and watched the empty lands fly past.

Logan, reaching the peak of excitement over having

some ears to butcher, increased the tempo of his incessant rambling. Unsurprisingly, once Logan reached the gory details of his last sexual encounter in Brady Crossing, Jake's stomach turned. However, despite this discomfort, he did manage to catch some sleep.

In his dream, he lay side by side with Piper Goodwin in her home in Blue Falls. He turned onto his side and, starting at her collar bone, ran his fingertips down her naked body, over her breast, before laying the palm of his hand on her navel. He leaned over and kissed her and, for a brief moment, felt happier than he'd felt in so many years.

"I'm falling in love with you," Piper said.

"I already fell in love with you," Jake said.

MERITHEW LOOKED DOWN at the newborn baby settling in his arms.

Maybe it is true what they say, he thought with a smile. *Despite my ridiculous size, maybe I do have a calming, reassuring presence?*

He'd heard some of his people refer to his deep voice as being able to vibrate the air around them in remarkable ways; he'd heard others speak of his eyes moistening and softening as he listened to them, welcoming them into his confidence rather than judging and condemning them, as so many of Merithew's predecessors had done.

It seemed most did appreciate him as a leader. *Most*, if not *all*.

To date, since Althea had founded the community, every leader had been a direct descendant, Merithew included. Qualification didn't only come from being in the bloodline; if necessary, the elders could vote for a change in

The Rotten Core

leadership. This quirk allowed those who became disgruntled a forum in which they could express their discontent. Presently, some of his people were taking that opportunity. However, that was a concern for another day. The concern now was this newborn girl swaddled in a blood-stained towel.

Mindful of his great strength and not wishing to scare the child, Merithew knocked gently on the door of Sumner's hut.

Sumner was smaller than Merithew, but this did not make him a small man. He filled most of the frame.

Merithew regarded him. "You look troubled, Sumner."

Sumner bowed his head. "I'm happy, Merithew. I assure you."

Merithew nodded. "Good ... it's the way. You know this." He looked over Sumner's shoulder into the shadowy hut. "So dark in here."

"We thought it better for the baby. The sun can get bright late afternoon."

"Yes. The baby. Have you not got a name yet?"

"We have some ideas. But we wanted to meet her first, see which fit most appropriately."

"Good idea." He knew Sumner was lying.

In the shadows, Merithew saw Corrie, Sumner's wife. She was a beautiful woman, but right now, he couldn't see her for the dark. She was standing far back, beside a window closed off with blinds. She was beside her fourteen-year-old boy, Marston, whose head was lowered. He was a quiet boy who didn't favor the company of others.

"Corrie, how are you?"

"Good, thank you." Corrie slipped her arm around her son.

"And you, Marston?"

"Fine, thank you," Marston said, without lifting his head.

Merithew handed the newborn to Sumner. "A gift."

As soon as the baby left Merithew's hands, she started to cry.

"Thank you." Again, a lie. He wasn't grateful. Not really.

The baby started to wail, and Sumner stroked the child's face to settle her.

Merithew took two steps backward. "It is the way."

"I know," Sumner said. "Goodbye, Merithew." He took a step backward and closed his cabin door.

Merithew walked away, allowing his mind to turn from the newborn to the discontent that was blossoming in the Nucleus.

First stop after checking into the Brady Crossing motel was the bathroom, where Jake could take a cold shower. He'd read somewhere that cold showers helped with injuries, and following his stint in Blue Falls, he had a fair number of them.

He wasn't sold on the cold shower. To be honest, he wasn't sold on any process that made him gasp out loud, but he had to admit he was feeling marginally better these last couple days—or, at the very least, less like a worn-out punching bag.

He'd been careful to check in under his pseudonym, Frank Yorke, and had waved off calls for his passport with a handful of green. He'd already made the mistake of using his real name in the last town he was in—a mistake that had brought those he'd run from to his door, or, at least, some assassins hired by those he'd run from.

That encounter had cost those assassins big. Unfortunately, Jake had also been billed for the experience with the deaths of two innocent people who lived in Blue Falls, who were also two of the best people Jake had ever met.

He rubbed his eyes, determined not to cry. He had spent so many of the days since his retreat from Blue Falls out at sea in a storm of melancholy, drowning in both guilt and self-loathing. It was time to get a grip. There were people out there he owed it to.

He headed out of the bathroom, checked that the curtains were closed, and unzipped one of his duffel bags on the bed. As always, the first thing he checked was the money he'd stolen from the organized crime outfit, Article SE, in England. Without this money, he was well and truly fucked. As long as he kept finding places to exchange it, he could survive without work. Work brought unnecessary attention. He stowed the money behind the wardrobe.

He pulled out the other thing that kept him going—not physically, like the money, but emotionally—his photographs. He looked down at the two people he cared most about in this world—two people he thought about every waking moment, and every moment when in the dreamworld for that matter.

The first was a young boy wearing a Southampton FC shirt—the team he had worshipped with his own father and should have continued to worship with this young child, his son Frank. The second was the most beautiful woman he knew, with long dark hair, green eyes, and a killer smile, standing alongside him. *With him. Loving him.*

The very people he wanted to stay strong for reduced him to tears again.

2

JAKE'S EXPERIENCE WITH small towns to date had led him to believe the recession had spared no one. He'd clearly been mistaken. Not only had the recession taken a sharp left before entering Brady Crossing, but it appeared as if a wealthy benefactor had come in through another entrance.

As Jake walked Main Street in Brady Crossing, he couldn't help but recall the boarded storefronts, blown streetlamps, and cracks in the sidewalk that had littered Blue Falls, because it stood in stark contrast to what he was seeing now.

The fresh and colorful storefronts looked as if they'd been painted yesterday. The first three stores—the grocer's, the butcher's, and a shop selling vinyl records—gleamed and wouldn't have looked out of place on Queens Boulevard, unless one paused to look through a window. Then they would see the vinyl store was completely empty, while the butcher's had an extremely small line of customers. The place, despite being heavily funded, lacked custom.

Jake recalled the Welcome to Mossbark County sign

coupled with a population count of just over two thousand. What he saw now really didn't make a great deal of sense. This place couldn't be funded by trade; it *must* be coming from elsewhere—some local millionaire, perhaps, who had great sentiment for the town he came from and was content to let it feed from his pit of cash?

He remembered nearly jumping out of his skin the first time he'd heard a pickup hit a pothole in Blue Falls; now, he watched with awe as a hybrid car slid silently past on the smooth road. He shook his head in disbelief when he counted three bars in total: Brady Inn, The Half-Moon, and the Old Forest. Had tourism brought this investment? But wasn't it tourist season right now? And, so far, all he'd seen was a couple of small lines, a hybrid car, and very few pedestrians. Hardly a holiday spot, was it?

He looked between the three bars. Logan had said he would stay above one of them. *"Less distance to travel when, you know, I hit gold."* Jake wondered which one Logan had opted for so he could steer clear. Realizing he had no idea, he decided his visit to Brady Crossing would have to be a dry one. Which meant, of course, this visit wouldn't be long.

When he turned the corner, a young girl accidentally barged into him.

She turned around, walking backward, with her hand held in the air to apologize. Jake assumed her to be late teens, but the copious amount of black eyeliner and black lipstick could be hiding a younger age. She held up a black leather jacket. "New jacket, sorry, was trying to get the price tag off it."

"It's okay," Jake said. "It's refreshing to see an accident caused by a leather jacket than a cellphone, but still, be careful crossing the road." He pointed ahead at the hybrid that had parked outside the butcher's. "You can't even hear them coming around here."

She flashed him a confused look before turning and walking away.

Jake smiled. *"The youth of today,"* he heard his father say in another life.

He passed several more stores before reaching Hardy's Convenience Store. It proudly claimed to have been established in 1854, but, considering its neighboring buildings, the year came across as more of an excuse for its peeling paint and crumbling exterior. Oddly, Jake found this more appealing. Policing the less affluent parts of Wiltshire had certainly made him au fait with the rougher, more downtrodden establishments, and maybe, he now felt some nostalgia?

"Yes?" an elderly man said from behind the counter.

"I was hoping to buy something," Jake said.

"What exactly?"

"With such affectionate customer service, anything I can get my hands on, really."

The man furrowed an already wrinkled brow.

Jake paused for a response that didn't come, and rather than suffer the painful silence, he conceded to the hostile questioning. "A can of Coke, perhaps?"

The old man nodded at the fridges along the back.

Jake passed the Diet Coke and went straight for a can of the full-blooded stuff. These days, following Blue Falls, his limbs ached, and he was always on the lookout for an energy boost. When he reached the counter and saw the way the old man was regarding him—like some pest that had thrived in the dirty corners of his shop and would require an exterminator—Jake couldn't help himself. "Judging by the competition around here, I would probably give some time to your sales pitch for when someone chances by that front door. A front door, by the way, which makes you a candidate for a robbery when everyone else down the street has their shiny new shutters on show."

The old man raised an eyebrow, took hold of the can, and scanned it. He pointed at the price on the register.

Jake handed over a bill. "Keep the change. Call it a tip for suffering my bad humor."

As Jake turned away, the man said, "Do come again."

Again, Jake couldn't help himself. He turned back. "Yes, I'm from out of town. Yes, I have an unfamiliar accent, but come on, is this not overkill? I get the sense that you don't know whether to refuse service, warn me out of town, or worst-case scenario, pull out a shotgun."

"You'd do well to listen to that sense, young man. And if you do so, I'd be doing you a service, after all."

Jake left the store, drank half of his can, and belched. He hadn't realized how thirsty he was. He sighed as he traversed Main Street. Well, if the old man really was warning him out of town as a service, maybe he should just go? After all, there was plenty of small towns, and if there was even a sniff of trouble here, he'd be best to avoid it. He eyed the bars and sighed again. Looks like he would have to visit one of them tonight and hunt down a ride somewhere tomorrow—somewhere farther north, or farther inland perhaps? Who knows, he may even end up with Logan again.

He turned the corner where the teenage girl had almost knocked him over.

She was now sitting on a bench several yards ahead, wearing her new leather jacket.

Jake took a seat beside her. "A bit hot for that. You got the tag off, then?"

The girl nodded. "Even with these." She showed Jake long, fake black fingernails.

"I couldn't imagine being able to do anything with them. Anything that doesn't cause bodily harm anyway."

"Are you forgetting that me and you don't piss the same way? I've nothing to fear."

Although he found this amusing, her bluntness had stunned Jake so much that he didn't manage a laugh. "I was just about to say, don't worry, I'm not a creepy stranger, and I'm only sitting here to finish the rest of my Coke, but something tells me you're not someone who gets concerned easily! Anyway, just be careful you don't draw blood when you scratch an itch."

"Watch this." She ran her fingers and those dangerous-looking nails through her hair and, pushing it back over her ears, revealed a shaved undercut. She lowered a hand. "And not a scratch on me."

"I'm impressed."

She laughed. "Why do we feel it's necessary to yak about bullshit in order to be comfortable?"

"Sorry ... I didn't mean—"

"No, you say, 'I don't know. That's a good question.' And I say, 'And that's when you know you've found someone special. When you can shut the fuck up for a minute and comfortably enjoy the silence.'"

Jake smiled. "*Pulp Fiction.*"

"Mia Wallace and Vincent Vega."

"One of my favorites."

"A favorite of anyone who knows anything about anything."

"Agreed."

"I'm Celestia." The young lady proffered her hand.

Jake made a performance of fearfully edging his hand

toward her. "Careful with those deadly weapons." He then shook her hand. "I'm Frank. Celestia's an interesting name."

"My father must have thought so. Your name is interesting too."

"Frank? I think it's fairly commonplace."

"Not round here, but then, nothing is commonplace about here."

Jake raised an eyebrow. "Care to elaborate?"

"You mean you haven't noticed?"

"Only that the shop owners seem to have a lot of money despite a population smaller than the cast of *Reservoir Dogs*. Oh, and the shop owner who seems to have noticed there was a recession practically told me to leave town!"

"You should probably listen to him."

"Strangely enough, that was exactly what I was thinking just a moment ago."

"Loved the *Reservoir Dogs* namedrop by the way."

"I thought you'd appreciate it." Jake smiled.

"So, you're British, in the middle of nowhere. I don't actually know where to start with that."

"Don't start, then. One of the reasons I'm here is so I don't have to talk about it. I'm on holiday."

"A vacation? Well, you should be enjoying yourself! In which case, I definitely would give this place a miss!"

Jake nodded. "So, Celestia, apart from buying a new jacket, what're you up today?"

"The same as every day. Sitting here and watching the world go by."

Jake looked around and clucked his tongue. "There's not that much going by."

"Hence, my boredom and the resulting obsession with my appearance. Nothing else to do round here."

"Your appearance is nothing out of the ordinary for a teenage girl where I come from."

"Are they all bored there too?"

"No … I mean, yes, probably, but that's not the point. Your look usually does the rounds with rather emotional youngsters who have a tendency toward a certain kind of music."

"Sounds like you come from a place rife with stereotypes. Believe me, this appearance *is* very out of the ordinary for Brady Crossing."

Jake focused on a middle-aged couple walking past, sharing the responsibility of one of the smallest dogs he'd ever seen. The man looked over, and Jake expected a greeting. There wasn't one. Instead, the look was rather solemn, as if perhaps he was seeing the ghosts of someone he had once loved on that bench rather than a colorful young lady in conversation with a much older stranger.

"Hi," Celestia said, waving her black fingernails.

The man looked away. It was either sadness or disgust; Jake couldn't discern which, so he concluded it to be a combination of both.

"Well, he certainly considered us out of the ordinary."

"Yes. That was a look of fear."

"Remember though, people are always curious of strangers—"

"Not you. Me. Everyone gives me the same look."

Jake thought before asking, "Is there any particular reason that is happening, other than the gothic-stroke-emo look, which I really don't see as an issue?"

"Yes, there's a reason. A very good one."

Jake waited.

"Favorite film?"

It was a sharp change of subject. He clucked his tongue. "*2001: A Space Odyssey*."

"HAL 9000." She put on a soft, calm voice. "'This mission is too important for me to allow you to jeopardize it.'"

"Wow, you sounded just like that batshit computer! What's your mission, then?"

"To get drunk."

"How old are you?"

"Nineteen."

"Too young to get drunk. At least in this country."

"You forget we are in the middle of nowhere. Plus, I started hunting when I was nine."

"Bloody hell! What did you hunt?"

"Deer, elk—the usual. Hated it."

"Why?"

"I like animals. Besides, my point is, if you are old enough to kill something else, you are old enough to kill yourself with alcohol if you so wish."

"It's not a philosophy I'm familiar with."

"Are you going to help me then or what?"

"No! Besides, I don't even think you're nineteen."

She smiled. "You're right. I'm seventeen."

"Why lie?"

"Because I thought you'd be more likely to help me get drunk if you knew I was more mature. You might have thought you'd have a chance."

Jake guffawed. "Celestia, I'm old enough to be your father."

"Well, no need to be so horrified! Anyway, don't let it go to your head. Even if you were some creepy old predator, you're not my type anyway!"

"Good! What's your type anyway?"

"Not men."

"Okay ... you have a significant other in your life?"

"Nothing worth mentioning. As I said, most people steer clear of me. Told you that already. They're scared."

"That's ridiculous! There's nothing scary about you."

"Second favorite film?"

"You're relentless," Jake said, smiling. "Clue: 'You're gonna need a bigger boat.'"

"There's no challenge in that!"

"Well, it's my second favorite film, so like it or lump it. Now, why're you scary?"

"Tell me why you're here."

"I guess this will be a stalemate."

"Seems that way. Worst ever film?"

The conversation continued at a relentless pace, mainly about films, and Jake found himself smiling. This was significant, because he'd yet to really smile since leaving Blue Falls, and that was over a week ago. It was amazing what frivolous conversation could do, especially with individuals with similar interests.

During the afternoon, several more locals strolled by, all wearing the same troubled look that had possessed the shopkeeper and the man with the small dog earlier, but each time he questioned Celestia as to the reason behind this, he was promptly batted away with more film-related trivia.

After a much-needed afternoon had passed, Jake felt disappointed when she stood to leave. "I was just about to ask your top ten favorite foreign movies."

"Have to be tomorrow. I've got to get home."

"Which is where?"

"Not in Brady Crossing."

"I'd offer you a ride, but I hitched into town."

"No worries. It wouldn't be a good idea."

"You're very secretive."

"And a middle-aged British man hitchhiking into Mossbark isn't?"

"Less of the middle-aged, I'm still in my thirties."

"You don't smoke, do you?"

"You've been sitting with me with a fair chunk of the day; surely, it would be obvious I don't."

"Just checking."

"You know it kills you?"

She leaned in, pinching her eyes, regarding him. "I didn't think you'd be so concerned about that."

"And why wouldn't I be?"

"You know why."

"Elaborate."

"The sadness, Frank. Around your eyes. There's a lot of it."

Jake raised his eyebrows. "I could say the same about you, Celestia."

Celestia smiled. "And you'd be right."

"What does a seventeen-year-old girl have to be sad about anyway?"

"What does a thirtysomething man thousands of miles from home have to be sad about?"

"It's that stalemate again, isn't it?"

Celestia backed away. "Nice to meet you, Frank. Same time tomorrow?"

"I was thinking of leaving tomorrow morning."

Celestia nodded. "Well, I'll be here in case you change your mind."

Jake nodded and smiled. "I'll think about it." But he was lying. He'd already changed his mind.

* * *

Sheriff Gordon Kane picked up his *I love New York* mug—a souvenir from a bygone era. He steadied his trembling hand by taking hold of his wrist. Spilled coffee blurred the words on the newspaper spread on his desk.

Continuing to support his wrist, Gordon took a mouthful of coffee. He placed the mug next to a framed picture of his wife in her twenties. She had been beautiful at that age. However, this wasn't the reason behind this selection. He still considered her as beautiful now as the day he'd met her. He'd chosen this one because this had been a far happier time in their marriage and evoked some good feelings; incidentally, it was the time they had taken the trip to New York and purchased his cherished yellowing mug.

He did a quick calculation in his head. Thirty years ago! Christ!

Only this morning, Susan had admitted to another brief affair. He'd responded with a sigh and a weak nod before leaving for work. His days of exploding were over. He had learned early on what little purpose that served. Tonight, when he arrived home, she would have prepared him a feast worthy of a king, just like she had done the previous times she had cuckolded him. It was this show of guilt, and the fact she did still love him—although not physically—that always fooled him into believing it would change. I mean, she was into her fifties now, and the desire to play away would wane at some point. Surely?

He stroked the picture frame with his twitching finger. He could never leave her. They'd spent most of their lives together now, and it would be impossible for him to embark on a whole new life. He wouldn't know how to. Anyway, in a roundabout way, this was all his fault, really. He should have given her children, given her something else to do while he invested nearly all his waking hours in the Mossbark County Police Department. But he hadn't been able to —firing blanks. Not the scientific terminology but just as accurate. She had wanted to adopt, but he'd dismissed the idea with a single sweeping statement many years back. *"I'm a policeman. The things I've seen. You can never know for sure what the child has been through ... I couldn't do that to you, Susan. I couldn't take the risk."*

The statement had certainly been sweeping enough to dismiss any protests and any resurrection of the request. He wondered now, as he'd wondered a great deal recently, if it'd been too sweeping. Was it this that had destroyed what had once been a sacred union?

He sighed and turned his trembling hand in the air before him. Nothing to worry about, according to the neurologist. Countless tests had shown him to be as fit as a fiddle.

Nothing to worry about! He snorted. Weren't frayed nerves something to worry about? Wasn't anxiety as debilitating as a degenerative disease?

A knock sounded on his office door. Scott, one of two identical twins serving as officers in the MCPD, poked his head around the door. The only reason Gordon knew it was Scott was because of the shaved head. Brad had grown his long and wore a ponytail.

"Sheriff. Hands have been shaken. The Crichton brothers are friends again."

"Was never in doubt, Scott, even after they practically killed each other."

"Wild animals. Well, after these last couple days, I'm not sure I'd ever chance a wife swap with Brad!" Scott said with a laugh.

"A bit hard to when neither of you are married."

"Well, if we ever are, I'd like to think we'd choose a different path than the Crichton brothers."

Drunk one night, the Crichton brothers, who were also identical twins but had opted for no distinguishing feature in outward appearance, had decided to experiment with each other's wives. The problem being that the wives hadn't been aware of this experiment. This may have ended better if one of the brothers hadn't opted out of a condom. Now one of the wives was pregnant, and family relations were at an all-time low.

Gordon clasped his hands together as he spoke to mask today's bad case of the shakes. "I don't even know why you're comparing yourselves, Scott. The Crichton twins are a totally different breed. What they got up to wouldn't find its way into the more civilized echelons of our small world."

"Yes, sir. Anyway, I think the bruises they've given one another will hopefully deter them from such experimentations in the future."

"Don't count on it, son, leopards and all that. But I guess the psychological scars that comes with having to DNA test your own baby might teach you something."

"Choose peace, sir."

"Choose peace, son."

Scott closed the door.

Choose peace. It was Gordon's mantra, and he had stood by it for most of his law enforcement career. For many of his earlier years, he'd watch his gung-ho seniors and colleagues chase crime with conflict. Time and time again, he'd watched them add fuel to the fire, bringing over short-term and volatile resolution. Sustained peace and calm formed the only route to tranquility.

It *also* won elections. Which was, of course, Gordon's primary concern.

Choose peace.

His cellphone rang. After hoisting the phone from his pocket, he was forced to hold his wrist again to keep his hand steady enough for him to read the blurring screen.

Pastor Frederick Deering.

His stomach turned. The cellphone slipped from his hand. Vibrating, it rattled a path across his coffee-stained newspaper.

Since his arrival, Frederick had changed Mossbark, had taken its god-fearing folk and made them more god-fearing. And god-fearing, in Gordon's opinion, did not make for peace. It made for the complete opposite.

However, throughout his career, Gordon had learned how essential it was to work with those in power, no matter how troublesome, to establish peace. And Frederick was a powerful man, far more powerful than him, and if he was going to win his election and maintain peace and calm in Mossbark, they needed a symbiotic relationship.

So, get a fucking grip, Gordon ...

He picked up the cellphone and answered it. "Pastor?"

"Sheriff."

"It's good to hear from you, Pastor, but you catch me with a foot out the door. How pressing is it? I could contact—"

"It's pressing, Sheriff."

"Ah, I see." Gordon clamped the cellphone hard against his ear.

"You remember our conversation, I assume?"

"Yes."

"You talked to me about peace, and I talked to you about cohesion."

"I remember."

"And we agreed we were following the same path."

An agreement you forced from me when you hinted at the next election. "Uh-huh."

"And now comes the time to truly test our partnership, Sheriff."

"I'm listening," Gordon said, clenching his fist.

"Something is about to happen in Brady Crossing, something for the good of Mossbark. It will draw you and yours out from the office, Sheriff, and here's how I want you to play it."

After Gordon had listened to the instructions and ended the call, he slammed his fist onto the table.

There was a smash.

He looked at the remains of his *I love New York* mug on the floor.

3

FOLLOWING CELESTIA'S DEPARTURE, Jake became restless.

Rather than follow his instincts and wander aimlessly around, before inevitably dropping into one of the inviting bars along Main Street, he kept himself rooted to the park bench and thought. Right now, he needed an alternative to self-pity, of which both mindless wandering and heavy drinking were symptoms.

But his options *felt* limited.

More than anything, he wanted to speak to his son Frank. But caution held him back. He was a dangerous man, and his son was clearly safer without him in his life. Also, what promises could he make? He couldn't ever return home to him, could he? Surely, it was better for his boy to move on with his life rather than live with the empty promise that one day he may have a father again.

Then there was Piper, a woman who had shocked his still heart back into life. How he longed for her now, knowing again it was impossible. He had spent too long with her in Blue Falls and those psychopaths back home had discovered Jake's location. It'd almost cost Piper her life. They'd still be there, watching, and if he ever returned, he'd be putting her in danger all over again.

His thoughts took him in a constant circle, because no solutions existed—at least no alternative solutions.

The fact is, he had to stay lost.

The sadness, Frank. Around your eyes. There's a lot of it.

Or could he be ready for the alternative? The darkness? The never-ending silence?

Jake was staring at the ground when he felt someone approaching. He didn't bother looking up until a pair of threadbare sneakers stopped in his field of vision. He lifted his head to the elderly man who'd served him earlier in Hardy's Convenience Store. "Here to apologize for the customer service?"

There was no reply.

Jake was in no mood for this man. "You're blocking the sun."

"I see you're not listening to that good sense of yours. You need to leave."

"Give me chance. I'm just having a little sit down."

"You've been here all afternoon. Sitting with one person you really shouldn't be sitting with."

"Explain to me how a girl of seventeen years of age came to be public enemy number one?"

"She's not the same as you ... she's not the same as any of us."

"The older we get, the more teenagers can sometimes come across like aliens. I get that. But she is the nicest person I've met in a good while."

The old man sighed.

"So you'll be pleased to know I've decided to stay another day."

The elderly man stepped backward. "I thought you had common sense. Seems I was wrong."

Jake snorted. "Come off it! You've hardly held me in high regard since we met."

"No, young man, you seem to have a good head on your shoulders, but you can't always believe what—"

"Good afternoon, Alb," a tall, wiry man wearing a business suit said and strolled past them just in front of the bench.

"Afternoon, Pastor," Alb replied, turning his head and nodding a greeting.

When the man had passed, Jake asked, "Bit hot for him to be in a suit, don't you think, Alb?"

"It's Pastor Alton Banks. He preaches at Sharp Point. And I'd keep your voice down. Tetchy bunch, those pastors."

"You're not a churchgoer yourself, then?"

Alb shook his head. "I like to keep myself to myself."

"And you struck me as a socialite—"

Wheels screeched, and Jake looked up as Alb faced the noise. A pickup truck had sped around the corner that led to Main Street. As the pickup tore down the street in their direction, Jake's gaze instinctively flew to where there should have been license plate. The pickup roared and plumed a black cloud in its wake. The driver was managing to keep their vehicle on the road, but they were swerving from one side to the other. Jake bolted up and yanked Alb backward from the front of the sidewalk toward the bench.

The pickup screamed past. Jake managed a look at the lunatic behind the wheel, but the windows were smeared with dirt, and he only managed to tell that the driver had cropped hair; he would guess on male but couldn't swear an oath on it.

"Crazy fucker," Alb said.

The prick mounted the curb just ahead of them.

With over six thousand pounds of metal bearing down on him, Pastor Alton Banks's eyes widened. He scurried backward until the shutters of a closed fishmongers ended all hope of farther retreat. The front of the pickup smashed into him at chest height. The sound of the buckling metal shutters drowned out any sounds of bone being pulverized. The shutters, probably installed at a great cost, held firm. Alton had time to look down at the vehicle crushing him, then up at Jake and Alb, the only witnesses other than the driver to his fate. Then the pickup reversed. Alton, still standing, surveyed himself, perhaps thanking God that he was still on his feet and, may yet, see another day, when his destroyed bones betrayed the lie, and he crumpled to the ground, as if he was made of jelly.

Jake made a move, but then was forced to halt to avoid being rear-ended by the reversing pickup. He bashed the side of the vehicle. "Stop! Fucking stop!"

The murderer sped off in the opposite direction from where he had come.

"Call an ambulance!" he shouted at Alb, then darted toward the felled pastor, who was wriggling in a growing pool of blood, like a boneless sea creature drowning outside of the ocean. Jake fell to his knees but fought his instinct to hold the damaged man, as if, by some miracle, he could be saved. Instead, he leaned over Alton's head so the pastor would at least know he wasn't alone. Jake expected terror in the pastor's eyes, but he saw only calm. Here was a man at peace with dying.

He tried to speak but coughed up blood instead.

Jake looked back at Alb, who had his cellphone pressed

to his ear. He was thankful to see this, despite knowing, deep down, it would do little good.

Alton coughed again, and Jake turned back to him. He was *trying* to say something.

Jake leaned in close to the man's bloody, frothy mouth.

"Jerimiah." Alton wheezed and coughed.

"Jerimiah?" Jake repeated back.

It sounded as if the pastor had said yes, but this could just be the hiss of air trying to break through the blood clogging his airways.

"Twenty-nine," the pastor managed.

"Twenty-nine what?"

"Twenty-nine," the pastor repeated.

"Jerimiah Twenty-nine," Jake said. Some kind of Bible reference.

"Twenty-nine ..." The pastor released another long hiss, and Jake suspected it was his final breath. He was surprised when a final word escaped at the pastor's last moment. "Seven."

Jerimiah 29:7

Feeling his knees burning, Jake sat on the ground and sighed. He glanced at the dead man's face and closed his eyes with his thumb and forefinger.

What a way to die ... He rose to his feet and took a deep breath. *Jesus ...*

It had only been a week since he was last standing over a body. Getting lost should have been the easiest thing in the world.

Not for Jake Pettman.

* * *

Frederick declined the offer of coffee as he sat down in Pastor Norman Banks's office.

"I have a new machine. It grinds the beans for you—"

"Please take a seat, Norman. My visit is fleeting."

Norman placed a hand on his bulbous stomach. "I'd prefer to stand. I have a new app to count calories, and I ticked the box that said moderately active—"

"Norman, now isn't the time. *Really*. Sit."

Norman's face reddened over his failure to read his boss's signal. "Sorry, Pastor."

"Don't be sorry, Norman. I am sitting here because I have every trust in you. Don't doubt that, but I need you to steel yourself for what I'm about to say."

Norman rolled his big shoulders, and his spine cracked. "Steeled, Pastor."

"I've had something done. Something necessary. You saw what happened this morning. It simply couldn't continue."

"Alton?"

"Gone."

"He left! Is that not dangerous? Does he not know too much? Did you tell him to leave?"

"Precisely, Alton. They were my concerns too. No need to worry though. He's gone to a place in which he cannot talk." Frederick looked down. "Ever again." He looked up and steeled his own weakening expression.

Norman paled. He opened his mouth to speak, but nothing came out.

"Take a deep breath, Norman, and consider. You yourself just pointed out the awkwardness of the situation. There was no other choice."

Norman followed the advice. He took a deep breath and nodded.

"Good."

"How?"

"To be honest, Norman. I don't know. It doesn't concern me, and it shouldn't concern you."

"And Merithew just complied with this request? Does he not worry about the anger it may draw toward the Nucleus?"

Frederick's nostrils flared as he took a deep inhale. "I didn't ask Merithew."

"I don't understand."

"I asked Lemuel."

Norman rose, not because of his calorie counter but because of a sudden rush of adrenaline. "*Griffin's son?*"

Frederick nodded.

"A dangerous game."

"It is."

"So, with all due respect, why are we playing it, Pastor?"

"Because, Norman, to achieve what many consider impossible, you have to be ruthless in its pursuit."

"We have a church without a pastor?"

"Our churches in Brady Crossing and Lewis are big enough. We can incorporate those of Sharp Point. They will need us, after all, to heal after this great tragedy."

Norman paced to the back of his chair, then marched back and forth.

"It's not sitting well with you, is it, Norman?"

"Merithew is a dangerous man, no doubt, but Griffin and his son Lemuel? They aren't just dangerous, they're ... you know ..."

"Insidious?"

"Yes."

"You think I've taken it too far, don't you, Norman?"

"No, Pastor. I'm not saying that; it's just—"

"Listen ..." Frederick rose and approached Norman. "Our endgame involves all these people. Merithew, Griffin, Lemuel—they are either with us or against us." He took Norman by the shoulders. "Unless they choose the wrong side, like Alton, they, and we, have nothing to fear."

Norman nodded.

Frederick embraced him. "Now, let us pray, Norman. Let us pray for the soul of our lost colleague, Alton."

* * *

Celestia leaned on the rising arm barrier at the southernmost border of the Nucleus. She eyed the wooden hut beside it, until the door swung open, and Lyman, the young man on sentry duty, came out with a rifle slung over his shoulder.

He paused at the end of the barrier, chewing a match. He lifted his top lip to flash his yellowing teeth. "Merithew won't like this." Lyman spat his match on the floor.

"My father doesn't like much of what I do. In fact, last time, he was annoyed I didn't check back in." She held her arms out. "So, here I am."

"Yes. Except you didn't check out."

Celestia smiled. "Well, at least I got it half-right this time."

Lyman tapped the barrier. "Why don't you just drive like everyone else, then you've no choice?"

"Are you going to teach me?"

The sentry smiled, flashing yellow teeth again. "Nothing would give me greater pleasure."

"My father may not appreciate my adventures, but he would appreciate that tone of voice a lot less."

His smile fell. "You think you're untouchable."

"It's what you think that matters."

Lyman narrowed his eyes. "I think I'll let Merithew know you're back." He disappeared into the wooden hut.

She heard mumbling from inside as he talked into his walkie-talkie but struggled to understand what they were saying.

After Lyman emerged again, he waved her through. "Get a car," he hissed after her.

She replied by giving him the finger.

As she wandered the dirt path through the trees, her leather jacket hung over her arm, and she thought about Frank. She couldn't recall ever having such an entertaining conversation. She hoped he'd stick around another day or so.

"New jacket, Celestia?"

A tall, red-headed man with long hair and a goatee stood before her, holding a walkie-talkie.

"Griffin, you startled me. I didn't hear you approach."

He smiled. One of his front teeth was black. "I've lived in these woods a long time. I understand it better than most. If I want to arrive unannounced, then I *arrive* unannounced."

She pointed at the walkie-talkie. "Lyman told me he was contacting Merithew."

"He contacted me instead."

"I see. Is there a reason you're standing in my way, Griffin?"

Griffin laughed, exposing more blackened teeth. "Always the feisty one." He stepped forward so barely a yard separated them. "Yet sometimes I wonder." He tilted his head as he looked down on her; his long red hair covered one side of his face like a curtain. "If maybe it's just an act. A teenage girl playing sassy."

"Come any closer, Griffin, and I'll show you how much of an act it is."

He ran the tip of his tongue over his rotting teeth.

"Do you wish to upset my father?"

Griffin knelt and placed the walkie-talkie on the floor. He stood and put a large, bony hand on her upper arm.

She felt her blood run cold, and she shrank away.

"And how would you do that, Celestia? What would you tell him I did?"

Her chest tightened as adrenaline flooded her body. "Get your hand off—"

"*Nothing.* You know why?"

She gulped back the bile rising in her throat.

"You no longer have the big man's ear."

"You don't know what you're talking—"

"Too much wandering. Going here and there. The disappearing child. He can't trust his little acorn anymore, can he?"

She tried to pull away from him, but the grip on her arm tightened. Another wave of nausea passed over her as she looked Griffin up and down. She could try to break his balls with her knee, but if she messed that up, he was large enough to crush her. Steeling herself for this confrontation, she issued one more warning. "Get your hand off me."

He withdrew his hand and showed her his palms. "Relax, Celestia. I meant no harm. I'm simply out here to hunt." He reached for the sheath around his waist and withdrew a long hunting knife. "I came for a *close* kill today." He turned the knife in the air in front of him. "Nothing's like being close when you take a life." He smiled again. "A kind of intimacy, don't you think?" He turned the point of the blade toward Celestia so it pointed at her face.

Anxiety swept over her, but logic dictated he wouldn't do this. "My father will kill you if you hurt me."

"Merithew?" He smiled again, then clacked his unpleasant teeth together. "Can you remember the last time he killed? I can't, Celestia. A shame, don't you think? He was a good killer. The best, some would say. But alas, no, he has lost his taste for it—"

"He will find it again if anything happens to his only child," Celestia said, glaring at him.

"*Only?*"

"The only one he loves."

"Ah, that is true enough, Celestia." Griffin turned the blade downward. "He loves you dearly." He lowered the weapon. "And that will be his undoing." He slid the hunting knife into his sheath. Griffin focused on his sheath as he fastened it, and Celestia took the opportunity to take another step backward.

"There is someone else that loves you too," he said, looking up.

"I need to get back. Father will have heard about my return and will wonder where I am."

He smirked, keeping his ruined teeth hidden for a change.

She spied the walkie-talkie Griffin had deposited on the ground. Her father didn't know, did he? For sure, Lyman had *only* contacted Griffin. What was happening around here? Things seemed to be changing. And fast. She looked up at Griffin.

"Lemuel loves you."

"Good for him."

"I have promised you to him."

"I am not yours to promise to anyone. That is not our way."

And there were the decaying teeth again, and the obscene tongue running over them. "You will sire his children."

She ran a finger down her stomach. "I will slice open my guts and pull out my womb before I let that happen."

"Nice." He grabbed his walkie-talkie and turned to leave. He didn't bother to avoid the broken bark and brambles, making his exit a far cry from the silent approach. Several yards away, he turned his head and said, "Stop wandering, Celestia. It is a concern for us all. Who knows what ill you'll bring down on our tranquil little spot?"

4

DESPITE BEING one of two witnesses to murder, Jake spent a long time sitting on that bench on Main Street, waiting to be interviewed. He sighed. The incompetence and corruption in Blue Falls had risen to new levels, and he hoped to God he wasn't about to see more of the same in Mossbark.

Eventually, long after the police had scraped the remains of Pastor Alton Banks from the shutters and had cordoned off the area with cheap tape, and the limited forensics had taken far too brief a glance at a scene of carnage, a squat cop, bald on top and with a face that looked as if it had been mauled rather than aged by time, slowly approached the bench.

Jake stood to greet him. He offered to shake his hand, but the cop opted to thrust his thumbs into his belt and looked off toward the side to pretend he hadn't received a greeting.

"I'm Sheriff Gordon Kane. And you are?"

"Frank Yorke."

Gordon eyed Jake. "What're you doing so far from home, Mr. Yorke?"

"Hunting."

"You can't hunt in England? I heard you like to hunt foxes."

"The laws are more relaxed here."

"Not so relaxed that you don't have to check in. You should have registered yourself at the station."

"I only just got here. I was about to," Jake lied.

"Still. Seems odd that a man from the other side of the world comes to America just to visit Mossbark. Is Mossbark on many people's bucket lists back in the UK?"

"You'd be surprised."

"I'd be astounded."

"Look, Sheriff. I'm on a road trip. Hitched in, and I'll be hitching out soon enough. I'm not here to cause any bother."

"Yet, here we are. In the midst of bother. And with blood on your shirt too." The sheriff unhooked a thumb from his belt to point out the stain.

"The man was dying, Sheriff. Believe me; who I am is unimportant. Surely, you are more interested in what I saw?"

"I already *know* what you saw."

Jake raised an eyebrow. He tried to hold back but couldn't. "Telepathy, eh? That would certainly make Mossbark a place of interest globally."

"Nothing that colorful, I'm afraid, Mr. Yorke. We simply spoke to Albert Hardy immediately. We're not incompetent, you know. He saw exactly what you saw, Mr. Yorke, and, with all due respect, he's more trustworthy."

"How so?"

"Because we know who he is."

"The dying pastor didn't speak to Albert Hardy; he spoke to me."

"He spoke to you?"

"He managed a few words."

"What did he say?"

"So, you're interested now?"

The sheriff puffed out his cheeks. "Listen, Mr. Yorke. Our community has just lost a very respected man. Nobody has time for conflict. I apologize if I came off abrupt; the whole incident has shocked me somewhat, and when news of this breaks, there will be a great sadness in these parts for the foreseeable future. The focus now must be on healing. I will send over someone to take your statement just as soon as you tell me what Pastor Banks said. You know, this isn't the first hit and run from someone out of town, and it won't be the last. We've come back before, and we'll come back again."

"This wasn't a hit and run."

Gordon leaned backward so he could more easily look up into Jake's eyes. "What makes you say that?"

"Just the fact it was very intentional. No accident here."

"I see. And what qualifies you to make that judgment?"

"Eyes in my head!"

"Well, that isn't—"

"I'm also ex-police."

"Ex-police ..." Gordon raised an eyebrow. "Well ... the plot thickens. Alb thinks it was a hit and run, and, as I said before, he is an extremely respected member—"

"It *was* intentional." Jake pointed at the sidewalk. "He mounted the curb there and chased down his victim."

"A man, you say?"

"It was fast, and the windows were dirty, but I'm fairly sure it was a male."

"Fairly sure? To be honest, Albert spoke with far more confidence. He assured us the driver was male, and he has also assured us that this was a hit and run. Unfortunately, if he's right, as I'm sure he is, catching an out-of-towner will be extremely difficult, if not impossible."

Jake laughed.

"Is something funny, Mr. Yorke?"

"Not really, Sheriff. Anything but. I just watched a man get murdered. I'm laughing over how strikingly similar the situation is in this particular town to the one I was in before."

"And where was that?"

"The name escapes me now."

"Well, you might want to start remembering. When you check in, we'll need to know where you've traveled from."

"I'll be sure to look it up when I get to my motel." Jake looked skyward and sighed.

"Good. Anyway, Mr. Yorke, you had something to tell me?"

Jake looked back down at the sheriff. "Sorry?"

"What Pastor Alton said before he, you know, passed."

"Oh yes. He said, 'Jerimiah twenty-nine seven.'"

Gordon creased his brow. "Jerimiah twenty-nine seven?"

Jake nodded.

Gordon pulled out a notebook and wrote it down. "I'll look into it."

"Sounds like something from the Bible."

Gordon nodded. "Well, he was a pastor. Stands to reason he had something religious on his mind as he embarked on his final journey."

"Judging by the state of him at the time, I doubt it was anything that reflective."

"Well, I'll look into it." He thumbed at his officers behind him. "As you can see, Mr. Yorke, we are very busy. Could you pop into the station to give your statement? You could register to hunt while you're there too."

"Okay," Jake lied, knowing they wouldn't even care less if he showed up to make a statement. He looked down, trying to hide his disappointment. The police were about to sweep this poor man's death, brutal in nature, under the carpet, and he couldn't really do anything about it. But that was the way it had to be. Jake could ill afford to get involved in something like this again.

"And one piece of advice, Mr. Yorke?"

Unbelievable ... "Get out of town, by chance?"

The sheriff smiled. "Not at all. Enjoy the hunting, after you register, but maybe keep your head down? People around here will be sore for a few days, and although they know it wasn't you, well, some of our folk tend to look toward the unfamiliar when troubled, if you catch my drift."

"I caught it, Sheriff. You sure you don't want my statement right now while it might do some good?"

"No, son. You go back to your motel and sleep it off. You've had quite a shock."

As Jake walked away, he took one last look back.

Several officers were huddled together, laughing and joking, while the sheriff took a phone call, pacing around the crime scene, as if forensic investigation was yet to be invented.

Jake sighed and turned. *It was the way it had to be.*

* * *

Shaken up by her experience with the malevolent Griffin, Celestia was glad to reach her home in the Focus: the residential area of the Nucleus. She waved to her neighbor, Gillie, who was tending her garden. She was one of the oldest members of the Nucleus and often spoke fondly to Celestia of a bygone era. *"There was a time when folk from Mossbark appreciated the peace and stability that we, the Nucleus, brought to their lands. Now many of them seem to have forgotten the sacrifices we made and see us more of a burden. An entity to be feared rather than appreciated."*

As Celestia's hand closed on the handle of her cabin, she paused, feeling a familiar cold sensation. *Guilt.* She loved the Nucleus. Many of the people in her community were altruistic and kind and not, as Gillie often lamented, to be feared. Yet, here she was, Celestia, the black sheep, *always* running from her true home, as if this was a place to be shunned.

The problem with Celestia was her curiosity. The world was a big place, and the Nucleus was tiny. Minuscule, in fact. Her desire to know more, see more, *experience* more drove her outside their borders almost daily. Her affliction befell none of the others. She was alone in her excuses, and she knew that many, including the barbarian, Griffin, feared her actions would eventually have consequences.

Readying yet another apology for her father in her head, she opened the door. Seeing he wasn't in, she sighed with relief, despite knowing it only stalled the inevitable.

Onto one of the few items of furniture in the cabin—a hand-carved dining table—Celestia threw down the leather jacket Merithew would almost certainly disapprove of. The people of the Nucleus were minimalist. Both their homes and their clothing were basic. Everyone in the community wore simple cotton shirts and pants, reserving woolen legwear and jumpers for the colder months. Celestia's outfits, including her striking use of dark makeup, were out of the ordinary. Despite their silence, she knew many in the community minded; she saw it in their darkening expressions when she passed them. If her father wasn't the leader, she'd have been confronted long before now.

For years, Merithew had tried to tame her, bend her to their ways, but as she grew older, he'd succumbed to the fear of losing her. After all, she was bold enough to wander Mossbark daily now, so there was nothing to stop her fleeing the county completely if she wished. He would be lost without the person he cherished the most. He never said as much, but she could sense it in his submissive demeanor, and on more than one occasion, usually after he'd been drinking, he'd plead, beg, in fact, for her to 'please settle where she belonged.'

Two mugs sat by the kitchen sink. One was empty, but the other had been left out for her. Tea. Cold, now, but that was exactly how she preferred it. Her father knew her well. She drank the tea and felt both refreshed and calmer after that cold confrontation with Griffin.

She considered telling her father about the encounter, but there seemed little point. Griffin was one of the Nucleus's elders and, as such, was an important figure. Merithew was the leader, but it wasn't a dictatorship, and although a proper council didn't exist, many elders would gather to discuss important matters. Griffin and her father rarely saw eye to eye, but they worked hard to maintain a level of decorum in each other's presence. Her father had once told her that peaceable discussions were the only way a place such as the Nucleus could prosper—at least within the community borders. Outside the borders, however, the Nucleus did whatever it deemed necessary to keep the community alive. Celestia wasn't privy to the details of these 'necessary' actions and was promptly rebuffed whenever she quizzed her father about it, but she'd heard enough rumors to know the methods by which they preserved the Nucleus were not always 'peaceable.'

As she approached her bedroom door, she cast her mind back to Frank Yorke and smiled. It was rare for anyone outside the Nucleus to greet her, never mind engage in a conversation. Of course, it was because he was from outside Mossbark and wasn't aware of her origin, but that was unimportant to her, *simply* because she didn't want to be defined by where she was from. She wanted to be her own person, not just a part of this mysterious community hidden in the hills and trees.

And how entertaining that conversation had been. Movies. Her greatest love. In her early teenage years, it had been her only way out of the Nucleus. The films she'd lost herself in had sustained her wanderlust.

She smiled again, feeling somewhat excited about tomorrow's meeting with Frank, then opened her bedroom door. Her television, one of the few in Nucleus, brought to her by Merithew after she had begged for it on her twelfth birthday, was switched on. The DVD player wasn't on though, and the snowstorm on the screen cast the room in a flickering glow.

Merithew was sitting on the edge of her bed. He looked hypnotized by the screen.

"Merithew?"

Her father turned to look at her. His eyes reflected the glow from the television. His face seemed to sag, and he seemed older and more troubled than she'd ever seen him. "Where've you been today?"

"Brady Crossing."

"Any farther?"

"No, of course not."

The Rotten Core

"Are you telling me the truth, my acorn?"

"Yes, Merithew. I wouldn't break my promise to you."

He touched the bed beside him. "Sit with me, please."

She sat beside her father, and he put an arm around her. The security of his strong embrace was especially welcome following her turbulent experience on returning.

"They are becoming more and more concerned." Merithew sighed.

"Who?"

"The elders."

"But you're their leader?"

"It is hypocrisy. How can they see it as anything else? It's not—"

"The way?"

Merithew nodded. "No, it's not."

"The way! Things can't stay the same forever! Life is not static. Human beings are not static."

"My daughter, the philosopher." Merithew kissed the crown of her head. "But you know, my little acorn, I know all of this. Change is necessary. But it must be for all, not just for the one."

"What do you suggest? What do you want me to do?"

"You know what I want you to do."

"I cannot. You know this. I will not pretend to be like everyone else. If that is what you expect, if that is what you need from me, you know already what must be done."

"Stop, child."

"No. You will hear it again. If I left for good, if I ran from here without your blessing, then you would not be to blame. You could take one of your other children. Start again. Mold them exactly how you want them—"

"Stop, my acorn. Stop, please," he said calmly, but his eyes had widened to show she'd struck a nerve. "Please, stop." He pointed at the television. "It's this, I blame. The ideas it has given you. You should never have talked me into it."

"I didn't talk you into it! You did it because you used to like the fact that I was different, that I was interesting, that I stood up for myself and what I wanted."

Merithew sighed. "Yes, but now you are getting older. It is getting more and more ..."

"Dangerous?"

He nodded. "You speak of my other children, but they aren't my other children. I chose you. And those others have good lives. I made sure of it."

"You sound downbeat. Why today? Why *now*?"

"There are things I've done ... I'm having to do. It doesn't feel right. But it's about that change we spoke of earlier. We cannot remain static."

Celestia sat by her father and put her head on his broad shoulder. "All leaders have to do things they don't want to do to maintain peace. You told me that once. Do you not remember?"

"Yes, acorn, but these things ... well, it's too much. I just don't think I have the stomach for it anymore."

She recalled Griffin's words in the forest. *"He was a good killer. The best, some would say. But alas, no, he has lost his taste for it."* She smiled. She was glad. The thought of her father as a killer was not something she'd ever relished. She wasn't ignorant enough to think his past wasn't checkered, but the atrocities he'd committed had been against those who meant the Nucleus harm. She knew he was a good man at heart, and she really did hope his killing days were behind him. "Is there anything else you want to talk about, Merithew? I'm tired."

He kissed her forehead. "I must ask something of you."

"I've told you, I—"

"Not that, Celestia. Something else."

"Okay, I'm listening."

"Griffin has asked that his first born, Lemuel, be given your hand."

Celestia lifted her head from her father's shoulder and regarded him. So, there was truth to what Griffin had been saying in the forest? She shook her head.

He had tears in the corners of his large eyes. "He's my second-in-charge, and you are my first born, as Lemuel is his. It's an expected union."

She grimaced.

"This is the way."

"I will not ... I *cannot*."

Merithew nodded. "That I know, acorn."

She wiped away tears. "Please, Merithew, *Father*, I'd rather die."

"It won't happen. Between you and him. I promise you that. As I've said before, ways are for changing. It is a lesson I'm learning, rather late it seems, but I'm learning, nonetheless. I believe a good leader adapts to the world around them rather than tries to adapt the world to their needs. You *will* not marry Lemuel, but I'm afraid you must give the impression you will."

"I don't understand."

"To keep the peace, we must establish a pretense, but, acorn, it will never come to pass. I will not let you marry him."

"But how can you stop it?" She was crying more freely now.

"I am the leader."

"The Nucleus will turn on you if you reject its traditions, and that will give Griffin the power he needs to take over."

"I already know how I will stop him."

Again, she heard Griffin's words from the forest: *"He was a good killer. The best, some would say. But alas, no, he has lost his taste for it."* Maybe Griffin had been wrong after all. However, if her father was prepared to do the unthinkable to spare her Lemuel, then let him. She could not bear the thought of spending more than ten minutes with the boy, never mind the rest of her life.

She came in close to her father and let him embrace her. "Thank you, Father."

"You don't need to thank me, acorn. Things are happening now that will change our community forever. For the better, I believe. But, for now, we must ride out the turbulence. No matter how distasteful that might be."

"I love you, Father."

"I love you, acorn."

* * *

Griffin was leaning against an old tree in the center of the Nucleus, rolling a cigarette, when he saw Merithew pass. After placing the end of the cigarette to his mouth, he rose his hand to greet the leader he so despised, but he was too lost in his own world to notice.

Which, of course, is your greatest problem, Griffin thought, lighting his cigarette.

Merithew had always been a slave to his thoughts, and doubt and delay would always be his greatest enemy. *Problems,* Griffin thought as he inhaled from his cigarette, *I do not possess.*

The Rotten Core

He watched Merithew hang a left into a small patch of trees. *To the dwelling again, Merithew, eh? To your bones and your rats. To the history of our beloved land. To a place of dead girls. To a place where you are trying to give birth to change.*

He blew out a cloud of smoke.

Over my dead body.

He took another deep inhale.

Or maybe yours?

* * *

In the far corner of the dwelling, Merithew's pets expressed their frustration by throwing themselves against the side of the cage. The scent of fresh blood in the air had robbed them of all control.

He checked that the dwelling door was locked behind him, glanced at the bed where Sophia Stephens had died earlier, and headed to the display case that contained the bones of Hamlin Smith. He pressed his hand against the plastic case, nodded in respect, then turned, ripped the sheet from the cage, and stared at the hungry rats that were descended from those that had taken Hamlin's life.

He looked between his dead ancestor and the dozens of rats in the cage, knowing this union, no matter how unsavory it may seem, had been a blessing. It had given birth to the Nucleus—a place which, for many years, until recently, had known peace and prosperity.

He looked at the cooler on the bed. Thaxter, one of his most trusted friends, had always excelled at preparing the meat that was hunted in the forests. The responsibility for preparing Sophia now had fallen to him. Merithew had told Thaxter that none of her should be wasted. She had provided for the Nucleus, after all, and deserved the honor of continuing to do so after her death.

This cooler would only contain some of Sophia. The rest would be on ice until the rats were ready to feed again.

He saw the plastic gloves sitting behind the box. "Thank you, Thaxter." This was not a task he particularly relished, and anything that made it more tolerable, even by a mere fraction, was greatly appreciated.

He slipped on the gloves and opened the cooler. Sophia Stephens's remains were organized carefully into tied see-through plastic bags. His hand moved over several bags containing internal organs before stopping and hovering over one that contained thick chunks of carved flesh, which could very well have been taken from Sophia's thighs or breasts. He plucked out the bag and untied it. The smell was overwhelming. Last time, he'd made a mental note to request some nose plugs from Thaxter. This time, he made a mental note not to forget last time's mental note.

The smell had intensified the rats' frenzy. Merithew watched as they scurried over one another to get to the bars of the cage. Some even leaped, but this was a futile endeavor, as Merithew had kept the cage tall enough to prevent escape. As much as he loved these rats and what they symbolized, letting them get free would be a disaster. They were vicious, bloodthirsty creatures; they had been born in captivity and must, under any circumstances, die incarcerated.

He opened the top of the cage and studied the multitude of faces. Their black eyes widened. Their lips curled back to expose their jagged teeth. Some continued to leap, others scurried, while many rose on their hindlegs, now becoming aware that they had to wait for their master's graciousness.

The Rotten Core

Merithew dropped Sophia's flesh into the cage and watched the rats close over it, forming one furry writhing mass. He turned back and waited by the cooler, listening to the rats' squeaks and grunts as they consumed. When they started to settle, he reached into the box for a bag containing the eyes, nose, and other parts of Sophia's face, turned, and threw them to the seething carnivorous mass.

5

THE SOUND OF laughter awoke Jake. As he wandered to his motel window, he checked his watch—1:03 a.m. He pulled back the curtains.

It appeared as if Logan had been successful in his hunt for companionship in Brady County. The rig driver was stumbling through the motel parking lot. The only thing keeping him upright was his prey—a woman far taller and far older than Logan. She also looked completely sober. When she saw Jake staring out his motel window, she winked at him. Jake then realized it was she who was the hunter and not the naïve widower.

Are you searching for something that cannot be found, Logan? He closed the curtains. *Is that me too? Am I desperately trying to find something that cannot be found?* He returned to bed, trying to answer the question. *No, Jake, you're just trying to stay alive and keep those closest to you alive. Except,* he thought, falling asleep, *I always fail.*

* * *

The Rotten Core

Two people Jake admired were dead: Lillian Sanborn, a young, enthusiastic Blue Falls Police Officer, and Peter Sheenan, a Vietnam War veteran and a lover of dogs.

"I failed you both," Jake told them as they sat together in a dream.

Peter stroked his beloved lab retriever, Prince, and allowed the big dog to lick his face. "Everybody here made their own choices, son."

Lillian nodded. "That's right, Jake. I *chose* to join the police. I should have seen the place was full of swinging dicks and turned the other way."

"No, Lillian. That's what made you great," Jake said. "You made yourself heard, loud, and very fucking clear."

"I did, didn't I?"

"You did, and I miss you for it." He turned to Peter. "And you too, old man. You sat down for no one!"

Peter laughed. "I sat down for you, son. About the only time I ever did."

Jake had tears in his eyes. "And I wish you hadn't. How I wish you hadn't."

Peter leaned forward. "It was my fucking pleasure. Now listen here, you self-pitying fool. We're not dead. Because of you, we're very much alive."

"That makes no sense."

"Think legacy, Jake."

"No ... you've lost me."

"Think about what we achieved."

"Yes, but—"

"Together, we got rid of Jotham Macleoid."

Lillian nodded. "And together, we stopped Gabriel Jewell."

"And don't forget," Peter said, "don't *ever* forget that together we brought Kayla home."

A tear formed in the corner of Jake's eye.

"Now, that's one legacy I'm happy to be part of," Peter said.

"Me too," Lillian said.

"So, now, son, you need to get that big dumb head of yours back in the game."

"How? I'm a human wrecking ball."

"Jerimiah twenty-nine seven," Lillian said.

"What about it? I'm not interested!" Jake said.

"No, son," Peter said. "Don't lie to me and Lillian, and *certainly* don't lie to yourself."

"Jerimiah twenty-nine seven," Lillian said again.

"What does it *even* mean?" Jake asked.

Peter winked. "The beauty of you, Jake Pettman, is that—"

"You'll work it out," Lillian said.

"It's not a good idea."

"Not a good idea?" Peter said. "You're wasting air, son. This isn't here for contemplation. It's simply here. And if that's not enough for you, Jake Pettman, just think of Celestia."

"Celestia? Why?"

"Do you not see the way they all look at her?" Lillian asked.

"Yes, but—"

"We've come a long way, Jake," Peter said. "All of us here in this room. We've certainly come too far to bow down to coincidence. Jerimiah twenty-nine seven and Celestia are linked."

"It's time to pick yourself up," Lillian said.

"Damn right," Peter said.

* * *

The Rotten Core

After waking, he cast aside bedsheets and brought himself back to reality by hydrating himself with a quart of water, then took a cold shower. As the cold stream bit into his bruised and damaged skin, he tilted his head back and nodded, hoping that somewhere, somehow, Peter and Lillian received this acknowledgment.

Mowing someone down in cold blood was unacceptable. Attempting to brush it under the carpet as a tragic accident was equally abhorrent.

It would be wrong of him not to ask a question ...

Or two.

* * *

Jake was surprised by the simplicity of the church in wealthy Brady Crossing. Even in poorer areas, churches tended to thrive well from donations and would offer the locals a warm and pleasant distraction that often went with the ruggedness of smalltown life.

The breeze outside rattled the wooden slats, and Jake felt cool air on his skin. Jake had never felt welcomed in churches because he had no time for religion. These days, he felt *even* less welcomed, because he had no business in a place which celebrated goodness—not after the things he'd done.

He walked down the aisle to a man sitting on the front pew with his head lowered. "Hello? Are you in charge here?"

The man sat upright and faced Jake. "That would be me. Welcome. Can I help you, sir?"

"Are you a priest?"

"I'm a pastor."

"You don't have a collar on."

"This is not a catholic church. The pastors in my church do not wear collars."

"I see. What kind of church is it?"

The man rose to his feet and approached Jake. "This is the Mossbark Bible Fellowship. We believe in the word of God, and we believe in love. Our faith is simple, and all are welcome. I am Pastor Frederick Deering. What brings you to my door today?"

"Something I saw ... yesterday."

"So, you are the gentleman who witnessed the tragic passing of Pastor Alton? Frank Yorke?"

"Yes." Jake was unsurprised; word got around these pokey towns like lightning. "Although passing wouldn't be the word I'd used. It was quite a turbulent affair."

Frederick approached and placed a hand on his shoulder. "Sometimes we're tested."

"Me more than most, I can assure you."

"How so?" Frederick withdrew his hand.

"Ignore my self-pity. However, I *am* struggling with what I saw."

"You have come to the right place, then. Here, you can talk, and we can listen."

"I was hoping you would talk too. I have some questions."

"I see. What about?"

"I'd like to try to get to the bottom of what happened."

"Bottom of what happened? A drunk driver ran over Pastor Alton. A tragic occurrence to be sure—"

"Your pastor was run over intentionally. That was no accident—drunken or otherwise."

"Really? The police have said it was. They've told me the driver will be found, and justice will—"

"I've had this line already."

The Rotten Core

"I understand you have come to me with a different perception." Frederick turned away to behold his statue of Christ on the cross. "And it has made you quite distraught."

"Anyone who saw what I saw would be distraught."

"Yes. So, may it explain this clouded judgment?"

"Listen, I've been around the block, Pastor. Many times. I'm also an ex-detective. I'm not in shock by what I've seen—not even close. My judgment is clear. It was murder. And I was hoping someone, *anyone*, perhaps you, might start listening."

"I am openminded, but what you're saying seems to contradict what Albert Hardy observed."

"I've not spoken to him myself."

The pastor continued to admire the shrine that formed the heart of his church. "I'm sorry to disappoint you, Mr. Yorke, but you have come to the wrong place. My loyalties lie both with God and with the people in Mossbark. I have spoken to the sheriff—or rather, he spoke to me. The last thing we need to do is contaminate the passing of such a wonderful servant of the Lord with suspicion and controversy."

"This doesn't sound openminded."

The pastor turned to glared at him. "It was an accident, and when the person responsible for driving inebriated is found, then justice will be swift, and then we will forgive him—just how Pastor Alton Banks would have intended."

Jake sighed. "I thought it best to at least try. It seemed the appropriate thing to do."

"I appreciate your concern, Mr. Yorke." He seemed to calm, then placed his hand on Jake's shoulder. "Is there anything else I can help you with?"

"Yes. Maybe you could offer me some closure in another

way, Pastor. Could you tell me a bit about him? Put a face to the tragedy, as it were?"

Frederick smiled and dropped his hand again. "Ex-detective, you say? It certainly shows. Why are you so far from home anyway, Mr. Yorke? Are you running from something?"

Jake gulped. This was exactly what had gotten him in trouble in Blue Falls: sticking his nose where it didn't belong. Would listening to Peter and Lillian in his dream backfire on him again? "My story is not important."

"Don't belittle yourself. Everybody's story is important."

"Anything you can tell me about Alton Banks?"

"I'm not sure that's my place to discuss him, not when the sheriff is investigating the hit and run."

Jake sighed again.

"We lead simple lives, as you can imagine. We are servants of God, and Pastor Alton Banks served him impeccably."

"Did he preach at this church?"

"There are three churches in Mossbark County: one here in Brady Crossing, where I preach, one in Lewis, under the leadership of Pastor Norman Flagg, and one in Sharp Point, which, alas, is now leaderless." He shook his head. "Until we can find a worthy successor, Lewis will take the flock from Sharp Point under its wing. Tell me, Mr. Yorke, are you a churchgoing man?"

Jake shook his head. "I've seen too much, you know?"

"Seeing too much often strengthens one's faith."

Jake shrugged. "It didn't with me. Does Alton have relations?"

"All three of us share similar existences in that regard, Mr. Yorke. We are not native to the area. We came alone to

Mossbark County because we knew there was a need for faith. There is a manse behind each of the churches we erected."

"A manse?"

"A clergy house. There we live alone, and we work hard, tirelessly in fact, to build our community. Socially, we meet once a week for a game of bridge at one of the manses, but all our other meetings are purely to support our calling. We are here to heal Mossbark. Faith is a powerful medicine. And we will not stop until we have succeeded."

"Heal? It seems to be doing quite well for itself. I have been to several small towns on my travels, and none of them are thriving like Brady Crossing. And with such a small population too, it also doesn't look much of a draw for tourism. How is it so wealthy?"

The pastor placed his hands to his chest. "I really don't know. Unlike you, Mr. Yorke, I'm not here to ask questions. I'm here to build and spread God's word."

"Yet, you have noticed the peculiar wealth and the lack of people?"

"I have and assumed the town's history as a prosperous mining town has protected it from economic downturns."

Jake raised his eyebrows. "Is that really how it works? I'm sure we can point to other mining towns that have seen better days."

"Maybe they didn't keep hold of their wealthy benefactors and fortunes? Look, these are questions you should really be putting forward to the council. Whether they answer your questions is anybody's guess. Our church preaches kindness, love, and acceptance, but you know yourself, I'm sure, how many small towns respond to outsiders and their inquisitive natures. But, Mr. Yorke, if you will excuse me now, I must visit a member of my congregation. She is due to pass very soon, and I want to be there to keep her positive for that final journey."

Jake nodded. "That's good of you. It's a shame no one offered your good friend, Alton, that same positivity in his final moments."

"On the contrary, I heard you were there, Mr. Yorke. I am sure Alton would have been appreciative."

"He didn't really get around to being appreciative."

"I'm sorry," Frederick said, turning. "I really am pressed for time." He started to walk away. "Feel free to stay. The doors are always unlocked. Some time to reflect may bring you some peace and—"

"Jerimiah twenty-nine seven."

Frederick stopped. "Sorry?"

"Jerimiah twenty-nine seven—can you tell me what that means?"

The pastor turned.

Jake immediately noticed his face tightened. "Of course, but why do you ask?"

"This is what Alton said just before he died."

"He did?"

"Yes."

"Interesting. And rather beautiful."

"How so?"

"It's one of our core beliefs. It's fitting he should pass into the warm bosom of our Lord with such a wonderful thought in his mind."

"I'm sorry, Pastor, if I continue to struggle with your poetic description of that violent murder, but please enlighten me as to what this core belief is."

The pastor turned and regarded Jesus again. He seemed to have forgotten all about his urgent appointment and spoke slowly and gracefully, emphasizing his words and adding intonation, as if he was currently addressing a congregation. "Also, seek the peace and prosperity of the city to which I have carried you in exile. Pray to the Lord for it, because if it prospers, you too will prosper."

"What does that mean?"

"Love between places will bring prosperity and joy."

Jake nodded. "Any idea why they would be Alton's final words?"

The tightening in Frederick's face relaxed. "Because of their importance to him. To us. It has been our life's work to unify."

"Well, you seem to be succeeding. You have a church in every town in Mossbark."

The pastor nodded and took several steps toward Jake. He stopped and squinted. "Your face ... why are you so tired, Mr. Yorke?"

"I don't sleep much. I was hoping it didn't show."

"I mean no disrespect. I just wanted you to know I understand. Your exhaustion ... and your pain? There is pain there, isn't there?"

"You don't have to worry about me—"

"We have a place for you. Here. You know that, don't you?"

"Thanks, but no thanks. I won't be staying around here long enough."

Frederick reached forward and cupped Jake's hands in his own. "These are not clean."

Jake's blood rushed to his face. He heard his own voice in his head. *You don't belong here. You're responsible for the death of others, a little boy included. You've killed people too. Bad people, yes, but they're still people, so you don't belong here. You truly don't belong here.*

"Let me help you. Let *us* help you."

Jake recoiled his hands. "Thanks for talking to me, Pastor, but I will leave you to your duties now."

"As you wish," Frederick said, and smiled.

As Jake walked away, taking deep breaths, trying to slow his fast-beating heart, the pastor called out after him, "Our doors are always open."

* * *

After Frank Yorke had left, Frederick didn't go to see the dying member of his congregation; instead, he sat alone.

His manse, like his church, was modest. However, the room he now sat and drank whiskey in was anything but. He surveyed the riches around the room: a framed handwritten scroll from Uruk, a pressed opobalsamum plant from Jericho, a decorated pot from Mari, and an inscribed tortoise shell from Yinxu. They were some of his most prized possessions—relics from ancient, glorious cities that once shone brightly.

He put the whiskey tumbler on the coffee table and reached forward to stroke the leather-bound book on the table. He ran his fingers over the emblazoned golden letters on the front. *Jerimiah* 29:7.

"We seek to love our God and neighbors by partnering with others to bring about a city that is thriving and a good place for all to live."

He lifted the cover and looked at the first photograph in the scrapbook. Three fresh-faced pastors stood in front of the newly built church in Brady Crossing. Norman looked far thinner and was pumping his fist in the air. A smiling Frederick was exposing teeth far whiter than they were now. And Alton, well ... Alton was alive.

Frederick closed the book and rubbed at his eyes.

Success and greatness came at a cost. He removed his shirt and reached for the scalpel on the table. He preferred a blade he could sterilize easily between uses and would cut with little fuss.

He stared at his exposed right arm. Starting at the thick white scar just beneath his shoulder, he counted the lines his scalpel had made in the years gone by. Each line was redder than the one before due to its freshness until the final lines, which were still bloody and sore.

"Forgive me, Sophia." He sliced his arm just below the elbow. The scalpel glided smoothy with little resistance. "Forgive me, Alton." He added a tenth cut.

He leaned forward on the chair, put the scalpel on the table, and let his right hand dangle inside a bucket he'd placed at his feet on the floor. Blood bubbled from the slices, drew dark lines down his arms, and fell from his fingertips. He listened to the steady drip-dripping. After he'd let out a suitable amount, he reached for a towel on the table and wrapped his wounds. He leaned backward and looked at the cross on his wall above his historical relics. "Forgive me, Father."

He rubbed at his eyes again. This time, there were tears.

6

JAKE BARGED THROUGH the door of Hardy's Convenience Store. "I've come to finish our conversation, Alb."

Albert Hardy kept his head down behind the counter as he scanned products into his system.

Jake waited for a reply. Instead, he was met by a loud beep as the elderly man registered some detergent. "Our conversation? By the bench ..." Jake continued, striding to the counter.

Albert looked up. "That conversation was finished."

"That's not how I recall it. I recall it being *interrupted* by a violent murder."

Albert pushed the detergent aside. "I tried to be subtle, but—"

"Alb, you're a lot of things, but subtle is probably not one of them."

Albert placed a clenched fist on the table. "I told you to leave. I *warned* you to leave."

"And I was all set to take your advice, but then I watched someone have the life crushed from them by a fair few tons of metal, and seeing that, well, it makes you feel some kind of responsibility."

"You have no responsibility here. None whatsoever. Pastor Alton Banks lost his life, tragically, to a drunk driver, and now it's up to the law to—"

Jake slammed his hand on the counter next to Albert's fist. "It's up to the law to do the right *fucking* thing! And that's where my sense of responsibility comes in, because I can't turn a blind eye, like the sheriff can, like Pastor Frederick Deering can, and like *you* can."

Albert glared. "It's not like that."

"It's very much like that."

Albert turned, leaving Jake to stare at the back of his balding head. "You really don't get it. Not at all. I'm trying to help you."

"Help me by telling me what is going on around here."

"Nothing. Seriously, nothing."

"I know a lot more than you think I know, Albert. But it doesn't take a genius, does it? Mossbark, or at least Brady County, from what I've seen, is rolling in it. Someone is furnishing it with money. Illegally, probably. Whoever is doing that has something to do with that murder yesterday, and so it is imperative that anyone who lives here and enjoys the benefits of wealth brush it under the carpet."

Albert spun, arms outstretched, and raised his voice. "Does it look like I'm enjoying the benefits of wealth?"

Jake felt flecks of spit hitting his face. "That's what makes it more curious," Jake said, leaning in. "Why are you the only person in this town not enjoying those benefits?"

"I won't accept any of them!"

"Because?"

"It's dirty money." Albert sighed and lowered his head. "Mr. Yorke, you're going down a dangerous path."

"I live on that path, Alb. Have for a long time now. Also, call me Frank."

"The Nucleus."

"Sorry?"

"I'll tell you about the Nucleus, and then you leave. No good can come of you sticking around to meet them. None at all. I won't take their filthy money, but that's as far as resistance can go if I want to keep breathing. That tragedy was a hit and run, and you're going to have accept that, and move on."

"Who are the Nucleus?"

"The Nucleus sits at the center of our three towns in the hills. Some would call it the fourth town in Mossbark, but they wouldn't be talking sense. That ain't no town—not like any town I've seen before, anyway."

"What does the council have to say about a fourth town?"

Albert laughed. "Nothing. Mossbark officially has three towns. It's the way the council wants it, and it's sure as hell the way the Nucleus wants it."

"What's the Nucleus look like?"

"No idea. Never been. There are rules, you see. You can't just wander up there unannounced—not that I would want to, anyway." He leaned in. "You think you live in modern times, Frank. You don't. That place is full of savages."

"How would you know if you've never been up there?"

"Don't need to. They come down here. For supplies. And to give money to the locals to furnish their stores. Money from criminal activities elsewhere, I'm certain. This keeps the peace. Turns the animals to kings!"

"Making the locals happy to ignore this cult sitting at the heart of their county?"

The Rotten Core

"Happy to ignore, but not happy. I'm sure you know as well as I do that the average man is born hypocritical. They take their money, smile, follow the rule to never disturb them, while ruthlessly cussing them behind their backs. The rotten core—that's the name some of the folk would use to describe them, as long as nobody from the Nucleus was in earshot, for that would be suicide!"

Jake smiled at Albert. "You're no hypocrite though, are you?"

"No, but nor am I a fool. I value my life. What little I have remaining. If they stay out of my way, the world can keep on turning the same way as far as I'm concerned."

"Hardly staying out your way! They killed someone a stone's throw from where you stood."

"Who's to say it was the Nucleus anyway? And it's a question best not asked!"

"What's the population of this cult?"

"They prefer to be known as a community. Dunno, and you'd be hard pressed to find someone who could tell you. The unknown keeps them fearsome. I guess if someone discovered there was less than ten, certain people in the town would have attempted to rub them out long back."

"Are they Native Americans?"

Albert laughed. "Native Americans were driven out long ago when Uncle Sam discovered our coal."

"What do they look like?"

"How you'd expect savages to look and behave. Unkempt, rudimentary clothing, and a lack of manners. They are hunters and gatherers, nothing more—except for one fundamental difference. The society is not patriarchal. Men and women are equal."

"A forward-thinking group of savages?"

"Maybe. Although this is just a rumor, fueled mainly by

the females who also come down from the hills for supplies too." Albert raised an eyebrow. "The ladies have a real swagger about them!"

"Good on them. How does the good sheriff, Gordon Kane, feel about a criminal enterprise in his hills?"

"Sheriff Gordon Kane feels about them as he feels about everything else." He smirked. "They are part of the status quo, and the status quo is to be maintained. It keeps things calm, and it keeps things peaceful."

"Keeps his job easy, more like."

"Maybe. There is a lot more to Gordon Kane than laziness though. His tenure has overseen the quietest and calmest years Mossbark has ever known. I guess it does take some sort of talent to do that, especially considering a rather rocky past. And there is another thing which keeps the sheriff sweet."

"Go on."

"Well, head off to other local towns, Frank, and you will see communities ravaged by opiates. Not here. Not here in Mossbark. If I didn't think you would actually do it and cause a stink, I'd challenge you to find someone with a drug issue. You won't. For whatever reason, the Nucleus demands purity in its surrounding towns, and it gets that. A couple years back, some young drug dealers were found swinging from branches. The verdict was suicide. They'd decided to take their own lives together, at exactly the same time, from adjacent trees."

"Seems like the hit and run isn't the first piece of bullshit to spew forth from the Mossbark Police Department."

"Nor will it be the last. But, as I said before, if it keeps Mossbark clean and tidy, then who is the sheriff to argue?"

"Surely cartels sniff around small towns like these?"

"Maybe they do." He shrugged. "Maybe the mystery

over how populated the Nucleus is just convinces them to walk away."

"The rotten core! Maybe it is actually the Nucleus keeping the rot from Mossbark?"

"They've been here a long time. Since the eighteen hundreds. You've only been here a day, Frank, and it's definitely time for you to leave."

Jake sighed. "You'll be pleased to know I will, but first, I want to say goodbye to someone."

"Not that girl from yesterday?"

"Celestia, yes."

Albert shook his head. "You're not listening to me, Frank. The longer you stay, the shorter your lifespan."

"I'm listening, but I want to say goodbye."

"She's one of them, you know?"

Jake was taken aback. "How? You said they were savages. She seems like a normal teenager to me: emotional, an issue with fashion ..."

"The fact that she is talking to you when no one else from that place would is a very good reason to steer clear! You don't know what she's up to!"

"Maybe she needs help? Maybe she doesn't truly belong there?"

"Oh, she belongs there, alright."

"How can you be so sure?"

"Her father is the leader, and that makes her heir to that fucking throne."

A knock sounded on the shop window. Jake turned to see Celestia at the glass, smiling and waving him out.

"Spend another day in this town and you'll be dead this time tomorrow," Albert hissed.

Jake turned back to him. "There's that subtlety shining through again, Alb."

***

Jake kept his cards close to his chest as Celestia took him on a hike to the outskirts of Brady Crossing. She was leading him from the central hillside, where Albert had said the Nucleus resided, toward the more mountainous region that framed Mossbark.

"You are quieter today," Celestia said.

"I don't remember saying that much yesterday either. I seem to remember you were doing most of the talking!"

She punched him in the arm.

"How do you manage to clench your fists with six-foot fingernails?"

She showed him her hands; the fingernails were gone. "You see the impact your relentless bullying had on me?"

"Give over," Jake said and wondered if she knew anything about Pastor Alton Banks's death. If she did, she was also keeping her cards very close to her chest. And if she knew Jake had witnessed it, she was probably the best actress Jake had ever met. "Where are we going?"

"Not much farther." She skipped ahead down a dirt track.

"I hope you're not leading me to my death."

She turned, walking backward, and waved him toward her. "Funny you should say that, Frank." She stopped and pointed to her right. "A lot of people died there, or at least as a result of being there."

Jake reached the end of the dirt track and followed her finger to the mountainside where someone had tunneled an entrance into the rocks. The timber that held up the roof, then extended to support a small wooden tunnel that had seen better days, and Jake was glad an iron door closed off the mine. *If you went into that mine now, you may very well end up staying there for good.* A steel track led out of the tunnel for the minecarts, and Celestia was already hopping down it. "I think that's far enough, Celestia."

"Don't worry. The door is locked. I've already tried."

"Good. Nobody should be going in there. In fact, no one should ever have gone in there."

"That's the truth. Ever wonder why there's hardly anybody in Mossbark?"

"I had, actually."

"Well, imagine what that kind of pollution does to the gene pool—infertility, among other things. It's also turned them all into rude idiots."

"I don't think that's pollution. I think that's just people in general—at least a fair chunk of them, anyway. But let's stay positive. There're still good people left out there."

"Well, there's you, I guess, but I've yet to meet any more."

Jake noticed the sun was coming in strong over the mountaintops. Who'd have thought a place of such natural beauty could end up being a place of such unnatural human suffering? "Celestia, we have to talk."

"That's what I thought we were doing!"

"No. Talk ... *seriously.*"

"Serious as in ranking Martin Scorsese films?"

Jake pointed at the hill back in the other direction. "Do you have a cinema up there?"

Celestia turned her head to the side. "If you know about that, why are you standing here?"

"Why wouldn't I be?"

"When people around here know you're from the Nucleus, they never give you any trouble, which I guess is a good thing, but neither do they want to talk to you."

"I'm not from around here, and I'd like to know about your home."

She looked back at him, opened her mouth to speak, then closed it. She thrust her hands in the pockets of her jeans. "Can we just go back to ranking Scorsese films?"

Jake shook his head. "I'm sorry, Celestia."

"You know I can't tell you anything ... not really."

"Why?"

"Because that is the way."

"The way? Whose way?"

"It's what we say. We are a very traditional outfit, you know."

"Is that traditional?" Jake pointed at her black T-shirt with, *Today is a lovely day for you to fuck off*, written across it.

She smiled. "Not in this color, no. Let's walk back. I'll try to give you the basics, although you do know how to take the fun out of an afternoon, Frank."

As they wandered back, Jake realized she was right. He certainly had taken the fun out of the afternoon. The conversation was somber, and she avoided eye contact as they spoke. Was she ashamed of something, or did she fear revealing something sinister about her home?

When they reached the outskirts, Jake realized he'd learned very little else about the Nucleus from Celestia, if anything, Albert had come across as more knowledgeable about the people he'd never visited.

He stopped, turned, and waited for her to look at him. "Do you know someone died in town last night? Murdered, in fact?"

Her eyes widened. She shook her head, slowly.

"Right in front of me, where you left me on the bench."

"Who? How?"

The Rotten Core

He explained, toning down the grislier details.

"I didn't know him." She paled. "That's horrible."

Jake nodded.

She looked down, shaking her head and reflecting, then glared at him. "And you're bringing it up with me? Why?"

"Because of everything I've heard."

"I just told you that my people are good, that they're *misunderstood*. Why, then—"

"Not just what you told me, but other things I've heard."

"What? From whom?"

Jake sighed. "Celestia, that's not fair on them—"

"Why not?"

"Because I'm completely in the dark about what is going on here! And just remember what I saw yesterday. Forgive me for taking a little caution. I don't want to put anyone else in danger."

Her eyes narrowed. "You're just like the rest of them!"

"The rest of who? Mossbark? Believe me, I'm not like anyone from around here, or any of the small towns I've visited, for that matter—"

"Well, you certainly sound like them. Something tragic happens, and it's immediately down to the Nucleus."

"I never said—"

"A car is stolen. Blame the rotten core. A purse is lost. Blame the rotten core. A cat dies. Blame the rotten core. The beer runs out at the bars. Blame the—"

"I get your point, Celestia, but believe me, I'm not blaming you or your people. I'm just asking you to tell me more about where you come from."

"Why? You'll be gone tomorrow anyway."

"Yes ... maybe ..." He put a hand on her shoulder. "I want to know you're safe."

"My father is their leader." She looked up at him. "So, yeah, I'm safe."

Jake nodded, pretending this was news to him, and removed his hand. "Thank you for telling me that. He must be a good man to have a daughter like you."

"He is. The best. He *understands* me."

"I'm glad to hear that."

"He doesn't smother me. Trap me in the woods. He trusts me enough to give me my freedom. He knows I'll come back. He *knows* I'll never betray the Nucleus."

"Is it like that for everyone?"

She flinched. She didn't respond.

"Celestia, is everyone allowed their freedom?"

Still no response.

"I see. Doesn't that make you feel bad for the others?"

"Others don't feel as I feel. They don't feel trapped like I do."

"*Everyone?*"

Celestia nodded.

"Do you truly believe that?"

Celestia avoided Jake's eyes, making him suspect she didn't believe it.

"What's your father called?"

"Merithew."

"I'd like to go with you and meet Merithew."

Celestia shook her head. "That can't happen, Frank."

"Why not?"

"You have to be invited. You can't just show up."

"So, invite me?"

"If I invite you to the Nucleus, I betray the trust my father has given me."

"Ask your father, then?"

"How do you think he will feel about an older man

taking an interest in me?" She smiled, but she didn't look amused. Not really.

"It's a fair point. What would actually happen if I just called in?"

"You would be treated like an intruder."

"And?"

"Well, how are intruders usually treated when they go onto someone's land?"

"Depends. In my country, you can't really do what you want to them, if that's what you're getting at."

"This is a different place."

"Yes, but your country still has laws."

"It's not our country. The Nucleus is not America. It has its own rules."

Jake sighed. "So, what you are saying is I cannot see where my new friend comes from?"

"It is the way. Remember?"

"Where's your mother?"

"Dead."

"I'm sorry."

"Childbirth. I don't remember her. I'm not sad."

"You can still be sad about it."

She flinched.

"Has your father remarried?"

"No. His relationships are purely for practical reasons."

"I don't follow."

"He takes partners in order to grow our numbers."

"So, you have brothers and sisters?"

"Yes. I do, but I cannot be sure who."

"Would you like to—"

"No, I wouldn't." Again, she avoided eye contact, and again, Jake suspected she was lying.

They entered a small park which was richly decorated

with flowerbeds. They sat on bench overlooking some orchids.

"Tell me more about your life."

The Nucleus was a secretive community. Of that, there could be no doubt. But Jake could feel his bond with Celestia growing and strengthening, and so she punctured her clandestine world and let the secrets seep out. At first, they came slowly as she discussed her childhood and the clear division of her life into two responsibilities: learning to hunt and gathering food for her community, and attendance at school for reading and writing. Eventually, the puncture expanded, and she discussed her relationships with others in the community. She shared close bonds with several elders, most notably an elderly woman named Gillie, and often spent time gardening with her when she was less plagued by her natural calling to venture out and explore other lives. She also spoke of arranged marriages and her distaste for them, especially considering her own potential plight in her promised marriage to an obnoxious youth named Lemuel.

This concerned Jake, and he had to look in the other direction. He didn't want her to see anger in his face. This was not his world, and he had to control his emotions regarding it or risk driving her away. Also, involving himself was a path he'd trodden before. And with that came costs. He *must* be disciplined to avoid this path again.

"Lemuel won't happen," Celestia said.

Jake nodded.

"Merithew won't let it. He has promised me. And when he promises me something, he means it."

"I'm glad," Jake said. And he really was.

After Celestia had finished telling Jake about the Nucleus, he had to admit that, apart from the arranged

The Rotten Core

marriage, the core sounded anything but rotten. However, this was only one perspective, and it belonged to someone under a privileged umbrella held up by a leader. Not only was it likely to be rose-tinted, but she may also be protecting her father, who was, in turn, protecting her from a grotesque union.

"What about the money that keeps this town ticking?" Jake asked. "The money that keeps the people of Mossbark so passive?"

"I don't know the details of that."

"It doesn't matter how altruistic and kind the Nucleus seems if it is taking from other communities—communities who also need money."

"We're not vampires," Celestia said, looking at her feet. "We take what we need, but we take from many, not the few. We don't damage other places."

Jake sighed. "If you take, no matter how much and no matter from who, you will damage. That's inevitable."

"No." She raised her heels off the ground as she studied her feet. "No one is ever hurt. My father assures me of that."

"And you believe him?"

She looked at him. "He has never lied to me."

"You told me that your community hates organized religion. That you only believe in one another and the togetherness that brings. Yesterday, a pastor died—a symbol of organized religion."

"You're wrong, Frank. My people don't kill. Not unless they have to."

"Maybe they had to?"

Celestia shook her head. "This pastor has no relevance to the Nucleus. As I said before, blaming us is always the easy option. Maybe the sheriff should look elsewhere."

Jake sighed. "He doesn't seem that bothered about looking anywhere, to be honest."

"Good. At least for us, anyway. We are a peaceful community. There are problems, but there are always problems, I guess."

"How was the Nucleus founded in the first place?"

Celestia told him.

After she was finished, Jake stood and circled to the back of the bench, taking deep breaths. He felt nauseated; moving and filling his lungs was the only way to prevent himself from succumbing to it.

"From tragedy, we were born."

But that wasn't how Jake saw it at all. The Nucleus had been born from blood. And if his many years of experience had taught him anything at all, it was that this wasn't a good thing. He recalled Albert's words and Celestia's tales and realized there was a cauldron here—a bubbling cauldron.

Set to boil over.

He opened his mouth to tell Celestia he didn't think she should go back there. That her future—her safety, in fact—lay outside a community with a barbaric heritage. He prepared to tell her that she could stay with him for as long as she wanted. Forever, if necessary. He would be her father. He would protect her ...

But something stopped him.

The realization, perhaps, that staying with him was probably just as dangerous as returning to a community born from blood.

She looked around at him. "I need to go. I promised Merithew I would be back by now."

Jake nodded. He opened his mouth to speak again, but nothing came out, and he simply nodded.

The Rotten Core

"Same time tomorrow? A lighter subject, perhaps?" She smiled.

Jake contemplated it. He knew he should decline. This was his cue to say farewell, to wish her great happiness, to walk away from problems that weren't his own.

"Yes," he said, returning her smile. "Any problems, day or night, you come to room one-oh-five at the motel. Okay?"

She continued walking.

7

BRITTANY HIRST had experienced far worse than a dark, rough neighborhood in her eighteen years of life, but that didn't stop her feeling particularly vulnerable this evening. She accelerated her march toward the homeless shelter, with the small rucksack containing her whole world bouncing on her back.

She wiped another tear from the corner of her eye and cursed under her breath. She was stronger than this. She'd *always* been stronger than this. Being betrayed by Terrence, the man who had welcomed her into his apartment after her first and only month sleeping rough, had really left her in a wobble.

Betrayal! Maybe to her! To Terrance Bishop, it would simply feel like moving on. Hadn't her relationship with him started the same way? She recalled the skinny brunette leaving his apartment in tears when Brittany had first turned up with the same backpack she wore now. Four months later, it was her turn to leave in tears, while a new, fresh-faced homeless girl sought salvation in the arms of the handsome liar.

"Get a grip," Brittany told herself. "What did you expect?" What made her any different from any other young, naïve street urchin? Had she really believed he would fall so deeply in love with her that he would abandon his wandering eye?

She wiped at her eyes with the back of her hand and turned left onto Lunis Road, the grubby heart of Petel—or Petal, as some had ironically nicknamed it. Nothing was fresh, beautiful, or flowerlike about Petel.

She recalled her visit to this homeless shelter five months back. That night, she had felt more defiant than vulnerable, because it was her first night on the streets, the first night after telling her bitch of a mother that she was done, that she would never see her again. Her mother had called her bluff, of course. *"Close the door behind you, dear. See you in two days, when the winos start touching you while you sleep."*

She smiled. *"Try five months, bitch!"*

However, although she wanted to feel proud that she had lasted longer than two days, she felt anything but. To find herself in this same predicament again five months later filled her with shame.

She passed two people huddled in the doorway of a boarded-up convenience store and sighed. That didn't bode well. It suggested the shelter was full—unless they had been turned away for being drunk or high. She didn't wish ill on anyone but really did hope this was the case.

"Hi, darling," a deep voice said.

She spied a tall, scantily dressed prostitute, who looked disarmingly female, despite not sounding it.

"You okay, dear?"

"Yes, going to check the shelter."

"Good on you, girl. Try to get one of the top bunks.

They've had a problem with rats recently." She held her hands open. "Big ones."

"Will do."

"And if you see any tricks, send them this way. Been quiet as anything tonight."

"I will—"

The beep of a car horn interrupted Brittany.

"Thank the Lord," the prostitute said and broke into a small jog, her high heels clicking against the sidewalk.

As Brittany walked away, she cast a look back at the prostitute outlining her terms through the open window of a pickup truck. Suddenly concerned it may be her stepfather, Ben, she took a deep breath. *Calm down, girl!* That dog lived for picking up prostitutes and never bothered to cover his tracks, so why would he be here, fifty odd miles from home?

Still, the mere thought of him had made her feel physically sick. Tragically, the man was never far from her thoughts, but how could she forget a brute who had first raped her on her eleventh birthday, then continued to do so weekly—sometimes twice weekly—until she turned seventeen and escaped through the door? Hence why she spent most of her life in this state of nausea and sported an anemic, emaciated appearance.

"Close the door behind you, dear. See you in two days, when the winos start touching you while you sleep."

"At least it won't be your husband!" Brittany had shouted back.

Her mother had smiled and slammed the door. She'd never believed her and wasn't about to start then.

"Fuck off!" A deep voice bounced from boarded front to boarded front.

Brittany glanced over her shoulder at the prostitute

kicking the pickup's door, her short skirt riding high and exposing her panties. It was a ridiculous sight.

The pickup took off; its fender hung loose, as if it had recently been involved in an accident.

"*Sick fuckers!*" the prostitute shouted.

The pickup passed with its window open. She saw two men laughing. The one driving had his eyes on Brittany rather than the road. The pickup turned left onto a side street without indicating. It was the direction of the shelter, but it wouldn't matter. The creepy bastards would be gone before she got there.

Just before the turning, she had to bypass a man huddled in the center of the sidewalk. He had his knees to his chest, and he had a hood over his head. He had an empty bottle of spirits beside him. It seemed like he was sleeping, so she was startled when he looked up as she passed.

"Any change, ma'am?"

She noticed his face was a mess of eczema and sores. One of his eyes was glued shut. His lips were bloody and cracked. "I'm sorry, no."

"Sit with me a while."

"I can't—"

"I'm dying, you know."

"I'm sorry."

"Sit with me ... Please."

Part of her really wanted to sit with him, simply because it seemed and felt like the right thing to do. Despite her turbulent life, she'd always held close to the belief that one should do what was right. But she was ashamed to admit the man repulsed her. And even though he didn't appear to have enough strength to threaten, she felt scared. "I'm sorry."

She turned and accelerated toward the side street. Her heartrate increased, and she cast a few worried glances behind her. He remained sitting, and after one final look at the turn off, she breathed a sigh of relief that he'd not stood and chased—

Adrenaline seized her. She saw the pickup parked against the sidewalk several yards from the shelter's entrance. The right taillight was busted, but the other made the spiraling exhaust fumes glow. Brittany looked left at the despairing drunken beggar, then forward at the stationary pickup standing between her and the shelter. Neither looked appealing, but neither were any of them definitely dangerous. Outside her mind and vivid imagination, there could be no problem here.

She moved deeper into the shadows of the boarded-up properties at a steady rate—but not running so as to attract attention—and approached the shelter. When she drew level with the pickup, she didn't look.

"Hey there, beautiful."

She felt her heart up-tempo and suddenly wondered, with the bitter taste of acid rising up her throat, whether she should have stopped to sit with the sick beggar instead. She kept walking.

"How much, beautiful?"

She took a deep breath, considered, and made a quick decision. Ignoring him may antagonize. Best to dismiss, politely. "You've made a mistake. I'm just going to that shelter." She turned to look at him.

A man stared at her from the darkness of the vehicle. He had sharp, angular features, which made him look somewhat devilish, but she took another deep breath and tried to reassure herself that it was the limited amount of light which accentuated the contours of his face. "Everyone is for sale, beautiful."

"I'm really not, sorry—" And her breath caught in her throat for a second time when she realized the seat next to him was empty. There had almost certainly been someone else in the vehicle when he'd driven past her. She turned and made for the shelter.

"I did ask nicely," the man from the vehicle said as someone stepped from the shadows to block her escape.

In contrast to the other, facial hair and a long black fringe hid most of this man's face. He was also bigger.

She tried to slip around but couldn't avoid her ambusher's long arms, which darted out and snaked around her chest and back from the side.

"Get off me!" she shouted, writhing, but the man was squeezing tightly, restricting her movement. He had pinned her arms against her side, crushing her breasts against her chest. "Get the hell off me!"

She heard the clunk of the other car door. Seconds later, the other man was standing in front of her. His long, sharp features remained clear; they hadn't been a trick of the light. Smiling, he ran a hand over red hair cropped short to his head.

She tried to kick out at him, but he easily evaded her.

He lifted his fist in the air so it hovered just in front of her. "I will ask again."

"Fuck you—"

He rabbit punched her. Everything flashed white, and she felt burning in her cheek bone.

The other man gripped her. "We're not supposed—"

The redheaded man opened his fist and put a finger to his lips, then closed it into a fist again. "How much, lovely?"

"Please ... you're mistaken—"

Another rabbit punch. More white. This time, her nose burned.

"Please ..." she murmured.

Punch. Whiteness. Burning lip.

She tasted blood and felt the strength draining from her. If the other man hadn't had her in such a tight grip, she'd have slipped to the ground. "Please ..." She could still see his fist hovering there. She let her eyes close.

"How much?"

"I—"

This time, it felt as if a sledgehammer had struck her around the side of the head. Her head hung forward.

"How *much*?"

She lifted her head and looked at him with tears in her swelling eyes. She let blood dribble from her mouth. "Whatever ... you ... want ..."

"Didn't I say it, beautiful? *Everyone* is for sale."

Darkness closed around her.

For most of the day, Jake had toyed—or rather, *toiled*—with the idea of confronting Sheriff Gordon Kane at the station to insist, yet again, that Pastor Alton Banks was not a victim of a hit and run but had been assassinated.

However, reason won out in the end.

One didn't have to be a local to realize the sheriff wouldn't be doing anything to jeopardize that fragile relationship with the Nucleus. The town was financially better off for peace. There'd be no quicker way to end prosperity than law enforcement marching all over that hidden community, guns drawn.

And if they did, then what? He'd be putting Celestia in danger.

Yes, there was a question mark of an arranged marriage with someone who repulsed her, but she claimed to be safe, and she did have her father, the leader, protecting her. If the Nucleus were responsible for the pastor's death, and it was all brought crashing down by some cowboy law outfit, that would leave Celestia lost at sea.

So, all in all, despite the encouragement of Peter and Lillian in the land of nod, reason still dictated that he leaves well enough alone.

That in mind, he was doing the only thing he could think of doing in his paralysis.

Drink.

The Crown looked like the royalty of bars in Brady Crossing. Still, if The Crown was indeed royalty, someone had failed miserably to get that message out. It stood, like Brady Crossing did in general, empty.

But Jake appreciated the quiet. He drank IPA in the snuggly atmosphere by a fireplace, which would see little use this time of year. The bar reminded him of home. It had wooden-paneled walls, a cluttered assembly of portraits, and glass tankards to drink from. The wooden oak table even wobbled every time he put down his glass. He sighed, closed his eyes, and imagined for a moment he was home.

"Hello, stranger."

Jake opened his eyes. "Hello, Logan." He felt a mixture of disappointment and curiosity over the rig driver's continued presence in Mossbark.

"Can I sit with you, Frank?"

"Yes." He pointed at the bottle of Budweiser in his hand. "As long as you opt for a different drink next time."

He nodded from the comfort of the fire. "I have a reputation to uphold."

Logan scanned the bar. "With whom?"

"The bar staff?"

"Staff? You mean the bartender?"

"Yes, him."

He sat.

"What're you still doing here, Logan?"

"Good question."

Jake drank the remains of his third glass. He caught the bartender's eye and pointed at his empty cup.

The bartender nodded.

He looked back at Logan. "You fall in love?"

"Eh?"

"I saw you last night at an ungodly hour, walking home with someone."

"Oh ... Cindy ... yeah."

"You and her together?"

"God, no."

"Shame. She could really help you out of bother when you need to get to the cereal on the top shelf."

Logan laughed. "Because she's tall or I'm short?"

"Both. So, back to my question, why're you still here?"

He sighed. "Just feeling kind of lost. I get that sometimes."

"Lost? Really? You sounded anything but, last time I saw you. You were howling like a wolf at the prospect of coming to Mossbark. Although, I have been rather confused as to why since we arrived. There's hardly anyone here."

Logan nodded.

"You told me it was the single man's dream!"

"Well, in a way, it is. There's not much competition. Not many men, you see."

"Or women either."

"There's women, in The Oak. It's a bit more sophisticated here in The Crown. The Oak is a rowdier place. Draws folk and women in from all over Mossbark."

"How rowdy we talking?"

"There were close to twenty folk there last night."

"Heaving!"

"Heaving with loneliness," Logan added, then took a drink. "Lonely folk like me."

"Cindy feels like this?"

"Cindy's married."

"What she doing in The Oak, then?"

"The man she married, he's a piece of work."

Jake raised his eyebrows "Sounds like she met the right man to whisk her away?"

"Nah. We're not suited."

"Ah, okay."

"I don't really think I'm suited to many people, to be truthful."

"Why're so down on yourself tonight, Logan? You were the picture of joy, driving me in."

"Remember what I told you on the way in? My wife. Sometimes, I miss her. A lot, actually."

The bartender put the drink in front of him.

"Thanks."

The bartender didn't even look at him. He was as rude as the next man. He'd probably espied him chatting with Celestia. *Fraternizing with the rotten core.*

"Thank you for your service!" Jake snorted.

The bartender walked away.

"Jesus," Logan said. "I thought I rubbed people the wrong way."

"You do. It's not a competition. We're both very talented people."

Logan smiled.

"I'm sorry to hear you're feeling down."

"Losing someone you love sucks. Has it ever happened to you?"

"No," Jake lied. "I've been very lucky."

"Not a day goes by that she's not on my mind. What shirt would she be wearing today? Where did she want to walk the dog today? And ..." He smirked. "What grief would she give me about being on the road for over a week?"

Jake nodded. "It must be hard."

"Hard, but necessary. I'd hate to forget her. That would be worse."

"I don't think there's any danger of that."

"I wish I could be so sure. I'm always looking for distraction. Trying to give my head a rest. What if one day I wake up and, you know, I'm over it? And I don't spare a single thought for—"

"You *won't*. Trust me." Jake stared at him for a moment, then looked away, realizing he risked betraying his own secrets.

Logan nodded. "You're all right, Frank, you know that?"

"Thanks," Jake said, smiled, and took a drink. "You're not so bad yourself, Logan. Yes, you really need to work on that gender and racial stereotyping and that woeful first impression you present, but deep down, you seem a different kettle of fish."

"Deep down, I'm miserable."

"I was going to say reflective, sounds better."

The Crown door opened, and Sheriff Gordon Kane entered, closely followed by a taller, younger uniformed deputy. Gordon approached the bar and greeted the bartender. "The usual please, son. I've got a thirst on."

"Of course, Sheriff. Been a busy day?"

Gordon laughed. "Always, son."

Doing what exactly? Jake thought.

The bartender placed two Budweisers on the bar.

Do people lack tastebuds around here?

"On the house," the bartender said.

"You spoil us, son."

The bartender leaned over the bar and whispered something to Gordon that Jake couldn't quite hear, but it quickly became obvious what it was about. The sheriff turned his head toward Jake and doffed his hat.

Jake raised his hand in greeting, then faced Logan to continue their conversation about life and loss. Their discussion grew more upbeat as Jake worked his way through his fourth drink. With Gordon and his man chortling away from the other side of the bar, it was hard to keep their own interaction serious and somber.

When Jake reached the end of his glass, he stood to leave but felt Logan tug his arm. "One more, Frank. On me."

Jake looked down and smiled. "I'm tired."

"Please. This is the first decent conversation I've had in … God knows. One more before I take my desperate, melancholic ass to The Oak."

"You still heading there after everything we just talked about?"

"Did you doubt I would?"

"Not for a second. I'm no fool. I know seeing the light takes a long while."

"A lifetime, perhaps?"

Jake smiled. "In some cases, longer, I expect! Okay, one

more, after a toilet stop."

After Jake had finished with a urinal that was surprisingly clean for a bar—probably because of its dire custom—he washed his hands in the sink and examined his face in the mirror. His eyes were worn, and his hair was graying in patches. He looked as if he'd aged a decade since leaving the UK. He heard the door behind him open and saw the face of Gordon's man in the mirror. He lowered his eyes as he rinsed his hands, and when he looked back up, he saw the man still behind him, staring at both their reflections.

"Can I help you?" Jake said.

"You're still not checked in at the station. When were you thinking of hunting?"

"Changed my mind, actually." Jake turned to the side and pulled the towel through the dispenser on the wall. "Seeing all that blood yesterday put me off hunting for a while."

"So, why're you still in town, then?"

Jake shrugged. "The local beer?"

"Treat yourself to a few bottles of it from the convenience store, consider it a souvenir, and then leave."

Jake smiled, dried his hands, and turned to face him. The toilets were small, and the space between the sink and the urinal was narrow. They were barely a yard apart. "And who am I talking to exactly?"

"Can't you see the uniform?"

"A uniform is not a name."

"You don't need a name."

"Actually, I do. To report you."

The deputy smiled. "Why's that?"

"Harassment."

"You think *this* is harassment?"

"Where I come from, if you get this close to someone in

the urinals without permission, it would definitely be harassment."

The deputy sneered. "You think you're smart, don't you?"

"No, I just feel somewhat threatened by your proximity."

"My name is Deputy Scott Derby. Feel free to file a report."

"You needn't worry. I won't be hanging around long enough to do so."

"Thank the Lord."

Jake shook his head. "What have I done, exactly? Anyone'd think I slept with your sister."

"I only have a brother."

"Brother, then."

Scott inched closer to Jake with a disgusted look on his face. "There's no place for people like you here!"

"Like what?"

"Troublemakers." Scott's top lip curled.

"Is that you talking or your sheriff?"

"Me."

"Funny that."

"Why?"

"Because you came in so far up Sheriff Gordon's ass that I—"

Scott's hand shot out and grabbed the front of Jake's shirt. "Shut the hell up."

Jake looked down at the gleaming white knuckles. "Really?" He raised an eyebrow at Scott.

"You cannot talk to me that way."

"And you've no right harassing me."

Scott drew back his fist.

"A copper clobbering a tourist might bring some outside

attention. Good. You could do with some outside attention. Chase up on the murder I witnessed yesterday. So, go on, Deputy Dumbfuck, take a pop."

The toilet door opened. Logan entered, surveyed the situation, and adopted a pugnacious pose. "What's going on here?"

Clenching his teeth, Scott flitted his eyes back and forth between their faces. Realizing he was in a situation that could go one of many ways, all of them bad, he took a deep breath and released Jake's shirt. "Nothing. Nothing's going on."

"Doesn't look like nothing," Logan said. "Nothing is you taking a piss while whistling."

Scott took another deep breath and shook his head. "You both need to leave Mossbark."

Logan shrugged. "Why? Seems to me you could do with all the people you can get."

Scott glared at Jake one last time, then eyed Logan. "Out of my way, please."

Logan sidestepped. "Because you asked so nicely."

Scott stormed out.

Jake called after him, "Listen, I'm done! You can take your piss now if you want!"

There was no reply.

Jake laughed and looked at Logan. "I shouldn't really have enjoyed that as much as I did."

Logan raised his eyebrows. "No, you shouldn't have."

"Lazy cops really piss me off."

"No shit."

"Lazy but heavy handed too, which is why we should take their advice and probably leave."

"Yes, we probably should." Jake smiled. "You're all right, Logan, you know that?"

8

MERITHEW TURNED HIS back on the caustic father and his devious son, marched across the dwelling, placed the palms of his hands against the plastic case, and looked deep into Hamlin's dark eye sockets. "I'm sorry."

He turned and again scanned the battered unconscious woman on the bed, then stared long and hard at Griffin and Lemuel while his rats crashed against the side of the cage.

Lemuel, the sadist who had wreaked havoc on the woman's face before bringing her here, stared at the floor. Not that he was ashamed. It was merely pretense. Even with his head turned downward, Merithew could see his taut face twitch as he fought back a grin.

Alongside him, his father, taller with long red hair but possessing the same taut face, did not attempt to pretend. He stared at Merithew nonchalantly. At least, Merithew thought, he doesn't find it amusing, like his sadistic child.

"Have either of you anything to say?" Merithew asked.

"The situation is as it is," Griffin said, eyeing the unconscious girl. "And she is here, as intended."

"Half-dead!" Merithew stepped forward, shaking his finger. "That is *not* the way."

"But, you know, Merithew," Griffin said, "not many things are the way these days, as you well know."

"And what does that mean?"

"Interpret it as you see fit."

Merithew shook his head and turned to look down at Lemuel—the boy whom many would like to see united with Celestia. *Over my dead body.*

The girl moaned from the bed, and the smile broke on Lemuel's face.

Merithew clenched his fists and moved closer, but Griffin was quick and managed to come between the two of them. "Be still, Merithew."

Lemuel, the audacious little prick, turned his smiling face upward.

Merithew reached over Griffin's shoulder to strike the boy, but his second-in-charge shoved him in the chest, sending him stumbling backward. "You have no right to stop me!" Merithew pointed at Griffin. His heart bashed against his ribcage.

"He's *my* son."

"He's part of the Nucleus, of which I'm the leader!"

"And I accept that you're the leader, Merithew, but I won't accept you hurting my son."

"Your son is a monster."

"My son is part of our future."

"Maybe, but he will never lead. There are others more worthy."

"Celestia?" Griffin said.

"Among others," Merithew said.

"Celestia and my son will lead together."

"After what your son has done to this girl, you think I would ever let that union happen?"

Griffin nodded. "It is, as you so always say, Merithew, the way."

"As is the punishment for his unnecessary brutality."

"And I understand that." Griffin put his arm around his son's shoulders.

At first, Lemuel looked happy to receive his father's embrace and allowed him to draw Lemuel in close. He still hadn't dropped that irritating smirk, and now he regarded his father with it.

"As touching as this is," Merithew said, "we have pressing matters—"

"Merithew ..." Griffin raised a finger to silence him. "Be patient."

"You do not give me orders—"

Lemuel gasped. "You're *hurting*—"

"Be patient, Merithew," Griffin repeated.

Lemuel's eyes widened. "Griffin ... please ..." His words were suddenly strained.

Griffin kept his eyes on Merithew as he folded his son even tighter against him.

Lemuel continued to plead. "Sorry ... Griffin ... Father ... I'm sorry ..."

Griffin relaxed his squeeze.

"Thank you ... Griffin," Lemuel murmured, slipping free.

Griffin closed his large hand around the back of his son's head, turned him toward the wall of the dwelling, and slammed him face first into the wooden slats. "There are many methods to teach you self-control, Lemuel." Griffin slammed his son's head into the slats again. "But unfortunately, you only seem to understand one method."

As Griffin slammed his son's head against the wall, Merithew nodded, admitting to himself, deep inside, that witnessing such barbaric punishment on such an insidious individual was rather satisfying. A loud crack sounded, and Merithew wondered if it was the wood splintering or Lemuel's face. When Griffin turned him back round and Merithew saw the state of the Lemuel's nose and cheek, he reasoned it had probably been a combination of both.

On the bed, the stirring woman cried out as she woke. Merithew watched her gasp for air, looking from side to side, experiencing both the pain from the wounds inflicted on her and the sudden realization she'd been kidnapped and chained. She started to scream.

Lemuel moaned loudly.

And the rats, surely smelling all this blood in the air, snarled and crashed about in the cage.

There was too much noise, but Merithew didn't know where to start in bringing about silence.

Griffin, meanwhile, was still holding the back of his son's head and forcing him toward the chained woman on the bed. When they were close enough, Griffin hooked his son's feet from beneath him with his boot.

The boy howled again when his knees crashed into the floor.

"Apologize, Lemuel, for what you did to her."

"Sorry ..." his apology bubbled out with the blood from a split lip.

Griffin slapped the back of his son's head. "Like you mean it."

"I'm *sorry*." If he hadn't been instructed to say this, it would have been unclear to Merithew what words were really coming from the damaged boy's mouth.

The captive woman wasn't interested anyway. She

screamed and yanked at the chains that bound her wrists above the headboard to a bolt that had been fixed into the wooden wall.

Merithew came alongside the bed and withdrew a syringe from his jacket pocket. He held one of her chained arms steady and pressed the needle into her skin.

Her eyes rolled back, and then closed.

The rats were still making a racket.

Lemuel was gurgling and moaning as he swayed on his knees.

His father hovered behind him.

"That was quite a show, Griffin," Merithew said.

Griffin took a step backward.

"I supposed you saved me my energy," Merithew said.

Griffin regarded Merithew for a moment and grinned. "I keep my *own* house in order." He leaned down, slipped his hands underneath his son's arm, and helped him to his feet. Then, he stooped so Lemuel could get his arm around his shoulder. "The question is, Merithew. *Do you?*"

Bearing his weight, Griffin led Lemuel out the dwelling.

This time, Corrie opened the door to Merithew rather than Sumner.

She was cradling the baby they'd adopted the previous day. The baby was sleeping, and Merithew appreciated the quiet, having just come from the dwelling and the cacophony within.

"Have you named her yet?" Merithew asked.

"Inez."

Merithew smiled and nodded. "She's beautiful."

"Yes, she is. Thank you."

"No need to thank me, Corrie. The warmth you offer in your home made it an easy decision."

"I would invite you in, but it is late, and she really needs to feed and go down for the night."

"There is no need. I am here to see Sumner and Marston."

"Marston?"

"Yes, Corrie. It's time."

"Time? But Inez only came to us yesterday."

"These ways, these paths we have chosen to follow, Corrie, are not slow and ponderous. We have opted for progression and haste. Such dire times demanded it. I'm sorry if you were led to believe it would be longer than this. But your husband, Sumner, will be prepared. Please, could you summon him?"

"He's out with the charge. They're hunting coyotes in the darkness, yet again."

"I see. That's unfortunate because I wish the process to begin now. It is you who must come with Marston then."

She was shaking her head and backpedaling. "But Inez?"

"We will drop her with Gillie en route." Merithew smiled. "There has never been a better mother than Gillie, I can tell you. Growing up, I remember always looking to her for guidance. And Celestia, well, she is full of adoration for her."

"Inez is just a baby. She needs me close."

"Gillie has mothered three. Now, I wish to move quickly. Would you get Marston?"

"He isn't so well. He is out back, lying down. Do you maybe have another option? I don't want to disturb him."

Merithew sighed. "I'm sorry to be so demanding at such a late hour, and with such a kind, peaceable person such as yourself, but there are no other options. This is the way. Sumner would appreciate this." He leaned in, putting his hand on the doorframe. "But he may not appreciate so much your ... hesitation?" He regarded her with a serious expression.

She offered Inez to him. "Hold her ... please ... while I wake him."

"Of course." He took Inez from Corrie's shaking hands.

While Corrie went to fetch Marston, Merithew stared at Inez's beautiful sleeping face. "You are the future of the Nucleus." He kissed her forehead. "Althea would be so proud."

* * *

Celestia could barely concentrate during *The Godfather Part II*, which was peculiar, as it was one of her favorites. Her conversation with Frank had her shaken up—not because she had spilled secrets to him regarding the origin of the Nucleus and its 'ways' and was fairly certain she could trust his discretion, but because of the pastor's death. Frank had been right in his understanding that the Nucleus rejected organized religion in all forms, and the death of someone so representative of it would arouse suspicion in many. It had also aroused suspicion in her.

She paced her bedroom.

Other than Frank Yorke, very few people had given her the time of day on her many visits to Brady County. There had been one man though—a man who'd always had a smile for her, asked her how her day was going, and would happily relay anecdotes of how he too had enjoyed wandering as a young man, discovering new and exciting places.

Pastor Frederick Deering.

She'd never known Pastor Alton, but if, as many in town would believe, the Nucleus had struck out against organized religion, did that mean Frederick could also be in danger? She'd desperately hoped not. The man had been kind to her.

With her thoughts repeatedly returning to this during the past hours as the Corleone family descended into chaos, she eventually resolved to do something. She left her bedroom to talk to Merithew. He wasn't here. This wasn't surprising. He spent much of his time in the dwelling.

She slipped on her shoes and headed there.

Corrie held Marston's hand as they entered the dwelling.

Concerned about a reaction, Merithew didn't lead; he followed instead. It seemed he was right to be cautious.

After seeing the unconscious girl, Corrie turned, wide eyed. "By the soul of Althea. We're leaving." She pushed Marston toward the exit, but Merithew was already blocking it now, and the boy simply bounced off the leader's large body and into his mother's arms.

Merithew closed the dwelling door behind him, turned, and locked it. He slipped the key into his pocket.

"She would be ashamed of you," Corrie said. "Althea would be *ashamed* of you."

Merithew didn't immediately turn back. The words struck a blow. It took him a couple seconds to absorb it.

"Let us out," Corrie said. "I want no part of this viciousness."

Merithew turned. He took a deep breath and looked between mother and son.

Both trembled, although it was only Marston who appeared terrified; Corrie shook with anger. "Do the elders know about this?" Corrie asked.

Merithew nodded.

"How is this the way?"

"We have to adapt. And this is the way, *now*."

She shook her head.

"I'm sorry, Corrie. This is why it would have been best for Sumner to come. He knows. He *appreciates* the situation we are in."

Her face paled. "I don't believe this—"

"*Corrie*. It's very important that you start to believe. I brought you here, in Sumner's absence, to ensure your son Marston will do what he is expected to do."

"Which is?" she snarled.

He nodded at the bed. "She sleeps. She will feel nothing."

"I was led to believe they were willing!"

"And you believe it is so easy to find those willing to grow the population of a community that no one understands and most fear?"

"Is it any wonder that people fear us? Look at what's happening here."

"These actions remain in the dark. In the silence."

"How? You don't think she will tell?"

Merithew looked away.

Corrie gasped. "No, on Althea's soul, *no*."

"This *has* to be the way, Corrie. It is flourish or fade and die. With every new generation, fertility deteriorates. It is the curse of Mossbark. It cannot be the curse of the Nucleus. We will build toward a brighter and larger future. I cannot—"

"This is *not* what we are."

"Corrie," Marston said. "Mother ... please. I am willing."

She spun on her son. "Marson. You will listen to—"

"I am fourteen. I am old enough to support the Nucleus."

She grabbed his collar. "This is *not* right."

Merithew stepped forward and put a large hand on Corrie's shoulder. "I brought you here to be a soothing influence if your son was anxious or hesitant. It seems I made the wrong call. Sumner and Marston are both understanding of the crisis facing our world; it is you who question my judgment and the judgment of the other elders in the Nucleus."

"I question it alright!" Corrie hissed, releasing her son's collar and shrugging off Merithew's hand.

"But you know what happens if you question our ways?"

"Please," Marston said to her. "This is my decision. Please do not put our family in danger."

"Your son is wise beyond his years. You'd do well to listen to him."

Corrie shook her head and ran a hand through her short, cropped hair. "I cannot."

"Go back," Merithew said. "Leave Marston with me. He will be safe and will do his duty admirably. Think on our conversation. I believe that reflection will bring clarity which, in turn, will bring acceptance."

Tears welled in Corrie's eyes. "I cannot accept this. It is too ... too ... *inhumane*."

"Please ..." Merithew stepped forward and placed his hand on her shoulder. "Go. Wait for Sumner. Speak to him. I will return your son to you within the hour. He is part of the Nucleus, and through performing these duties, he will

The Rotten Core

ensure that he, you, Sumner, and Inez will always be part of the Nucleus."

* * *

Corrie marched past Celestia. Her head was lowered, and she appeared to be in some distress.

"Corrie?"

If Corrie did hear her, she simply ignored her and disappeared at a fair speed toward the focus.

When Celestia turned toward the dwelling and saw how close she was, she felt the cold of anxiety. *Had Corrie just come from there? What had she seen to make her so distressed?* There were her father's rats, but he always had the decency to keep them covered. Celestia, herself, found the vermin disgusting too but understood her father's need to breed and care for them. It kept him closer to his ancestry. She'd regularly warn him that she couldn't be relied on to continue, but he would simply shrug and say, *"I said the same thing to my father. His death changed my perspective. My death will change yours."*

So she knew it wouldn't have been the rats that had sent Corrie into a spin. Likewise, it wouldn't have been Hamlin's skeleton, because everyone had been and paid their respects to those remains before tonight.

She reached the dwelling door and went to knock, but that cold anxiety steadied her hand. She pressed her ear to the wood and heard muffled voices.

As a child, in the days before she was allowed to wander *beyond* the boundaries of the Nucleus, she'd instead wandered incessantly *within* them. She knew every inch of this place. She knew, also, the dwelling—not just the inside, but the outside too. Sometimes, as a child, she'd spied on him from between two uneven slats on the left side. At an early age, she'd understood very little of the meetings Merithew conducted in there, but she'd enjoyed the freedom and the power that spying on someone could bring.

She inched around the side of the dwelling to the gap between the slats. As a child, this had been at head height. Now, as an adult, she was forced to her knees to look inside. Her hand flew to her mouth to contain her gasp.

Celestia saw a woman on the bed. Her hands were above her head and chained against the wall behind her. Her top half was clothed, but her bottom half was not. Her father came around the side of the bed, facing his daughter's inquiring eyes, and Celestia ducked away from the gap, dropping her hand so she could gasp for air. The cold anxiety was now surging through her.

Merithew wouldn't? Not a prisoner? Surely? Clutching her mouth, she turned in for another look.

Merithew had lifted the woman's knees and slightly parted her legs, as if preparing her to give birth. The woman's head lay to the side, and even though Celestia could not see her eyes, she assumed her to be asleep. Merithew looked up and gave a nod. A naked boy strolled into sight and stood at the other side of the bed, opposite her father. The boy had long blond hair and broad shoulders. She needed a better view before she could identify him.

"Would you like me to stay?" Merithew said.

"Yes," the boy said. "I should be all right tomorrow. Alone."

Celestia recognized the voice. *Marston.* He must have only been fourteen!

"It could take many days," Merithew said. "Many weeks. Even months."

Marston nodded.

"She will always be asleep for you. She will never know you, nor will she feel pain."

"I understand."

Merithew handed him a tub containing a clear substance. "This will help. It will ensure she feels little discomfort when she wakes."

Marston took the tub. "Thank you."

Nausea overwhelmed Celestia as she turned from the gap and sat against the slats. She put her hands to her head. She didn't need to ask herself what this was. It was obvious —nauseatingly obvious.

How could you, Father? How could you?

She could hear the conversation continuing inside but struggled to focus on it now. Her father's previous words were on a loop in her head. *"Many days ... many weeks ... even months ..."* They were trying for a child.

And then she tasted bile in her throat and mouth because something started to make sense. After a barren period of decades with very few new births, a sudden peak had spiked in the Nucleus over the past three years. Gillie had referred to it as the Nucleus's baby boom. Did *she* know about this too? Did she know they were farming babies through ... through ...

She held her mouth, concerned she was about to vomit.

This was rape.

Then she heard the first of Marston's grunts, and she forced herself to her feet and into a run, because the vomit was already spilling between the cracks in her fingers.

* * *

As Celestia crossed the motel parking lot, she rubbed tears from her eyes with the back of her hand. She glanced at the vomit streaking her T-shirt. She looked a hot mess.

Good. Let Frank see what her discovery had physically done to her. It would be evidence enough that she had nothing to do with the atrocities taking place at the Nucleus.

She knocked on room 105.

There was no answer.

"Come on," she said, crying harder now. "*Come on.*" She sidestepped and knocked on the window instead. She waited. She hopped from one foot to the next. She knocked again and again.

A large woman, two doors down, poked out her head. "Keep it down, will you? It's obvious they're not in." She slammed the door.

Now what? She went to sit on the ground, but another option struck her. She turned and ran, recalling the pastor who'd had enjoyed wandering as a youngster, the pastor who'd always had a smile for her.

When she reached the door of his church, she knocked.

No answer.

Is no one in?

Before she finished her second knock, the door opened.

"My, my dear!" Pastor Frederick Deering said. "Come in."

9

A LOUD BANG at the door awoke Jake, and he winced. The noise didn't agree with his alcohol-induced headache. The second bang was on his window, and this one really threatened to split his temple. Rather than get dressed, he went to open the door only in his underwear, to prevent the visitor from demolishing him in this fragile state.

Jake poked out his head.

A large woman stood at his window in a nightie, looking pissed.

"Can I help?"

"How do you like it?"

"Like what?"

"Being disturbed."

"I haven't the foggiest what you are on about."

"Your booty call!"

"Nope. Still foggy." Jake stepped out.

She ran her gaze down his body, and her aggressive expression melted away. "Strike that. Feel free to disturb me any time you want!"

"Can you tell me what is going on?"

"Because your little girlfriend woke me up past ten last night. Mind you, can't say I blame her." She chewed her bottom lip.

"Little girlfriend?" Jake shrugged.

"Lots of makeup, dyed black hair, Marilyn Manson's wardrobe."

Jake's heartrate increase. "What did she want?"

"Didn't ask her. She looked like a trainwreck though. I Just told her to go."

"And?"

"She went."

"Shit." Jake turned into his room.

"There's plenty more fish in the sea. Sometimes it's looking you right in the face—"

Jake slammed his door.

* * *

Jake knocked on Logan's door, and Cindy answered.

"I'm here to see Logan."

"Not me?" she said, smiling.

"Don't you start."

She looked offended. "I thought you were supposed to be gentlemen where you come from."

"This is me being gentle. Logan?"

She stepped aside.

Logan peered at him from the bed with half-closed eyes. "Frank," he murmured. He eased himself into an upright position. "Come in."

"No time, Logan. I need a vehicle. Something's wrong. At least I think something's wrong."

"I only have a rig. Not the easiest thing to drive without experience."

"I know. I can't take a truck where I'm going. I noticed Cindy has a pickup."

"You did, did you?" She pointed at her chest. "Cindy's here, you know."

Jake looked at her. "I need to borrow your pickup."

"I've never seen you before in my life."

"Logan will vouch for me."

"A couple days ago, I'd never seen Logan before in my life either."

"He's a good guy."

She looked back at him.

He smiled.

"What do you need it for?" Cindy said.

He pointed at the hill in the distance.

"You've got to be shitting me."

"No. My friend lives up there. She came to see me last night, distressed I hear. I was out. She's young. And she's innocent."

"Do you understand what's up there?" Cindy asked.

"My friend."

"And the Nucleus. The rotten core? Have you heard of them?"

"Yes. In detail."

"So?"

"So, what?"

"So, why the hell would you go up there?"

"Listen, Cindy. Nucleus, rotten core, whatever. My friends come before everything. You too, Cindy, could be on that exclusive list if you lend me your pickup."

"You're insane. Completely. I give you that pickup, I'll

never see it again. Or maybe I'll see it again, minus the driver."

Logan was out of bed and padding toward them. "Cindy, honey, for me. Lend him the pickup."

"If he's your friend, Logan, I'd be trying to talk him out of it right now."

"Honey, can't you see he's made up his mind?"

"So, you wouldn't talk someone down from a ledge if they'd already made up their mind?"

"Anyway, what harm can he come to? I'm going with him."

Jake shook his head. "You don't have to do that—"

"My girlfriend's pickup, my terms," Logan said, nodding at Jake.

"Hurry up, then," Jake said. "Get some clothes on."

"I haven't even agreed yet," Cindy said.

"Thanks, Cindy," Jake said. "I'll be back. With the pickup."

Cindy handed over the keys. "I hope she's worth it."

Jake nodded. "She is."

* * *

The dirt track that wound up the hillside had seen better days, and the pickup clattered from side to side in the deep ruts. Never the most confident of drivers, Jake had asked Logan to do the honors, and he was glad of this when the track deteriorated even further and the drop alongside them became more sheer.

Jake peered out the window with wide eyes. "Forget the Nucleus. The journey there will kill us."

"I'm surprised the town council hasn't built them a decent road in thanks for keeping their economy afloat."

"Because it's probably the last thing they want. A treacherous journey up the mountainside will deter visitors. Imagine this in rainfall?"

"Let's hope it doesn't rain, then. We've still got to come back down. *Shit!*" His left-hand tires were taken by a particularly deep rut.

Jake bashed against Logan's side, then bounced against his door when the pickup cleared the hazard.

Logan laughed, then howled like he'd done several days earlier. "Makes you feel alive, doesn't it?"

Jake took a deep breath. "Yes, as well as making me realize how fleeting life is. Have you got a gun?"

"Yeah, but I left it in the truck."

Jake sighed. "Probably for the best anyway. Might antagonize them."

"Do you have any idea what to expect up here?"

"From what everyone has said, a hostile reception."

Logan smiled. "You really like her."

"It's not like that."

"Whatever, soldier!"

"Just drive, Logan. Enjoy the last thirty seconds of your thrill ride. I can't promise we'll be making the return journey."

* * *

Logan stopped the pickup at a sentry shack beside a rising arm barrier between two trees. A young man watched them from inside but made no effort to leave.

"What do you suggest, partner?" Logan asked. "Reckon this pickup could take out the barrier?"

"No time to play out your boyhood Dukes of Hazzard fantasies now. You sit tight while the grownups talk." Jake opened the pickup door and stepped out. He closed the door behind him and took several steps toward the sentry shack and the young occupant within.

The sentry didn't leave; he just kept his eyes firmly on Jake.

"Listen," Jake said, holding his hands in the air. "I'm unarmed. I just want to talk."

The sentry lifted the rifle and pointed it at Jake.

"There is no need for that."

The sentry stepped from the shack. "I'll decide what there is a need for. Is the other trespasser armed?"

"No. And we're not trespassing. We're still behind the barrier."

The man approached, keeping an eye pinned to the sight on his rifle. "Lie face down on the ground with your hands behind your head."

"Is that necessary?"

"Yes."

Jake laid down with his hands on his head. Fortunately, the ground was dry, so his chin pressed against solid earth. He kept his eyes on the sentry, who approached the vehicle, and then waved out Logan with his weapon.

Logan obliged, and then was given the same instructions to lie down.

Logan and Jake were on the ground a couple of minutes before several more guards arrived.

"Stand up," the original guard said, gesturing an upward motion with his rifle.

Jake stood and eyed Logan, who was also now on his feet.

A female guard patted down Jake, then backed away from him. "He's unarmed."

A male guard said, "This one too."

"All clear," the original sentry said.

"Thank you, Lyman." A hulking man stepped from behind the sentry shack. Like the other guards, he wore cotton pants and a cotton shirt, but that's where the similarities ended. His face was strong but weathered, and his eyes were calming rather than threatening. So, despite his size, this man seemed far less intimidating. "Why're you here?"

"We came to talk," Jake said. "We're not a threat."

The man raised an eyebrow. "Ah, I see. Now, that is good news for you. Because, as you can see, we don't leave ourselves vulnerable."

Jake surveyed the armed guards. "Yes. And we're not stupid men. I just came to ensure everything was okay with someone I met from here."

"Someone from here?" The man took several steps forward. "Someone from the Nucleus?"

Jake nodded. "A friendly interest. I just want to check on their safety."

"Why would any member of this community be in danger?"

Cult, more like, Jake thought. *And no member of any cult is safe.* "I'm sure that's the case. Although I like to be thorough. Her name is Celestia."

The man's eyes widened. His smile fell away. He looked visibly shaken. "Celestia?"

Jake nodded.

"I'm Merithew. I'm the leader here. I'm also Celestia's father. And, as a protective father, I do wonder what a man of your age is doing here, asking after a young girl." He nodded toward Jake's left.

He heard Logan gasp. "Easy, now!"

Jake turned to see that a guard had placed the muzzle of

the rifle against the back of his friend's head. Jake faced Merithew. "There's no need for—"

"You presume to know what is needed here?" Merithew walked forward. "In a place like this?" He lifted his hands to gesture around himself. "You understand how many wolves bay at our doors?"

"You keep those wolves well fed, from what I see. I don't think you've anything to fear."

Merithew stepped around the barrier. "Ahh, so you *do* presume to know?"

"I don't presume anything. I simply want to check that your daughter is safe. Killing me or my friend will serve no purpose for you."

Merithew nodded at his guard again.

"On your knees, fat man," the guard said. "I don't want blood on my face."

"Fuck you."

The guard slammed the butt of his rifle into Logan's back, and the truck driver fell forward and onto his knees.

"I'm going to ram that up your ass," Logan said.

The guard smiled and pressed the muzzle to the back of Logan's head again.

"This is a mistake," Jake said. "I'm asking you, begging you not to do this. We are harmless. There really isn't any purpose to it!"

Merithew lifted his finger in the air and held it there, indicating his guard should hold fire. For now. "Two trespassers came up the hill; only one returns. Please tell me how that doesn't serve a purpose?"

"All it does is turn you into monsters."

"Ha! And how do you think we are viewed already? Lambs? Do you think it's a bad thing to be viewed as monsters?"

"Yes, because it never ends well for them."

Merithew laughed. "The Nucleus has stood strong for almost two centuries, and up you stroll, asking us to be kinder and more peaceful."

"Okay," Jake said, staring at Merithew's raised finger, willing it to stay there. "You've made your point. We fear you, and fear makes you safe. Now, please."

"Any chance you can get your animal to back off?" Logan asked. "I'm getting neckache."

Shut up, Logan, Jake thought.

Merithew looked at his own raised finger. "No, I think this is best. The message is always the most important thing."

Jake realized that being on the back foot wasn't working, and he was running out of time, so he went onto the front foot. "You can never be truly safe in these circumstances. History will show you the threat doesn't just come from outside a kingdom built on fear, it comes from within them too. Show your own people you have mercy, and your community will be stronger."

"Your friend is facing the end of his life at the end of one of my guns, and you want to question my leadership?" He laughed. "Does your friend know how little you value his life?"

Jake's heart hammered as he studied Merithew's finger. Such power. The smallest of movements and a life would end. "I value life, hugely. But I'm taking a chance that a man who presides over a community which has had to fight for existence for centuries values it also."

Merithew looked at Logan. His head was forward, and he was continuously cursing his assailant and really wasn't making the situation any better. "Your friend presents an interesting argument," Merithew said to Logan. "He is asking me to reject our more traditional approach to trespassers. Do you have anything to add?"

Logan couldn't lift his head to look at Merithew, because the weapon was pressed so hard into his skull, but he managed to speak. "Would a *fuck you* do?"

Merithew refocused on Jake and smiled. "It seems he doesn't possess your talent with words."

"Get the gun off me, and I'll show you what I'm talented at," Logan hissed.

Jake forced back a sigh. *Shut up!*

Merithew smiled at Jake. "Lucky for him, I'm enjoying our conversation."

"So let him go."

"Maybe. But first, let's go back to that topic of purpose." Merithew leaned in so he could lower the volume of his voice. "Tell me, what is a man of your age doing here asking after a young girl?"

"It is nothing untoward, I assure you of that. It's just friendship."

"Friendship between someone of the Nucleus and someone not of the Nucleus is *very* untoward."

"Maybe so, but that's the way it is. We simply talked, and we got on well. That's as far as it went ... it's as far as it will ever go. As a father, I can understand your concern. But I would never have feelings like that for someone much younger than myself. *Never.* But I do like her, a lot, and I won't lie to you about that."

"There is a lot to like."

"There is."

"What's your name?"

"Frank Yorke."

"Well, Frank Yorke, I'm extending an invitation to you."

"I'm grateful."

"You ought to be. Without an invitation, you would, despite your arguments to the contrary, have to face the consequences."

"Does that mean the invitation extends to my companion Logan?"

"Of course. But he will wait in his vehicle while you walk with me."

"Into the Nucleus?"

"A short distance only. In that time, you will tell me your concerns, and I will attempt to alleviate them. Then you will leave here, and you will leave Mossbark. Is that clear?"

"If she's safe, I will leave."

"Good. Let's start walking."

As Merithew led him around the barrier, Jake heard Logan laughing at the guard. "Back on your leash now, eh?"

Jake stifled another sigh. *Just stay alive long enough to drive me back, okay?* "Will I be able to see Celestia?" Jake asked him.

Merithew clasped his hands behind his back and smiled. "Dogged, aren't you? No, of course not."

"There." Merithew pointed ahead toward several parked vehicles beneath a patch of trees. "That's as far as we go. There and back again."

"At least I can claim to have seen the Nucleus's parking lot."

"To whom? No one outside Mossbark will care. And that's where you will immediately be going: outside Mossbark."

"If she's safe, I will leave."

"She's safe, Frank, really. You have my word. What has brought you to our door so concerned anyway?"

"I don't want to get her in trouble here."

"If she was to be in trouble with me, she would have been in trouble long before now. Please tell me what has led you to risk your life this morning."

"Yesterday evening, she came by my motel room."

"In the evening?"

"Yes."

"Why?"

"I don't know. I was out, drinking in town with Logan. But someone in the room next to me saw her and said she looked distraught about something."

"What time was this exactly?"

Jake told him.

Merithew looked off, deep in thought. "Well, she returned."

"Are you sure?"

"Yes, because I checked on her before I retired, and she was sleeping." He eyed Jake. "She was also asleep this morning when I rose."

"That's a relief."

"Yes. You see, I always look in, morning and night. And she was in bed, I assure you."

"Could you reconsider me just saying goodbye before I leave Mossbark?"

"You already know the answer to that question. No matter how many times you ask, it won't change." Merrithew sighed. "I'm not surprised though that *this* volatile situation with you has arisen."

"I don't follow?"

"People like you are the reason we don't encourage our kind to spend time outside the Nucleus."

"People like me?"

"People who like to express an interest."

"I'm not sure your daughter received the message about spending time outside the Nucleus."

Merithew stopped by the vehicles. "Oh, you can be sure she did! However, although we don't encourage people wandering, we don't *prohibit* it either."

Jake stopped and faced Merithew. "But as the leader, surely you'd like your daughter to set an example?"

Merithew nodded.

"Ah, I see. Is this why you opted for the quiet word alone?"

Merithew avoided Jake's eyes.

"There have been rumblings of discontent, haven't there?"

Merithew met Jake's eyes with a smile. "Astute too. Dogged and astute."

Jake surveyed the vehicles. A battered, old Land Rover caught his attention. He remembered seeing it in town somewhere the previous day but exactly where he couldn't recall. He squinted and read the words on the sticker by the tailgate. *Love God and He will love you.*

He took a deep breath. He'd seen it outside Pastor Frederick Alton's church. *Was he here? Why? Didn't the Nucleus reject organized religion?*

"I'm afraid I have nothing more to say. As her father, I give you my word that she is safe. And now, it is time to leave, Frank, and fulfill your side of the agreement."

Jake nodded.

As they walked back toward the barrier, Jake tried to make conversation with Merithew, but his responses were always short and abrupt. He was struggling to push the image of Frederick's vehicle from his mind, and so his final line of questioning touched on that. "Do you believe in God, Merithew?"

The leader of the Nucleus snorted. "No. Why do you ask?"

"Sometimes communities such as yours can be very religious."

"The Nucleus is made differently, Frank. We believe in what is real, what is tangible. We chose not to opt for fantasy."

"Some would argue this fantasy, as you refer to it, brings peace, cohesion, and goodness to a place like yours."

"Some may argue the opposite."

"So, what *do* you believe in here, Merithew?"

"Ourselves. The Nucleus."

"But does that bring happiness?"

Merithew looked away. "Well, we're still here, aren't we? Almost two centuries later."

When they reached the barrier, Jake exchanged a wave with Logan, who was scowling in the driver's seat, no doubt because the same guard was still pointing a rifle at him through the window.

Jake turned to Merithew. "Thank you for speaking to me."

"No need to thank me. Just leave now. You were lucky today. You won't be next time." He nodded and turned.

Lyman, the original sentry who had greeted him, showed him to the door of the pickup.

* * *

Merithew's heart thrashed in his chest. Waiting until his visitors had driven down the hill was painful. But wait he did. He couldn't risk that fool turning back in his absence.

Once he was sure Frank was out of his hair, he turned and sprinted toward the focus. Merithew had seen Celestia in her bed at the exact time Frank had claimed she was in Brady Crossing. How could that be so?

Last night ... this morning ... I saw her!

Lungs burning, he bounded through the woodland.

But did I actually see her? The shape of her body in bed, yes, but her face?

He darted around the traps on their perimeter. He caught a foot on a broken branch, threw his other foot acrobatically forward, and went into a squat rather than fall.

Should he have kissed her forehead? Made sure? *But you sleep so light, my acorn ...*

He burst from the woodland behind two wooden cabins. One belonged to Gillie. How he could do with that reassuring hand on his shoulder this moment. As he bypassed her garden, he noted her absence, then weaved around several more cabins. The eerie quietness of a place usually bustling at this hour was peculiar.

Before reaching his cabin door, he prepared himself for the possibility that she wasn't there—and hadn't been there this morning or yesterday evening. Why had he not realized this before?

He saw clearly now, in his mind, the image of her lying with her back to him, warmed with a duvet and a woolen hat—an image that was *identical* on both of his visits. *I should have gone in close. By the soul of Althea, I should have gone in close!*

He reached for the handle but was surprised to find the door ajar. Rather than concern, he had a moment of relief. Was she home? Had she, in her usual haste, thrown the door shut behind her, then failed to check it was actually closed?

He went through the cabin door, scanned his empty

living space, and darted for Celestia's bedroom door. *Please, let me be wrong.* He entered her room.

She was lying with her back to him—the very same position.

He dragged the duvet off her and saw the body shape comprised of pillows and cushions. The beanie hat was pulled over a large stuffed toy, then tilted carefully away to give the impression it was a head.

"No!" He threw down the duvet. "No!" He scattered the cushions and pillows from the bed. "Celestia!" He snatched the stuffed toy and yanked his arm back to throw it.

"Merithew?"

He froze.

That infernal voice.

"Merithew ... something's happened."

Gripping the toy tightly, Merithew turned, snarling. "Where's Celestia?"

Griffin stood in the doorway. "You need to come with me."

10

"FOR A MAN whose just had a gun to his head, you seem rather relaxed," Jake said.

"Do you think that's the first time that's ever happened to me?" Logan asked.

Jake eyed his driver. "No chance. In fact, I bet you've lost count."

"Yes. And it thickens your skin. Anyway, don't plead dumb; it's happened to you before too, Frank."

"What gives you that idea?"

"Your skin is thicker than the bark on a tree—"

"*Logan!*"

They caught a pothole hard. The pickup made a sound like it had been split in two, while Jake felt the seat momentarily disappear from beneath him, and his head collided with roof.

Logan struggled to right the vehicle, and Jake saw the several yards of dirt between them and the drop quickly disappear. He felt fear whiplash in his stomach and closed his eyes.

When he opened them, Logan had regained control.

"Don't you dare howl like a fucking wolf," Jake said.

Logan smiled. "Maybe your skin ain't so thick after all!"

"We all have weaknesses. I'd go through yours, but it's a long list, and I need your eyes on the road."

As they neared the bottom of the hill, Logan said, "So, did you believe him?"

"He's the leader of a cult!"

"So, where does that leave you?"

"Well, I *believe* he loves her. That's clear. So if he's not worried, then maybe I shouldn't be."

"Good."

Jake shook his head. "Nah ... no use. I'm still bloody worried. I'll see if she turns up to meet me this afternoon."

"I thought we were off."

Jake looked at him. "We will be. This afternoon. After I speak to her."

"And in the meantime?"

"Go thank Cindy for using her pickup."

"Not sure she'll be best pleased when she sees the state of her suspension."

"I'm sure a charmer like you will get around it. You can drop me at the church."

"Didn't know you were religious?"

"I'm not. In fact, I trust the Mossbark Bible Fellowship even less than I trust Merithew and his goddamned Nucleus."

* * *

Jake read the sign on the front lawn: *The Mossbark Bible Fellowship*. He looked up and surveyed the decrepit structure. How was Pastor Frederick Deering connected to the Nucleus? This church was the only place, apart from

Hardy's Convenience Store, which hadn't benefited from the cult's healthy cash injection.

Remembering Frederick's claim that the door to the church was always open, Jake tried it.

It was locked.

Fairly certain that Frederick was in the hills, he knocked and took several steps backward until he was standing beside the shoots of some new trees marked with engraved plaques. When he was certain the place was unoccupied, he considered how best to get in. But other than smashing glass and getting himself even further into bother, there didn't seem to be one.

Jake circled around to the back to find a striking garden planted with blood-red flora. Just ahead, behind the garden, stood a small red-brick bungalow. Jake assumed this was the clergy house Frederick had been referring to as his manse. It was modest and couldn't have been larger than five hundred square foot. A white wicker fence surrounded it, with a gate in the middle.

Jake went through the gate and to the front door. Like before, he knocked for the sake of it, knowing there would be no answer. He shimmied along and, shielding his eyes from the glare, pressed his face to the glass. Following the impoverished look of the church and the underwhelming size of the manse, Jake was rather surprised to see a room kitted out like an expensive museum with indigenous-looking pots and statues, hand-carved stone arrowheads, rudimentary paintings of tribal activities, which were surely colored by the ink from plants and fruits. There was even an engraved tortoise shell.

"So, not only are you still in town, Mr. Yorke, but you continue to make a nuisance of yourself."

Jake pulled back from the window and saw in the reflection the diminutive Sheriff Gordon Kane, and standing beside him was last night's bar urinal aggressor, Deputy Scott Derby.

"Would you believe me if I said I'd found God?"

"Yes. In fact, I wouldn't be at all surprised by anyone finding God after an impromptu visit to the Nucleus."

"The Nucleus, or the rotten core?" Jake said, turning, "Which side of the fence do you sit on with that, Sheriff?"

"Smack bang right in the middle, Mr. Yorke. I'm trying keep the fence standing."

"I think it's starting to buckle under your weight."

He expected an angry reaction from Gordon—a curling of the top lip or a snarl; at the very least, a shake of the head. But there was nothing. He merely scratched his cheek, as if a fly had landed there and he was trying to brush it away.

His partner, Scott, on the other hand ... "You don't seem to do courtesy all that well, do you?"

"That's rather hypocritical, don't you think? Have you forgotten the welcoming party you laid out for me in the bar bathroom last night?"

Scott stepped forward.

The sheriff's hand darted out to stop Scott dead in his tracks. Neither his facial expression nor posture changed. It was rather like watching the tongue of a motionless frog spring out to capture a fly, only to remain motionless after taking in its kill.

"Sheriff—" Scott began.

"Back to the car."

"But—"

"Back."

Scott disappeared around the side of the church, grumbling.

"You need to keep that one on a tighter leash," Jake said.

"Son," Gordon said, holding up his hand. "Don't think you're anything special. You're not the first to come into Mossbark and cause rumblings of discontent. Nor will you be the last, I warrant. I will say one thing of you though, son. In my time, you are the only one stupid enough to go into those hills."

Jake nodded. "In retrospect, I can see how it would look that way."

"It was careless. It could have gotten you and the man you were with killed."

"True. However, there are other ways to die, aren't there? Take the pastor who was mowed down the other day, for example."

The sheriff sighed. "Enough. You may come from a good place here"—he tapped his heart—"or at least think you do. I get that. But you really don't know where you are or what you're dealing with."

"Who told you I went up there?"

"When someone heads up to the Nucleus, it's like a thunderstorm. You can't help but see the lightning, and you sure as hell can't help but hear the aftermath."

Jake smiled. "Not really an answer, but anyway, it's all in the past now. There really isn't any need for you to worry."

The sheriff snorted. "We are standing outside the pastor's house!"

Jake looked around. "Seems I am. I have a question about that."

"There's only one service I can provide to you, and that's pointing to the fastest way out of town."

"Answer me one question, Sheriff, with enough detail to make the answer worth listening to, and me and Logan will follow those directions."

"Tenacious, aren't you?"

"Astute and dogged, Merithew said. I'm going to have to write these down. Not sure I've ever had so much interest in my personality."

Gordon raised an eyebrow. "The picture of you and Merithew in conversation, now that right there makes my blood run cold."

"Wouldn't worry. Think he liked me."

"I doubt that very much."

Jake touched his chest. "I swear on this good heart, tell me about Pastor Deering, and I'll go."

Gordon shrugged. "Fine. Not much to tell, really. He came to us three years back. We had an Anglican church here, but it was on its last legs. Priest wasn't too popular. Used to drink quite heavily, and he wasn't restrained with some of his views. He often had both barrels pointed at the Nucleus! Considered them heathens. Happy to say so in his sermons. He didn't preach tolerance and acceptance anyway."

"You're not a religious man, Sheriff?"

Gordon shook his head. "Always found religion quite antagonistic, to be honest."

"How did the Nucleus feel about this priest's attitude?"

Gordon shrugged again. "Not a clue. It's you who seems to have Merithew's ear, not me. I do know the priest's viewpoints weren't too popular with our folks. Numbers dwindled fast."

"The amount of money the Nucleus funnels into your town, are you surprised? One word from the folk in the hills and I'm sure this lot would sell their grandmothers."

"I wouldn't know anything about money."

"I'm sure. What happened to this priest?"

"He left."

"You never thought that was strange?"

"People leave."

"True, but after angering a powerful cult? Were there no red flags for you?"

"Well, you're about to leave, and you probably have them pissed off too."

"Do you know where he went?"

Gordon shook his head.

"Okay, so Pastor Frederick Deering just turns up out the blue to pick up the pieces of a fractured town?"

"They have a way, don't they, these religious types. They seek out need. There was clearly need here, and the pastor sensed it."

"You make them sound like flies on shit."

Gordon put his hands in his pockets and shook his head. "Your choice of words! Good thing I'm not religious."

"We're all religious, Sheriff. We all believe in something, and we're all driven by something. For you, it's keeping the peace, maintaining the status quo."

"And you, Mr. Yorke? What's your religion?"

"I hope that me standing here asking these questions today gives you some insight into that."

"Oh, it does. Problem is, as we all well know, religion does get people killed."

"A threat?"

Sheriff shook his head. "No. And you know it isn't. That's not who I am. I want you gone so you can live."

"What do you think of this pastor, then?"

"And here's me thinking that I'd answered your question."

"Remember, you answer with detail, then I'm off." Jake crossed his heart.

"Frederick is good for Mossbark. He believes in unity

and bringing the towns together. The church attendance has grown quickly. I believe he has bought a positivity to Mossbark that was long absent."

Jake pointed at the old church. "Looking at the state of that, I'm concluding the Nucleus aren't that supportive of the Bible Fellowship?"

"The Nucleus doesn't believe in organized religion."

"However"—Jake pointed at the manse—"have you looked through that window? It's like a museum! Someone is obviously supportive of Frederick's expensive tastes."

"There's nothing to suggest that wasn't Frederick's own money."

"He comes from wealthy stock, then?"

"Well ..." Gordon scratched his chin. "He came from Redland, which is small and rather impoverished, so I would have assumed not. But people have histories—histories I'm not privy too."

"Or could it just be the Nucleus fed the pastor to keep the town at peace with their existence?"

"You are sounding farfetched—"

"Farfetched! I could phone someone back home right now, Sheriff, and tell them all about the Nucleus and your rich little town. How do you think they'd respond? With these very same words! I understand your situation, and I understand that the calmer, the better, but answer me truthfully; could Pastor Deering be connected to the Nucleus?"

The sheriff shook his head. "I genuinely don't know. But I know this, and I want you to listen carefully to the last thing I will say on the matter. Mossbark is a good place. Its people are decent, relatively happy, and there is very little crime. This hasn't always been true here. So, if Pastor Deering has money from an unknown source, I am not about to question it. And now, Frank, I am asking you, pleading with you, to just move on. I can assure you the people here are safe, that the people of the Nucleus, including that young girl you befriended, are safe. It is only your presence here that is creating unnecessary danger."

Jake nodded. "As promised, I will head to the motel and leave with Logan."

"Thank you."

Jake left Gordon sitting on the bench, staring over the flora. He wanted so much to leave the conversation there, move on, prepare for whatever the new town he drew into offered him, and try to plan his way out of the current mess of his life, but he couldn't help himself, so he turned back and said, loud enough for Gordon to hear at this distance, "If anything ever happens to Celestia, I will hold you all responsible. The Nucleus, Mossbark, and you, Sheriff."

Gordon continued to look at the flora, sadness on his face. He raised his hand in farewell but did not lift his eyes to the whirlwind that had finally agreed to leave his secretive little town.

* * *

As Griffin, Lemuel, and four others led Merithew through the focus at gunpoint, he sought out a friendly face in the focus but found only empty lands and closed cabin doors.

"Where's Celestia?" Merithew asked yet again.

"I have assured you she is safe," Griffin said.

"Where is she?" He clenched his fist.

"Be calm, Merithew. Don't lose dignity in front of your people."

"Where are all the people?"

"They know what has come to pass and have been

asked to remain home. The elders voted earlier in your absence."

"Voted for what?"

"It has been acknowledged that *your* way has failed."

Merithew looked behind him as he walked.

Griffin and his son Lemuel walked in the center, while Lemuel's friends fanned out either side of them.

"Eyes forward," Griffin said, smiling.

"And you think things won't crumble under *your* reign, Griffin?"

"The respect I have will allow me to rebuild what you have destroyed."

"Respect! Your respect is no more than fear. Look at your son's face." Merithew glanced back again.

Lemuel looked ashamed and lowered his battered face.

Griffin snorted. "And look at your daughter. Look at what a lack of respect—or fear, if that's what you wish to call it—has done. It has destroyed her, it has destroyed you, and it would have, left unchecked, destroyed the Nucleus."

"Where is she?"

"She's safe. She's part of the future. You, Merithew, are not. And our first stop will show us why you have truly failed." He turned left and faced a large wooden structure with a cross mounted on the roof and pointed. "Hamlin, behold what your descendant has done." He spat on the garden that Gillie had arranged in front of the church. "Althea, behold what your descendant has done."

Merithew felt the butt of a rifle in his back and slumped to his knees.

"Merithew, this is your legacy, everything our ancestors chose to reject."

"You fool, Griffin. We cannot afford to be separate from the world forever more. We don't have enough people. We don't have enough security. This is the *only* way to preserve our future. The elders know this."

"The same elders who voted against you?"

The door opened, and Pastor Frederick Deering strode toward him, looking full of pride and purpose. Why was he not on his knees too, desperate to preserve what was about to fall? Frederick stopped at the garden and nodded a greeting to Merithew.

The bastard knew what was happening here.

"How could you?" Merithew said.

"I thank you for everything you've done. Together, we formed a special union. We have grown the Nucleus and started to solidify its status in this part of the world. Griffin will never thank you, but he knows and accepts that we must continue on the path we have started on. As leader of the Nucleus, he will learn to accept it. Prosperity awaits."

"Really?" Merithew said and laughed. "You trust *him*?"

"Yes. It is you who I do not trust. Your daughter came to me last night, speaking of your atrocities. You failed in control. It is time for someone else. Griffin may be hesitant about what we are building, but he is strong."

"You're deluded! This man behind me *won't* stand for it. He will not make the sacrifices I have made. He's not capable."

"In time, after you've gone, the Mossbark Bible Fellowship will become the Nucleus Bible Fellowship. And not only will we unify these lands, but the lands near to us, and then, one day, the lands far from us."

"The only certainty after I've gone is that you will quickly follow."

"Farewell, Merithew." The pastor turned.

"My daughter. Did you harm Celestia?"

"Of course not. The only person who has harmed

Celestia is you."

"What do you mean? What the hell do you mean?"

"She saw *everything*, Merithew. *Everything*. And it all came crashing down." The pastor walked toward his church.

One of Lemuel's men lifted Merithew to his feet.

As they approached the dwelling, Merithew visualized, time and time again, turning on the six rifle-wielding traitors behind him. In the visualization, he always came out on top and stood roaring over their broken corpses, while the people of the Nucleus emerged from their houses, pledging their allegiance and citing fear as an excuse for their temporary betrayal.

Of course, he never put this plan into action—not because he feared death, because he didn't and would happily die in combat than be slaughtered like an animal, but because he needed to see his daughter first. He needed to know she was safe and, if what Frederick had said was true, apologize to her.

"You bring me to the heart of the Althea, the bones of Lemuel, the soul of the Nucleus, to betray your own kind? You're an abomination."

"It is you who betrayed our kind," Griffin said. "As will become clearer, still, when you go into our center and see your daughter. Face the door, and I will tell you when to enter. Lemuel?"

"Yes, Griffin?"

"Take Orman and Vicie. Patrol the focus and ensure everyone is complying with the change in order. Both myself and Oshea will remain here where it all began ... and will begin again."

"Yes, Griffin," Lemuel said.

"Open the door," Griffin said to Merithew, "and after

you enter, you will be still. I am giving you a last moment with your daughter. Be grateful for that. Don't make me regret it, or your end will not be pleasant."

Merithew opened the dwelling's door.

The heart of the Nucleus was almost how he'd left it earlier—the covered cage, Hamlin's remains, the chained girl on the bed—but with one difference. A chair sat at the bedside where Celestia was slumped. Her arms were tied behind her back. Her ankles were also tied to the chair legs with rope. His daughter stared at him. He could see the hatred in her eyes.

"I'm sorry, Celestia, for what you thought you saw."

"I know what I saw."

He rubbed at his eyes. She was the only person who'd ever had the power to reduce him to tears. Even after his beloved wife's death, he'd been stone-faced. He turned to Griffin and Oshea, who had followed him into the dwelling and had closed the door behind him. "How dare you tie up my daughter!'"

"Rest assured she will be okay," Griffin said. "She is a part of our future."

Merithew thought of her arranged marriage to Lemuel. He felt every inch of his body scream out in despair. He'd failed her; by protecting her, he'd actually failed her.

He looked from one rifle muzzle to the next. The anger was such that he felt he could bend metal with his bare hands. He was becoming more tempted to try.

"How could you, Merithew?" Celestia turned her head from side to side. "How could you?"

"She deserves the truth, Merithew."

He glared at the smiling Griffin. "Fuck you for enjoying this." He turned back to his daughter. "I did what had to be done."

Celestia watched the young woman asleep on the bed. "She isn't much older than me."

Merithew moved toward his daughter.

"Stop, Merithew, that's far enough."

"I listened," Merithew said. "I listened to Frederick when maybe I shouldn't have listened. It felt right. In fact, it *still* feels right. Celestia, our people are dying out. The Nucleus will crumble. I did this for our future. For you."

"*Don't say that!*" Celestia hissed. "Don't say you did this for me. You could have let it crumble, for all I care. I never wanted any part of this. Haven't I made that clear enough?"

"Yes, of course, but I thought you would change. I thought that if I was patient, then one day your natural inclination to lead would manifest."

"She will lead one day, Merithew. You have my word," Griffin said. "With my son by her side, she will lead."

Merithew threw himself hard at Griffin, shoving his rifle aside.

The traitor hit the side of the dwelling, and air escaped his body with a whoosh. The rifle discharged. The bullet tore into Hamlin's plastic case and shattered the long-dead boy's pelvis.

Merithew slammed his elbow into Griffin's face twice, then turned for Oshea.

The fool was only now readying a shot.

Merithew charged, heard the crack of the rifle discharging, and felt the lead enter his ribcage. Using his adrenaline, he continued, fast and focused. He turned around Oshea, looping his arm around his neck, and applied a headlock.

Having recovered, Griffin approached, smiling, as blood snaked down his face. He lifted the weapon and pointed it at Merithew and Oshea.

"I'll break his neck," Merithew said.

Griffin continued to smile.

Merithew said, "You will let anyone die to get what you want. That's not how you lead."

"I'll do whatever it takes. If Oshea dies now, that is down to you and not me."

Merithew used his adrenaline and the remains of his strength to break Oshea's neck. The young man slipped from his arms and fell twitching to the floor.

"You always were a good killer." Griffin's smile broadened so Merithew could see his blackened teeth.

Merithew patted his chest. "Go on. I've had enough of listening to you."

"Please, no," Celestia said.

Merithew saw his daughter wrestle against the ropes around her wrists and ankles.

"You're finished already," Griffin said, nodding at Merithew's chest.

Merithew looked down and saw blood blooming onto his cotton shirt.

"Time for some fun." Griffin shot Merithew in his kneecap.

In his rage, Merithew had barely noticed the bullet in his chest. This was different. This was a blinding pain like no other. He collapsed to the floor, wailing. He heard the rifle fire again and felt his other leg being destroyed too. "Celestia!" he shouted through gritted teeth. "Celestia ... I'm sorry!"

The pain had reached a point where his vision was swirling, and clarity of thought was evading him, but he had a focal point. He had his daughter. He looked in her direction and pleaded. "Forgive me, Celestia."

"Please ... please, Griffin, don't hurt him."

Merithew felt the bastard's hand tug his hair. There was

a lot of blood, and it made it easy for the traitor to drag him over the ground. Merithew watched his daughter as Griffin pulled him.

A crash sounded when her chair toppled onto one side. She remained tethered to it and stared at him, crying and pleading for Griffin to show mercy.

"Forgive me ..." he tried again.

She shook her head. "Griffin ... please ..."

Griffin released his hair and, with a loud grunt, managed to flip him onto his front. Then the hand found his hair again.

Dragged ...

Lifted ...

His head hit the top of the open cage with a *thunk*. He stared down at the furry mass.

Countless faces turned and looked up at him. Many popped onto their hindlegs and lifted their twitching noses and sharp broken teeth.

"Get on with it," he hissed into the cage.

The first one jumped but didn't come back down.

He felt it swinging from the end of his nose.

The second rat failed to hang on, but the burning pain, followed by a ripping sound, indicated that his cheek had been ruined. One by one, they jumped to eat his face.

He had nurtured his pets since their birth, and he wished now he didn't have to see his pets driven mad out of lust for his blood.

He got his wish.

The next two managed to get his eyes, and he no longer saw anything.

11

AFTER CHECKING OUT of the motel, Jake joined Logan in his truck.

As they drove away from town, Jake waved from the passenger seat at Scott, who stood smirking by his police car.

"Can you believe he's smiling?" Logan asked. "The fucked-up world he lives in! It's us who should be smiling. We are getting the hell out of it. In fact, I am smiling!" He then made a point of showing Jake his grin.

Two minutes outside of town, when Jake still hadn't grinned—or even spoken, for that matter—Logan expressed his concerns. "She'll be fine. You know that."

"Really?" Jake threw a thumb over his shoulder. "In *that,* what did you just call it? Fucked-up world?"

"Yes, but she's the leader's daughter. That will keep her safe."

But something Jake had said to Merithew was continually plaguing him. *"You can never be truly safe in these circumstances. History will show you the threat doesn't just come from outside a kingdom built on fear, it comes from within too."*

"Change of plan," Jake said.

Logan scrunched his face. "What's wrong with the current plan? The one where we drive to the next town and have a nice drink."

"That plan is flawed. We need to go to Redland."

"What's in Redland?"

"A church."

"Never really gone in for confession."

Jake smiled. "Don't worry, ain't enough hours in the day for you to confess to everything, Logan. We are going to find out who Pastor Frederick Deering really is." *Or what he is.*

* * *

Redland wasn't far from Brady Crossing, but proximity wasn't a precursor to similarity. Redland was an impoverished mess. The locals may have disagreed, but Jake considered this a good thing; it provided reassurance that this place had no connection to the rotten core.

Ironically, the only church in this rundown place was in much better condition than the church in Brady Crossing. This structure was whitewashed, with a large ornamental cross at its summit.

"I don't belong in a church," Logan said.

"Couldn't agree more. Go and find us some lunch."

In the church, many candles burned at the front, while gentle orchestral music hummed in the background. He took a seat in a pew and waited.

Ten minutes later, a robed elderly priest emerged from a box at the front, and shortly after, a younger lady exited the one beside it. Jake assumed she'd been giving a confession.

The Rotten Core

The priest gave Jake a swift nod as he showed his guest out. Then he joined him in the pew. With greetings out of the way, and after a heavy nod of acceptance when Jake admitted he didn't have a religious bone in his body, the priest offered to help him in any way he could.

"Do you remember Pastor Frederick Deering?" Jake asked.

The priest gave another heavy nod and looked away, clearly reconsidering his foolish offer of help. "Been a long time since I heard that name."

"I take it, then, it doesn't evoke good memories?"

"He left under a cloud. Left a few behind under a cloud too, truth be told. It has taken a long time for those to heal."

"I didn't expect this to be positive. Do you know what he's been up to at Brady's Crossing?"

"Heard rumors, stories, but, you know, he's chosen a path to try to do some good. It would be unfair of me to question that."

"I don't know when you last checked, Father, but he's strayed from that path."

The priest sighed. "For many years, Frederick was part of this church. He's part of the history of our church actually. He was one of my altar boys—a good boy too. I always harbored a hope that maybe he would follow in my footsteps."

"And become a priest?"

"Yes. But it soon become obvious that priesthood wasn't for him. I can understand that. He wanted a family, children. Like most people, I guess. We're not the most fertile of places—similar to some of our neighboring towns—so that never worked out well for him either. One night, he told me that he was sterile. It was the first night when I saw a real change in Frederick. Not long after, he decided to become a pastor."

"Must have bothered you."

"Anyone can do good no matter the label. I gave him the benefit of the doubt, and even gave him advice when he set out to build his own church. He succeeded too, for a time. Managed to draw several of my own strong congregation away with his sermons. A powerful orator is Frederick. More so than I will ever be. Other people were suffering with infertility and the pains of a diminishing town. He knew how to tune into them because he felt the same agony."

"What went wrong with his church?"

"Nothing much, really. As is always the case with these bombastic movements, they burn bright, but then burn out fast. He focused on unity and bringing lands together, but he was speaking to a town who had already experienced unity under Catholicism. Eventually, he saw fit to travel away and find somewhere new for his beliefs—one that *really* was desperate for unity."

"Brady County, Mossbark?"

"So the rumors suggest, but it seems you know more than I do about that."

"That can't be everything. I've yet to see you smile, Father."

"I wish it was the full story, but no, unfortunately not. The tale thickens with tragedy, I'm afraid." The priest focused on the statue of Christ. "He had a wife. A *young* wife. Catherine. Innocent. Naïve. She was well-liked. Well-loved actually. It was partly the truth of what he did to her that led to the collapse of his church."

"I don't follow."

"She had three children."

"He was sterile."

"Yes, he was." The priest looked away from Christ and stared at Jake.

"So, he didn't father the children?"

"No, he did not."

Jake said. "She had an affair?"

"He had members of his congregation father his children. Three members."

"Like, artificial insemination?"

"Nothing was artificial about it. He used her as a vessel."

Jake scoffed. "And she consented?"

The priest shook his head. "She never said, but her subsequent actions suggest otherwise. She certainly was not happy."

"Subsequent actions?"

"Suicide, I'm afraid. Her and the children. Carbon monoxide poisoning in her car."

"Shit ... Sorry."

The priest shook off the expletive.

"*Three* children?"

The priest nodded.

"Jesus! Again ... sorry."

The priest sighed and looked down; he was in no mood to be concerned with etiquette. "After their deaths, the truth quickly came out. What *he* was doing. How *he'd* been using his wife."

"Disgusting."

"Believe me, everybody agreed. But there was no real evidence that she didn't consent, and the men involved, the biological fathers, would never admit to the abuse, so the law never got involved."

"So, he was run out of town instead?"

"Not really run. He left in sadness. He was meek and weakened by his great loss. Despite his foul treatment of Catherine, he did love her. He was broken. That's why I'm surprised at how he's managed to build himself up so much again. The rumors suggest he has built a strong community."

"Don't believe everything you hear. That isn't any community—at least not one any sane person would want to be part of." Jake looked up at Christ and across at the confessional booth. He thought of the many friends he'd lost and wished, momentarily, he had somewhere he could find relief from his own great sadness. He studied the floor, then realized his salvation wasn't in a confessional booth or with a false God, nor was it in the process of running away. He regarded the priest and smiled. His salvation lay on a different path. "But don't worry, Father. I intend to do something about it."

* * *

With tears in his eyes, Thaxter dragged Merithew's body across the dwelling floor.

Lemuel smirked over the scene of Merithew's closest friend experiencing great sadness. Despite loving the dead man, here he was, disposing of the body. There were no loyalties, were there? Not really. Even in the Nucleus, people always put themselves first. To protect himself, Thaxter would obey Griffin to the letter in making this corpse disappear.

Behind him, Lemuel heard Celestia crying. His future wife's anguish didn't shake his smirk. And, when he saw the state of Merithew when he slid past, he actually burst into laughter. "Fuck. Those hungry little bastards have eaten his whole face."

He turned to Celestia. Griffin had righted her chair before leaving, and she hung forward as far as her arms, bound behind the chair, would allow. "You cry for him now? Why? I thought you were disgusted with him! It was pathetic too, watching him beg."

Celestia shook her head, and between those gulps of air that come after a long bout of hard crying, she managed to say, "He *was* my father ... He did what he thought was right ... He loved this place."

Lemuel's smirk sharpened; it blended well with the many other pointed features which comprised his face. "He brought organized religion to the Nucleus." He gestured to the sleeping girl. "He made us bring women to rape ... and then kill. If you are as moral as you claim to be, Celestia, you should be disgusted. You should be *glad* he's dead."

She raised her red and blotchy face. "Fuck you."

"Big words for a little girl."

"Yes, you sick animal! A little girl. Go find yourself a woman."

"A woman?"

Behind him, Thaxter grunted as he worked hard to negotiate Merithew through the dwelling door.

"Yes," Celestia said between spasms. "Can you manage that?"

The dwelling door closed behind him. Thaxter had made it out with Merithew's body.

Lemuel gestured again at the woman he'd kidnapped. "Like this one?"

Celestia glanced at her, then back at Lemuel. "No."

"What's wrong with Brittany?"

"Nothing's wrong with her. She doesn't belong to you;

she's not from here. You should release her. Find someone more like you."

"Someone like me?" He touched his chest. "How do you know she's not like me? She's asleep, and you have never met her." Lemuel took a deep breath through his nose, puffed out his chest, and approached the bed. He leaned over and stroked Brittany's face. "Such beautiful skin." He looked up to catch Celestia watching from the corner of her eye and was pleased to see her trembling. "I chose her. Did you know that?" He leaned down and stroked his nose over her forehead. "But I wasn't allowed to have her. Your father saw to that. Gave her to that little shit, Marston." He kissed her soft lips. "Should I take her now, Celestia? Do you not think that would be appropriate?" He noticed Celestia shaking her head, trying not to look. "There's something about all of this blood." He nodded at the trail on the floor where Merithew had been dragged. "It gets you going, you know? Maybe we're just like all those rats in that cage." He took a handful of Brittany's hair and sniffed it. "Animals. All of us."

Celestia muttered quiet pleas to leave Brittany alone.

"Are you jealous? Or are you naïve enough to think I'm disgusting? Death inspires us. Makes us want to fuck. Nothing's more natural."

Celestia murmured something, but her weeping drowned it out.

"You are beautiful, Celestia, but I must admit Brittany here is more so." He kissed her soft lips again. "She's *overwhelming*, don't you think?" His hand slid over his body and brushed against his erection. There, he let it linger. His hand trembled as the urge to free himself from his cotton trousers burned through him. He ran his other hand over her body, stroking her breasts. "I've never been a good one for control." He groaned as he slipped his hand beneath her shirt and let his fingers roll over a nipple. He closed his eyes, and his head lolled back. "Griffin will tell you that." He groaned again as he worked his hand over her breast, his erection becoming more swollen. He opened his eyes, straightened his head, and withdrew his hand from her shirt. "But I'm changing. My father will be proud. You, my future wife, Celestia, will be proud." He smiled, then kneeled, lifted his cotton trouser leg, unclipped his hunting knife from his calf, and stood. "I can control myself now. I won't be like those rats in the cage." He heard Celestia plea again. "I do not belong with her, Celestia. I belong with you. Brittany doesn't belong here. *Never* belonged here. That was down to your father, and things now are about to change. We will grow now *without* these outside pollutants. We will cut out the organized religion." He stroked Brittany's hair and kissed her one last time. "And we will cut out the genes diluting the Nucleus." He sliced her throat and stepped backward.

"*No!*" Celestia tried to pull free of her ropes. "You monster ... you *fucking* monster!"

Lemuel watched blood bubble from the gaping wound in the dying girl's neck.

Her face contorted as she gasped unsuccessfully for air.

Lemuel cleaned his knife on the bedsheets, kneeled, and clipped it back to his leg. He approached Celestia, drinking in the sounds of Brittany's death behind him and letting the back of his hand stroke against his erection.

Celestia began to scream.

Lemuel waited until she was out of breath, then said, "No one will come to you, Celestia. The dwelling is now under Griffin's care. You think anyone around here will question Griffin? Your father's frailties were there for all to see. My father has none."

"Your father is evil!" Celestia hissed. "As are you. There is no greater frailty."

Lemuel slipped down his cotton trousers and exposed himself.

She tasted bile, looked away, and gagged.

"There is no greater time for our beginning." He edged forward so his erection was inches from her face.

She leaned back, creating more distance between them. "*Just* get away from me!"

He edged nearer. "Can you not think of anything more beautiful? If you prove to me that you are ready, I will release you. Take me into your mouth, and then we can begin."

She was leaning back so hard that if she hadn't been against the wall, she would surely have gone over. "I will bite. I swear. I will *fucking* bite you."

"Your acceptance would merely have been a bonus." He pressed himself against her face. "If you must be taught to be with me, then you shall be taught—"

The dwelling door opened.

Lemuel retreated, cursing, and turned his head.

Nile, one of his closest friends, stood surveying the room. If he was horrified by either the dead woman on the bed or Lemuel's nakedness, he didn't show it. He simply said, "Griffin has sent for you. It is time."

Lemuel hoisted up his trousers, still cursing. Once he was outside, the disappointment of not being satisfied quickly subsided. They were about to tear down Merithew's disgraceful legacy, and what would provide greater satisfaction that that?

12

PASTOR NORMAN FLAGG stared across the congregation of thirteen—thirteen from the Nucleus. What percentage of the reclusive community this was, Norman had no idea. Even though both himself and Frederick were regulars in these old woods, their passage within was limited. They had no idea of how many truly resided here.

"Welcome," Norman said, moving his smile back and forth between those on the pews who had chosen to accept the Bible Fellowship into their lives. "The Lord welcomes all of you this morning." He nodded down to the front pew and to the man he respected most in this world—Pastor Frederick Deering.

Frederick returned the nod.

Norman could see pride in the older pastor's eyes, and it filled his heart with joy.

Thirteen worshippers weren't many, but thirteen was more than zero, which was how it had been many moons back, when Gillie, the eldest member of the congregation, had led in some of her kin one windy afternoon. Gillie was one of the Nucleus's elders, and so, thanks to her, they were quickly in business.

Despite her eighty-plus years, her words had been strong and unwavering. *"It was I who lent the deciding vote to your presence here."* She'd held out her frail arms to gesture the old barn they'd provided to the pastors. *"This can be your church here. You come to a fractured community. Many here would disagree with me and find your presence here abhorrent, but their ways are no longer the right ways. They bare their teeth, fight, and shed blood, and to what end? To draw us further into isolation. Merithew understands, which is why you are here. I listened. I listened to your every word, Pastor Deering, Pastor Banks, and Pastor Flagg. We seek to love our God and neighbors by partnering with others to bring about a city that is thriving and a good place for all to live."*

"Jerimiah twenty-nine seven," Frederick had said with a nod.

"Do you believe what you preach?"

"We are not hypocrites."

"Good," Gillie had then led her people down the aisle for the first time.

Now, today, Norman was so thankful to be alive and part of the great change in this land. Since eleven years of age, he'd felt the calling and had passionately, *desperately*, wanted to unify all he could with his beliefs. Yes, the process had been fraught with challenges—the forced pregnancies, the sacrificed women, and, most painfully, the loss of his dear friend Alton—but change, when so bountiful and wondrous, always came with a cost.

To build a congregation to thirteen in a place which traditionally and vehemently rejected God would be a most enviable achievement by his peers, and today, as he led the service, he felt as he always did: ten-foot tall behind that pulpit. "Please join me in prayer—"

The two barn doors opened, and sunlight streamed in.

Norman shielded his eyes from the sudden glare, while two silhouetted figures marched inside. He took a deep breath.

Griffin and Lemuel—two men who had fought against the church's existence since its conception—had rifles resting on their shoulders.

Norman shrank back on the pulpit, that pride from a moment ago a distant memory.

Frederick rose, approached the end of his pew, stepped into the aisle, and turned.

Norman watched with envy as his senior pastor demonstrated confidence he could never hope to rival.

"Griffin, Lemuel," Frederick said with open arms. "We were just about to begin, if you would like to join us?"

Griffin eyed his son to his right, who looked uncertain how to respond, so he simply smirked. Then the tall intimidating man with the long red hair regarded Frederick with a creased brow and burst into laughter.

Norman couldn't see Frederick's facial response but wasn't at all surprised to see the experienced pastor march down the aisle toward the visitors. Frederick often spoke of conflict as a necessary part of unification. He didn't believe in meeting conflict with conflict, but he did believe in *meeting* conflict, because the suppression of it was the beginning of change.

When Frederick was a yard from the two intruders, he stopped.

Norman doubted he was afraid; he just wasn't suicidal.

"What can we do for you, Griffin?"

Griffin stopped laughing and focused on Lemuel, again,

who simply smirked nervously. Griffin looked back. "I think you've done quite enough for us."

"I don't quite follow—"

"*I said*"—he stepped toward the pastor, closing the gap—"you've done quite enough for us, Pastor."

"Again, Lemuel, I don't follow. We've an agreement, haven't we?"

"Oh yes, that." Griffin brushed long red hair from his eyes. "My deal with God. My first and only deal with God. Did you not suspect I would waver from it?"

"We all waver from time to time—"

"We all waver from time to time!" Griffin turned from Frederick with his hands raised, one of which was still holding the rifle. "The pastor says we all waver from time to time!" Griffin stood with his back to Frederick.

Norman scanned the congregation. Apart from Gillie, who stood with a stern expression, most sat with ashen faces.

"I never wavered," Griffin said with his back to them all.

"We understand," Frederick said. "You are a man with conviction. We all appreciate—"

"I ..." Griffin turned. His eyes were wild. "*Never* wavered."

Norman waited for Frederick to respond. He would undoubtably meet this conflict head on with reason. But time moved forward in silence, and Norman felt the dull ache of dread building within him. If the great man, Frederick, had been hushed, what hope did the rest of them have?

Griffin thrust a finger into Frederick's chest. "You should have listened to Merithew. He told you that I would not make the sacrifices he's made, and he was right. I am not weak. And it is now time for you and your other merry men to stop playing house in our land—"

"Griffin!" Gillie called out.

Griffin smiled. "I wondered how long it'd take before you piped up."

"Not long. Not long at all. And you know that when I pipe, Griffin, you stand to attention."

Griffin glared at her. "Do I? I'm no longer a child, Gillie!"

Gillie tutted. "Oh, but you are. You are that same angry, self-righteous little bully I had to watch like a hawk all those years ago."

Griffin laughed. "I remember you as a cranky old nag back then, and I guess you're the same cranky old nag now."

"I knew it was you who killed Margaret's chickens that time when you were ten. And I knew it was you who led little Cleon into that bear trap a year later."

Griffin looked away, betraying some guilt.

"Seven years old and he lost his leg. Did you laugh then, like you're laughing now?"

"You are deluded by age and desperation, Gillie. Why didn't you say anything then if you were so convinced it was me?"

"I loved your parents. They were good people. Losing you would have hurt them too much."

"You loved my parents! Really? They weren't that loveable."

"For you. It's hard to love with so much anger."

Griffin narrowed his eyes and chewed at his bottom lip. "This is not the conversation I came into the church to have today, old woman. Besides, I have no respect for anything that comes out of your mouth. You've been part of what is going on in this old barn. Did you know what your beloved Merithew was up to in the dwelling, by the way?" He tapped his chest. "The past years, he's been using our kind to find women for him to breed. Did you know that?"

"Lies, Griffin. Anything to justify—"

"Oh, and it gets better. After he finishes with them, he feeds them to his little monsters."

"Bull."

Griffin smiled. "Does God appreciate that language, Gillie! Mind you, those in God's home have been getting up to far worse than swearing, haven't they, Pastor Deering? How about murder?" He refocused on Frederick. "Why don't you tell your congregation about your role in this fucked-up affair?"

Frederick didn't respond.

"That's the first time I've seen you lost for words."

Despite being scared, Norman decided he owed it to Frederick to offer some support, no matter how pathetic it would be. "We've only done what God expects of us."

"Even if that were true, it's irrelevant." Griffin lifted his rifle from his shoulder and pointed it at Frederick's chest. "I'm not interested in what God wants. Never have been, never will be."

Frederick held up his hands.

Norman noticed he was trembling; this was unusual for the senior pastor. The situation was spiraling out of control.

"Where's Merithew?" Gillie asked.

"You mean, you don't know?" Griffin glanced at the elderly woman again.

"Know what?"

"Really?" Griffin grunted. "Where were you this morning, old lady?"

"I rose late and came here."

"Well, you missed all the fun. I would have thought someone would have told you by now."

"Told me *what*?"

"That the elders took a vote."

"Not in my absence, they didn't."

"But they did. It was deemed appropriate. We were voting against Merithew and his deal with organized religion. Your judgment would have been clouded."

She guffawed. "There is only one person with clouded judgment around here."

"The vote was taken. Merithew was deemed unworthy."

"No ..." The color drained from Gillie's face. "No, that cannot be."

"Afraid so. Which leaves us ... *here*. So, I come to give everybody here a simple choice."

Norman noticed Griffin's eyes move between the members of the congregation. An elderly couple were gripping each other's hands. A mother and father sandwiched their two young children.

"Walk out of this church," Griffin continued. "Turn your back on this false God. Do what our ancestors expect of you. Then, and only then, will you be welcomed back into the Nucleus."

Gillie shook her head the entire time Griffin spoke. It didn't take her long to issue her conclusion. "We've come too far. We'll not relinquish everything—"

"Really?" Griffin asked with a smile.

"Yes." Gillie looked over the congregation. "Do not be bullied into rejecting what you have found."

"You think God will protect them?" Griffin asked Gillie.

Gillie nodded. She regarded the congregation again. "Remember how it was before? Remember how fractured it was? God will protect us. Hold your ground."

The parents of the two children exchanged an uneasy glance, then held their children closer. The elderly couple gripped hands and nodded together, then flashed a respectful look at Gillie.

Griffin nodded. "Condemn them, then, Gillie. This is on you and your false God. Lemuel, bring Pastor Deering with us. There is a cost to what you have brought here, Frederick, and it is time to settle up."

Lemuel stepped alongside Frederick and pointed the rifle at the side of his head. "Forward, Pastor. Feel free to give me an excuse."

"You, Pastor Flagg"—Griffin pointed at Norman—"can stay. Continue your sermon. Ask God for protection. I'm curious to see if he listens." Griffin turned and followed Lemuel and Frederick toward the open barn doors.

Hoping Griffin had spared them all, for now, Norman straightened himself at the pulpit. He would do what he'd been instructed to do and continue the sermon, not because he was scared—although he most definitely was—but because it was the right thing to do. He had every faith in Frederick, outside, in talking sense into Griffin. It was what Frederick excelled at: talking people round.

His sudden confidence took a blow when he saw the silhouette of a third person break into the bright stream of sunlight and move quickly to come alongside the exiting men. Norman gripped hold of the pulpit. It was Nile, one of Lemuel's close friends.

The young man held a jerry can.

Norman stumbled away from the pulpit, gripped by nausea, when Nile hurled gas over the pews at the back of the church.

Gillie emerged onto the aisle and followed Griffin's

party at quite a pace for someone her age. "You wrong your people. You *wrong* the Nucleus."

Griffin turned.

"Your parents would be ashamed," Gillie said.

Griffin smiled. "And? They were always ashamed."

"You'll burn in Hell, Griffin."

"I think you'll find it is you who will burn, Gillie. And your friends." He pointed to the other twelve members of the congregation gathered near the front. "Because they chose to follow you."

"They followed their hearts."

"I guess it's all they'll have left to follow without you here." He lifted his rifle and fired.

Her head snapped back, and blood sprayed into the air. She dropped to the floor, with her head tilted back so Norman, now hyperventilating, could see the hole where her eye had been.

Griffin nodded at the congregation, who were now charging to the end of the pews. "Enjoy Heaven." He nodded at Norman. "Enjoy Hell, Pastor."

Nile, who had finished pouring, marched outside with Lemuel and Frederick.

"No!" Norman shouted before gulping back more air. He pounced from the pulpit. He landed well, but several yards down the aisle, he skidded over the puddle of blood gathering around Gillie's body and went face first onto the floor. He looked up from the ground to see Griffin drop a flaming lighter.

Several of the congregation were only a yard or so from Griffin, but the sudden whoosh of the pews erupting in flames sent them scurrying backward, shielding their faces.

"No!" Norman shouted again. "Please! Don't do this!"

But his screams of mercy were wasted on Griffin who,

aided by his two companions, managed to close the big doors, leaving the congregation to the flames.

* * *

It wasn't just the church burning before Frederick's very eyes. It was his entire world—his greatest achievement. On his knees, Frederick watched helplessly as Griffin slipped the wooden bar over four hooks across the barn door. "This is barbaric," Frederick said when he felt the muzzle of Lemuel's rifle press against the back of his head, then thought better of saying anything else.

The fire spread quickly, and the church groaned.

Griffin came over and squatted beside him. "I find it rather cleansing."

The thudding began, and the large doors pulsed.

"They're trying to get out," Frederick said. "Have mercy!"

"That's better," Griffin said, pointing up.

Frederick followed his finger to the cross on the church roof disappearing in the plumes of smoke.

"It really did spoil the view."

Frederick stared in disbelief at the throbbing barn door. The wooden bar was holding fast, but every thrust slightly widened the gap between the doors, releasing a belch of smoke. The shouting and screaming inside the barn were reaching frenzied levels, and Frederick had to raise his voice to be heard over the death cries. "If you're planning to kill me, what're you waiting for?"

"I'm waiting for you to see everything turn to dust."

Frederick could feel Griffin's eyes boring into the side of his face. The evil man wasn't interested in the burning church; he was solely interested in eradicating Frederick.

The Rotten Core

"Why do you not cry?" Griffin asked.

Frederick didn't respond. He had no reasonable response. He wouldn't cry simply because he never did. His personal emotions never seemed relevant. The picture was always much bigger than just him.

"You are harder inside than I am," Griffin said.

"You have ruined something wonderful."

The congregation, desperate in these final moments, strained against the inside of the barn doors, forcing the gap to stay open. Hands crawled from the smoky tomb. They scurried about, scratching at the wood and each other, relentless in their search for the wooden bar. From inside, the heart of the fire beat, and the glow and the heat worked its way to Frederick.

He coughed, then shielded his eyes from his heat.

"We will be wonderful again, Pastor. Ever so wonderful. Nobody will dare set foot on our land again after they learn about today. Nobody."

"Except, who is left alive to deliver your message?"

When he felt Griffin's hand on his shoulder, it dawned on Frederick the reason he was out here and not in the burning church. He was the messenger. What better way at ending the outside world's connection to the Nucleus than by using the fool who had initiated it? He would be sent scurrying down the hill, like a rat, to warn those of the atrocities that had taken place in the Nucleus.

Griffin squeezed his shoulder. "Your reward for your actions in our lands is the pitiful life I have allowed you to keep. Once your congregation down there learn what you are, what you've done, they will drive you from Mossbark. You will wander as a failure, with a God who has failed you, and soon, years from now, nobody will remember your name."

The screams had reached agonizing levels. Those inside who hadn't already succumbed to the smoke were now finding their end in heat and flames. The hands started to disappear from the gaps, until only one hung there and was crushed between the weight of the closing doors.

The fire broke through the sides of the converted barn, and flames licked one side of it. The loud creaking noise suggested the barn wouldn't hold out too much longer.

"Lemuel will escort you into town. He will take you to Sheriff Gordon Kane, where you will admit to everything."

"Is that wise? He may decide to tear you down himself."

Griffin laughed. "The sheriff understands what is best for Mossbark and what is best for the Nucleus. He will take your horror story and rebuild the fear you sought to crush. He may decide to run you out of town or dispose of you at the end of a rope in the drunk tank. Either option suits me." Griffin stood. "Lemuel, you know what to do."

"Yes, Griffin."

As Lemuel led Frederick away from the heat and fury of the burning wood, Frederick looked to the heavens, as he had done so many times before, and prayed for a solution. Several yards later, when the church collapsed behind him with a crash, he realized this time, for the first time, there really wasn't one.

13

"YOU'VE GONE ABOVE and beyond bringing me back to Brady Crossing, Logan, but I want you to get as far from this place as you can now." Jake opened the rig's door.

"I could just sit and wait here," Logan said. "For when you're fleeing for your life."

Jake climbed from the rig and looked back in, with his hand on the door. "I don't know how long I'll be. I'm not leaving Celestia here at the mercy of God-knows-what."

"Suit yourself."

"Thanks, Logan. You've been a good friend." He shut the door and patted the side of the rig.

Jake headed straight to Frederick's manse and, finding it seemingly unoccupied again, worked his way around the side of the property. He found a window, smashed it, and reached inside to unbolt the door.

Once inside, he armed himself with a kitchen knife, despite being confident he was alone. He needed to succeed here and couldn't take any risks, no matter how small. He had to return to the Nucleus, to Celestia, but simply approaching there was suicide and would not free his friend from her situation. No, this seemed his best, and only, option. Here, in the manse, there had to be some information as to how the Nucleus worked, information that would give him access some other way. And if the information wasn't within these walls, it would most certainly exist in Frederick's head; in which case, he would wait for the corrupt pastor's return.

It didn't take Jake long to check the rooms in the small bungalow. He was soon hovering in a room that had so intrigued him earlier when he'd been gazing through the front window. Again, he observed the scrolls, pressed plants, and decorated pottery that turned the living room into a museum before his gaze fell to a leatherbound book on the table. The golden letters emblazoned across the front threw his mind back to a pastor dying in his arms as his insides seeped out.

Jerimiah 29:7.

With a stone of hot dread in his stomach, Jake lifted the cover and looked at three pastors standing in front of the church in Brady Crossing. He recognized Frederick and Alton, the pastor who had died in his arms, but he didn't recognize the third one. After he turned the page, the stone of hot dread rose into his chest. "Jesus." He placed the book on the table and counted the photographs.

Nine. Nine newborns. Bloody and swaddled.

* * *

Leaning against his hood, Lemuel watched Frederick ascend the steps to the sheriff's office. He could only imagine the faces on those inside when the pastor gave a full confession, and then reported on the Nucleus's recent atrocities.

Barely twenty minutes passed before Sheriff Gordon Kane came to the door.

He stood at the top of the steps, crossed his arms, and stared over the road at Lemuel.

That's some mean look, Sheriff! Was my father wrong about you? Lemuel made a show of stepping in front of the pickup that had crushed the life from Pastor Alton Banks and stroked the ruined grill. *Isn't peace more important than justice?*

The sheriff stepped forward, uncrossed his arms, and clutched the handrail.

You really are thinking about it, aren't you? Lemuel thought about the rifle on the back seat and smiled. *Could be fun ...*

The sheriff nodded once, turned slowly, and headed back into the station.

To put Frederick to the sword ... He smiled. *And then release him or kill him, because you won't have the guts to charge him, will you? You won't bring that heat down on the Nucleus. That was your moment just then. I saw the temptation in your face, but you just don't have it in you, do you? My father was so right.*

Lemuel climbed back into his pickup. He looked out the window at the glow of the waning fire high in the hills and started the engine. He didn't turn back for the Nucleus though. That would be a waste.

Frederick's home was standing empty and unguarded. His collection was worth a small fortune, and Lemuel felt like being rewarded for a busy couple of days, as well as that beating from his father.

* * *

Frederick's book carried some weight. Jake was looking forward to throwing it onto the table in front of the ignorant sheriff. Let him just try to ignore this one!

But Gordon Kane came later.

First was Celestia.

The other day, on the walk by the old mine, she'd told him that she was on the verge of an arranged marriage—a marriage that repulsed her. Would she be forced into producing another of these bloody, swaddled newborns? Had her father, Merithew, consented to this?

He thought of his departed friend, Peter Sheenan. That man had been a tracker, an unbelievable one. He'd have found a route into the Nucleus, alright; they'd have been in and out like shadows—

"Don't move, or you'll be dead before you can look into your killer's eyes." It wasn't Frederick's voice. "Life has a funny way of figuring itself out, doesn't it? I was thinking about hooking up with you at some point."

Jake rose from the sofa, still holding the book.

"Thought I'd come in around the side of the house. And I saw someone had beat me to it."

Jake attempted to turn his head, slowly, to see who this was.

"Easy, beast. Both myself and my father are large animals too, but you, my friend, you're a whole new species. Keep still, or you'll hear this rifle before entering the big nowhere."

"Who the hell are you?"

"Let's stay focused on you, Frank. After all, you've been spending quite a lot of time with someone very dear to me."

"I haven't any idea what you're talking about."

"Celestia? You think we let her do all that wandering without keeping a close eye on her?"

"She's my friend."

"She's my wife ... or future wife. Not that it really matters too much to you. You are about to become completely irrelevant."

"Is this Lemuel?"

"Ahh, she told you about me?"

Jake detected pride. "Yes. Don't be excited. None of it was good."

"Good enough to make me a topic of conversation though."

"Repulsion made you the topic of conversation."

Lemuel laughed. "For a man staring down the barrel, you have some balls on you."

"It's not the first time I've been at the end of a gun."

"I can assure you this'll be the last."

"I've been assured of that before. Where is Celestia?"

"Where she belongs. Waiting for me to return. Her freedom has expired."

"What does her father have to say about that?"

"Nothing. He, too, expired."

So, it was the case, as was often the case, those within the kingdom had turned on their king. The place was in disarray. Celestia really was in trouble. "I guess it's true what they say, then."

"And what would that be?"

"The core really is rotten."

Lemuel snorted. "It was, but the healing has begun, outsider, and it's not something you will have the pleasure of witnessing."

Jake realized his time was up. It was now or never. "Would you pass a message on to Celestia?"

"Why would—"

"Tell her to hang tight."

"Hang tight?"

Jake spun and launched the heavy book at the man behind him. Having listened carefully to his voice, he was confident of Lemuel's location and that he was close enough for this to work. Jake fell to his knees as the heavy book crashed into Lemuel's face, and he discharged the rifle.

Having gone down fast enough to dodge the headshot, Jake now threw himself forward and looped his arms around Lemuel. Lemuel was, as he'd admitted earlier in the conversation, also a big man. It had been valuable information for Jake in determining how high to throw the book. It also ensured that Alton's murderer came down heavily onto the ground, which knocked the air clean out of him.

Jake grabbed the rifle and threw it behind him, then he scurried up Lemuel and delivered a hard blow to his face. He connected well. His knuckles burned, but the damage to Lemuel would surely be more significant. Confidently, he readied his fist for a second blow, but it seemed Lemuel was thicker skinned than he appeared and managed to deliver an uppercut to Jake's wide-open chin.

It was crushing. Everything flashed white, and he was brushed aside. *Get a grip, Jake.* He rolled, hoping to put some distance between him and his recovering assailant.

He rose onto his arms, jumped his feet inward, burpee-style, and came quickly to a stand. He glanced left at Lemuel, who was also working his way to his feet. He recalled the moment he'd first seen Lemuel behind the wheel of that pickup a second or so before he had crushed Alton Banks. He didn't recall his face being so battered. Jake doubted he'd just caused this with the book and his fist. He considered asking who'd done that to him but decided he didn't have time for it—nor did he really care that much. Instead, he glanced behind him at the rifle he'd slung behind him. Too far. So, instead, he reached for a large, decorated clay pot on a stand next to the sofa and threw it at his rising opponent.

Lemuel battered it a way with one hand, and it smashed against a coffee table.

Jake charged in, put his hands around Lemuel's throat, and squeezed.

Most men would have succumbed to Jake's strength, but Lemuel wasn't most men; he was almost as large as Jake and possibly in better condition. Lemuel grabbed Jake's wrists and pried them loose.

Jake slammed his forehead into Lemuel's nose, and the two men broke apart. Lemuel grabbed his face and moaned, while Jake stumbled backward unsteadily. The back of the sofa saved him from hitting the deck. Shaking off the dizziness, he sighted Lemuel snatching something from the wall and starting forward again.

A few yards away, Jake saw the ancient arrowhead in the his opponent's hand.

Lemuel came forward, slicing the air left and right, forcing Jake farther back.

Jake stopped at the edge of the sofa.

Lemuel flipped the arrowhead so it now pointed downward and went to hack at his face.

Jake threw himself backward onto the sofa.

The bastard's wide eyes fell to Jake's legs dangling over the sofa arm. His intentions were clear.

Jake snapped his legs back. The arrowhead sank into the arm of the chair. Jake thrust his legs out and hit home.

Lemuel stumbled backward, and Jake, riding a surge of confidence, swung his legs from the sofa and came to his feet. The remains of the broken pot crunched under his boots. He turned to charge down the dazed Lemuel, but his resilient aggressor had made another quick recovery and was coming again.

Jake ducked left and heard the arrowhead slice the air beside his ear. He sidestepped. A mistake. The coffee table took his legs. He crashed onto the other side, protecting his face from the wooden floor with his hands; however, the wind was knocked out of him.

He felt heavy pressure on the small of his back and the assailant's breath on his cheek.

"Game over."

It was a fair conclusion. This heavy idiot had him pinned to the floor. He felt the cold stone of the arrowhead against the side of his neck.

"Fortunately, the good pastor has kept this sharpened. Shouldn't be too hard to get it to slice deep. Might have to work pretty hard to get your whole head off though, as that's what I plan to do."

"Fuck you." Jake kicked his legs while trying to reach behind himself with one hand. He grabbed the coffee table leg but couldn't lift it or do anything meaningful with it.

"I'm going to present your head to Celestia as a wedding present just before consummation." Lemuel pressed one hand into the back of his head. "Now, hold still."

Jake felt the bite of the arrowhead in the side of his neck. He winced, struggled some more, and, as the pain set his nerves on fire, turned his mind to his son Frank, standing there in his Southampton FC shirt.

He stepped forward to embrace his boy.

14

ONCE THE CHURCH was ash, Griffin, Nile, and several other armed members of the Nucleus went door to door in the focus to inform everyone that there had been a change in order.

Having been instructed to do so, all the residents had kept to their homes this morning, apart from the churchgoers who'd left at sunrise. Watching dawn together with coffee was a ritual the congregation had embarked on weekly.

Griffin knew his tour around the Nucleus was not necessary. It was obvious what was happening, and who was about to challenge the state of play? No one would fancy keeping Merithew's vermin company. However, Griffin would be lying if he didn't admit to feeling proud over his elevated new status and, like any good emperor, wanted to show off his new clothes.

Scared, pale faces and erratic nods promising servitude quickly became old though. Reveling in power was one thing, but the conflict that came with a sudden challenge was unrivaled. Nothing could invigorate like that.

When it became clear that no one would be challenging today, Griffin sent away his other trusted followers, retaining only Nile's assistance. No king should be without a soldier, after all.

Nile knocked on the hut's door and stepped backward, taking the rifle strapped over his shoulder into his hands.

Unnecessary, Griffin thought, *but best to keep up appearances.*

Sumner, one of Merithew's most loyal followers, opened the door. This was one promise of servitude he would enjoy.

"Morning, Sumner," Griffin said with a nod.

"Morning, Griffin," Sumner said, nodding back.

Griffin told him about the change in order. "But I'm assuming you were aware."

"I was."

"Good."

In the background, Griffin heard a baby crying. "Is that the bastard that Merithew gifted to you?"

"Yes."

"She sounds unsettled."

Sumner averted his eyes from Griffin and nodded. "Yes."

Griffin creased his brow. "Is everything okay, Sumner?"

"Yes, of course." He nodded.

"Any reason she should be so tearful?"

"It's been a troublesome day."

"How so?"

"Sorry, wrong choice of words. Not a troublesome day, simply a day of great change."

Griffin nodded. "Nothing simple about it. But yes, I see your point. Babies are unsettled by change. I hope she settles soon for you. It must be a burden to have a child not of your making forced upon you."

Sumner nodded but didn't reply.

"Don't you think?"

"Yes," Sumner said.

"It's a shame that our community had to be weakened so. How many children did Merithew and that outsider, Frederick, inflict upon our sacred home, on *our* people?"

"I can't recall."

"Nine," Nile said.

"Nine children," Griffin said. "Some old enough now to run about in our lands and eat the food meant for our people. Do you agree?"

Sumner nodded again.

"No, really, Sumner, please. Speak your mind. What do you really think?"

"I think they will hunt, in time," Sumner said, not making eye contact with him. "And they still have Nucleus blood in their veins."

"Diluted blood," Griffin said. "An even greater tragedy."

Sumner nodded. He knew better than to continue this debate, no matter how gentle he kept his argument.

"I came today to ask if you were content with the change of order and willing to support the process of rebuilding?"

Sumner kept his eyes away from Griffin's. "Of course."

"You can understand why I ask."

"You have nothing to worry about here."

"I was never worried, Sumner." He was unable to resist a smile. "Not at all, but I must ask to speak also to your good wife, Corrie, and your son Marston."

"Of course." Sumner turned back. He called Marston and Corrie to the door.

Griffin briefly glanced at the fourteen-year-old boy and ran his eyes slowly up the full length of his mother. "Corrie, I hope you are well. I won't be long, as I know you're trying to get the bastard settled."

"Inez," Corrie said.

"I'm sorry ...?"

"Her name is Inez."

Griffin's smile broadened; she was quite the woman. He nodded. "Well, I hope you get Inez sorted soon. I was going to apologize for what my predecessor inflicted upon you and your family, but I guess, from your defensive tone, that you have made peace with that predicament?"

"Merithew inflicted a lot of wrongs on this family, but Inez was not one of them. She has not been a predicament," Corrie said.

Griffin watched Sumner look down, his face gray. *Do you realize what you have there, man?* Griffin studied Corrie and felt a stirring in his loins. *I believe we may have to continue developing this relationship at a future date ...*"I'm glad to hear it!" He glanced at the boy. "So, can I trust you, Marston, in your support for the rebuilding process?"

The boy, predictably, felt the weight of the situation and trembled. He managed a nod.

Griffin eyed Corrie. "And you, Corrie. Can we count on you as we revert to how things were? How they were always supposed to be?"

"You can."

He met Corrie's eyes. There was no fear there. The stirring intensified. Griffin turned and flashed a smile at the boy. "I hear you're a man now, Marston." He put his hand on the scared boy's shoulder. "It seems Merithew did you a service! I'll have space for men like you in putting things back together again." He smiled at Corrie. "Farewell. It won't be long before we talk again." He turned and walked away, the lightness in his step from an enjoyable interaction taking him several feet ahead of Nile.

It was this that saved his life.

He wasn't sure where the gunshot had come from, but upon hearing it, he was quick to react. He stooped, charged forward, and crouched behind a waist-high stone wall surrounding Sumner's property. He scanned for the source of attack but couldn't see one.

The groan from behind him informed him that Nile had been hit.

He saw his soldier writhing on the ground. He glanced to the doorway he'd just walked from.

Corrie and Sumner were wrestling Marston to the hallway floor.

Griffin stood and approached Nile as blood pooled all around him.

"My back ..."

"Be still," Griffin said. "Help will come." He looked up to see the soldiers he'd sent away minutes earlier charging to where he stood. Griffin grabbed Nile's rifle from the ground and looked to the doorway of the house again.

Corrie was now on her knees, cradling her crying son.

Sumner stood holding the gun Marston had shot Nile with. He kept it pointing at the floor. "Please ... I'm sorry ..." Sumner said to Griffin. "He isn't thinking clearly."

Griffin looked at Marston, inconsolable in his mother's embrace. "Why would you do that?"

"Because of Merithew!" Corrie said, glaring at him. "Because of what that monster made the boy do."

Between the wails of Inez and Marston, it was difficult to tell what anyone was saying, so Griffin moved closer. "So, why blame me?"

Marston was trying to say something, but he was spluttering, and his words were incomprehensible.

"Because he's confused," Corrie said.

"Shush!" Griffin pressed a finger to his lips. "I'm listening to the boy."

"I ... love ... her," Marston said.

Griffin smiled.

"Love ... her."

"I wasn't aware that you formed a relationship with her, Marston," Griffin said.

"He's a child," Corrie said. "Like I said, he's confused."

"But they didn't even talk?"

Corrie looked at her son, then up at Griffin. "No, they didn't."

Griffin's smile broadened. "This is priceless. He raped a sleeping girl, fell in love with her, and then blames me! I have seen it all now."

Marston turned and glared at Griffin. His eyes were red and puffy. "You'll hurt her."

"Not hurt her, no. Someone did a good job of that long before I became involved. However, I did consent to her end. She knew too much because of my predecessor, and so it was better for all concerned that—"

Marston raged, trying to tear from his mother's arms, but she held tight.

Sumner knelt to assist, pressing his hands firmly into his boy's chest to try to steady him.

"He's really got it bad," Griffin said and smiled.

"He's dead," one of Griffin's men said behind him. "Nile's dead."

Griffin held up his hand to silence those behind him and beheld the broken family.

Sumner looked up at him. "Please, Griffin. Do whatever you want to me. *Take* whatever you want from me, but do not harm my son. He's sick. He isn't thinking clearly."

"Oh, I see that. But don't worry; I don't intend to harm Marston. We'll need soldiers like him in the days ahead. Consider this his audition, and he's passed for sure! The last thing I plan to do is further *deplete* Nucleus blood!" Griffin took a deep breath and looked around, clucking his tongue. "However, I will take something now, for the inconvenience."

"Of course," Sumner said. "What can I give you?"

Griffin smiled and raised an eyebrow. He paused to listen to Inez crying in the background. He watched, with some pleasure, as Sumner's eyes widened.

The timid man shook his head. "Really? No!" He looked at Corrie. "I love her. She's everything to me."

"Not your wife, Sumner!" Griffin grunted. "What do you take me for? I mean the crying bastard in there. Let me take her off your hands."

Corrie rose from her broken son. "No. You leave her alone."

She really was something! "It's for the best, Corrie."

"*Why?* You don't want her. You're horrified by her existence!"

"You will thank me in time."

"I won't. Because you're not taking her!"

"I have asked nicely, but now I really must insist."

"You can't have her." Corrie moved forward, stepping over her son to fill the doorway.

"Corrie," Sumner said, placing his hand on her shoulder from behind, "be reasonable—"

"Get off me." She pulled her shoulder away. "You spineless fool. This is your fault. Maybe if you hadn't been so keen to please Merithew so much, we wouldn't be in the situation."

Spineless! How appropriate the words!

"But we are in this situation," Corrie said, refocusing on Griffin. "And we have made the best of it, and you are not taking Inez. I love my child."

Griffin looked between the faces of the distraught couple. "That is the cost for the attempt on my life. Would rather it was Marston?"

She shook her head. "I will die before you take them."

"There is no need to be so dramatic, Corrie."

She narrowed her eyes.

"But you must see how I cannot walk away now," Griffin said. "How can you expect me to undermine myself at the start of this new order?"

Sumner took her shoulder again. "We have no choice. We need to think of Marston—"

"Get the fuck off me," she said, trying to tear her arm away again. This time, she failed. Sumner was using some strength.

Sumner, finally showing some balls!

Sumner threw down the gun he'd taken from his son and tightly wrapped his arms around Corrie. "I'm sorry ... Corrie ..."

She struggled and writhed in her husband's grip. She kicked backward against his shins, but he held firm. Her betrayer yanked her out of the way and dragged her to where the son lay, distressed, in a heap.

"Do what you have to," Sumner managed to say while fighting his wife's struggle.

"Of course," Griffin said, stepping over the threshold. As he passed, the new leader glanced at the restrained woman he was coming to admire more with every passing second. Not only would she be useful to the Nucleus in the days ahead, but she'd be useful to him too.

Saliva frothed at the corner of her mouth as she shouted. If anything, this made her more attractive.

He approached the cot.

Corrie's loud distress had unsettled Inez further.

Griffin put his hand to the baby's scrunched face and placed his thumb in her toothless mouth.

She started to suckle and immediately settled.

He turned his head to wink at the distressed woman and the man destroying his marriage to protect his firstborn, Marston. "I have a few tricks up my sleeve. Believe it or not, Lemuel was a troubled young soul." He turned back and murmured, "Still is, truth be known." He scooped up the settling child. "Shh ... shh ..." He leaned forward and kissed Inez's forehead. "You may not be your mother's natural child, but you sure got that same go-get-'em look about you."

Corrie was no longer screaming but sagging in her husband's arms.

"I'm just putty in their hands," Griffin said with a second wink. While cradling Inez, who still sucked hard on one of his thumbs, Griffin walked to the front door. "Shh ... little one." At the door, he turned for one last look at the family he'd just torn to pieces. "The future I am offering you is greater than this moment. Remember that over the coming days. We will be strong again, and you will love me, as I love you, when everything is cleansed. Come on, little one."

He stepped outside, plucking his thumb from Inez's mouth, reached behind himself and closed the front door behind him. He shook his head at Nile's prone body, then waved Sullivan over. "Take Inez, Sullivan."

Sullivan wasn't the brightest among the Nucleus on

account of a fall from a tree in his childhood, but he was a reliable servant and tended to do most things without question. However, being handed a baby wasn't most things, and so did prompt him to ask a rather obvious question. "What do you want me to do with it?"

"Her," Griffin said with a smile. "*Her*. I was admonished back there for not showing the proper respect, and now that I have met the little princess, I acknowledge why. She's beautiful, yes?"

"Yes," Sullivan said, returning the smile. After a moment, he quizzically creased his brow again. "So, what do you want me to do with her, then?"

Griffin put a hand on his shoulder. "First, I want you to bash in her brains. Then I want you to round up the other eight half-breeds in the Nucleus and bash in their brains too."

Sullivan gulped.

"Do you understand, Sullivan?"

He opened his mouth to agree but couldn't produce the words, so he nodded instead.

"And after you do that, burn all the bodies by the old church. Then, with the past well and truly behind us, we can start rebuilding this place anew."

15

Thump.

The bite of the arrowhead in Jake's neck ceased.

Thump.

The weight was lifted from his back.

Thud.

Jake flipped over.

Logan stood above Lemuel's quivering body, holding the large shell of a tortoise in both hands.

Lemuel moaned.

Logan lifted the shell above his head.

Thump.

Lemuel emitted another pained whine.

Thump-thump-thump.

Out of breath, Logan hobbled to the sofa and collapsed onto it with the tortoise shell on his lap.

"That's ... inventive," Jake said.

After Logan had caught his breath, he said, "The heaviest thing I could find. You're bleeding."

Jake touched his neck. It stung. He looked at his red fingertips. "I'll be ... fine." He spied Lemuel's twitching body. "I got off much better ... than he did." Jake rose to his feet, also catching his breath. "He was about to get married ... You're a homewrecker."

"That's Lemuel?"

Jake nodded.

"I suddenly feel less guilty. I'm sure your friend Celestia will be devastated."

"Devastated she wasn't here to see it ... Logan! You're supposed to be miles away by now!"

Logan threw the shell to one side. "Is that your way of saying thank you?"

"You followed me."

"Luckily, I did."

"Sneaky."

"It's been said before."

Jake brushed the murder weapon onto the floor and sat beside Logan. "Maybe you could be quite useful."

Logan pointed at the body. "What? That not enough for you?"

"I have high standards."

"So, what next, then?"

"We wait for our host to get home."

"Pastor Deering?"

"Yes. He knows where Celestia is."

"We're going to end up back there, aren't we?"

"Yes."

"It's suicide."

"I just said my standards were high."

* * *

The Rotten Core

Judging by the muted response from Pastor Frederick Deering when he found his visitors in his living room—one of whom was dead—Jake assumed this man had been broken already. Hopefully that would make it all the easier for Jake to get what he needed: Celestia's whereabouts.

Frederick stood at the doorway to his lounge, surveying the mess. His gaze fell upon Lemuel's body on the floor, but he only looked visibly shocked when he saw the remains of the decorated pot beside the coffee table and the bloody tortoise shell lying beside it. He stumbled forward, and the ashen man slipped to his knees to pick up a piece of the pot. He turned it around to look at it from all sides. Then he cast it aside and ran his fingers over the bloody scuta on the tortoise shell.

Jake walked toward the kneeling man with Lemuel's rifle ready in his hands. He stopped a few yards from the distressed pastor. After everything he'd discovered, after what he'd seen in that book, Jake felt compelled to use the rifle. It was the only certain way to prevent Pastor Frederick Deering inflicting anymore pain on this world.

But the mystery surrounding Celestia steadied his hand.

Jake watched the pathetic man rummage through his broken ornaments. "They're things, Frederick. They're not people."

"They mean a lot to me," Frederick said.

"If people had meant as much to you as these useless objects, then maybe it wouldn't have come to this."

Frederick looked up. Last time, Jake had thought he'd looked grotesquely young for his age, like many a man who'd sold their souls to the Devil, but now he looked his age, and then some. "I love people."

"Your wife might have something to say about that if she was still alive, the children she took with her too. The priest from Redland doesn't seem to have good memories of you either."

"I adored Charlotte." A tear appeared in the corner of Frederick's eye. "But she never understood. *They* never understood."

"Add me to that list." Jake pointed to the leatherbound book on the floor with the end of his rifle. "That made for tragic reading."

"There is joy in those pages too."

"Whatever, Frederick. What is ironic is that great work saved my life, leaving me on the verge of ending yours."

"My life is over already. You are too late to claim that as your victory."

"Convince me of that."

"Surely that dead monster on the floor told you?"

"Monster?" Jake snorted. "Pot calling the kettle black, surely?"

"The world is full of monsters," Logan said from the sofa. "And Hell too. You'll find that out soon enough, Pastor."

"I will be judged on what I tried to achieve."

Jake lifted his boot and pushed Frederick backward.

He didn't fight and simply slumped back.

"What did you do with the mothers of those children in that book?" Jake said. "Did you take them to the Nucleus?"

"You wouldn't understand—"

"*Did you kill them?*"

"Throughout the history of man, all of our greatest achievements were built on the sacrifices of others—"

Jake leaned forward and struck him in the stomach with

the butt of the rifle. "I've heard enough." He paused to allow the winded pastor to catch his breath. "Now tell me what is going on in the Nucleus."

"Griffin overthrew Merithew." He pointed at Lemuel's body. "*That* man's father. Do you know that makes you a dead man walking?"

Jake grunted. "I've been a dead man walking for as long as I can remember. Now, before I use the butt of this rifle again, tell me what happened to Celestia."

Frederick sat upright and stared at his legs. "She's in the dwelling."

"The dwelling?"

"The heart of the Nucleus. It's where their founding ancestor is kept. His bones, at least. There are also rats. Disgusting feral things that have a taste for our blood. They were savages. *Are* savages. I was offering them salvation. I was bringing them into the fold, building their community—"

Jake struck him on the shoulder this time.

He slumped back, gripping his shoulder.

"Building their community by destroying other communities, very noble," Jake said. "Is Celestia safe?"

"She's captive, for now." He winced in pain and clutched his shoulder tighter. "She was supposed to marry Lemuel ... Whether she lives depends on whether Griffin can find another use for her."

"We haven't much time, then. You're going to take us up there, Frederick. To the Nucleus."

Frederick looked up with widened eyes and laughed. "You're insane. The man just burned thirteen people alive in my church. There are three of us against a community full of terrified people."

"Consider it your atonement."

"I'm exhausted and am currently being beaten to death. You aren't looking much better yourself with that neck wound, and as for the fat man on the sofa—"

"Hey!" Logan said, rising.

"That man just beat someone to death with a turtle shell," Jake said. "You may want to watch your choice of words."

"None of it matters," Frederick spat. "We'll be dead soon enough."

"Maybe if we go in the front way. I was thinking of skipping that prepubescent guard on the gate and going through the woods, straight for that dwelling you mentioned."

"Those woods are full of bear traps!"

"Do you know the route?"

Frederick sighed.

"Do you know the route?"

Frederick shook his head. "I've done it once before ... Not sure I'm confident ... There's a system, yes."

"Good. You've just bought yourself some more time, Pastor Deering. Now listen carefully, both of you. I have an idea."

* * *

All around the focus, families screamed as Griffin and his crew took the young half-breeds from their homes.

Griffin didn't fear any repercussions from his decision. Those eight families were in the minority. All the others, including those who had been wavering before, would now unequivocally serve him. Fear was a persuasive force.

Griffin was gazing at the smoldering church, feeling accomplished, when he heard gunfire and realized, with a

The Rotten Core

smile, that the minority objecting to him had just dwindled further. He turned to look at Sullivan, who stood a few yards ahead of him. He held his rifle backward so the butt pointed downward at the swaddled baby on the ground.

Inez cried.

Sullivan also cried.

Griffin wasn't concerned. If anything, the man's struggle was a good thing. Eventually, fear and a desire for self-preservation would break through his conscience, and he would strike. Then Sullivan would be different. He would be prepared for anything—to *do* anything. And when the lands in which they lived *required* such change, he would need men who could act without remorse.

More gunfire.

The screaming stopped.

Griffin smiled. The revolt was over. Those families who remained would appreciate the situation now. To survive, they must relinquish the children gifted to them.

From the focus, he watched his loyal soldiers lead the children toward him at gunpoint. They were of varying ages. Most toddled, while the soldiers held the ones who were too young to walk. He nodded to his tearful soldier. "Set the example, Sullivan."

Sullivan drew back the rifle.

Inez wailed harder.

Sullivan's face twisted as he fought his conscience. His hands shook. "I ... I ... I ..."

"Sullivan," Griffin said, loud enough to be audible over Inez's distress. "Be part of making the Nucleus whole again. Be part of our history."

Sullivan's red eyes met Griffin. He nodded and inched back the rifle a little more—

The sound of a loud explosion ripped through the

Nucleus.

Griffin stared toward the entrance and, beyond that, the black smoke rising thickly in the air.

16

GRIFFIN LEFT SULLIVAN and Thaxter to watch Inez and the other half-breeds at gunpoint. He wanted them kept alive until he returned; every man and woman in the Nucleus must bear witness to the eradication of Merithew's legacy. Of course, he didn't like to leave a volatile situation like this, but what choice did he have? The Nucleus was under attack, and, as leader, he was dutybound to lead its defense.

Speaking to Lyman through the walkie-talkie, he charged down the dirt path with his seven armed companions in tow.

"Lemuel was returning in his pickup truck with Frederick Deering's Land Rover behind," Lyman said. "About halfway up the hillside, on Netow's bend, where the rocks reach highest, the vehicles disappeared from view. Then ... well ... the explosion."

Griffin's blood ran cold. "Whose vehicle?"

"I don't know. No one has emerged from Netow since the explosion."

Had the decision to allow Frederick to live cost him so dearly?

"Fuck!"

When Griffin reached the parking lot near the entrance, he faced followers. "We'll go by vehicle. Whatever has happened, has happened behind the rocks at Netow's bend."

Everyone nodded. As the group clambered in and started up two pickups, Griffin radioed ahead to Lyman to request the raising of the arm so they didn't have to slow at the entrance.

Griffin rode shotgun in the front pickup, with a rifle across his lap, wondering what awaited them in the smoke cloud ahead.

After Logan had set fire to the rag poking from Lemuel's fuel tank, he dove into the passenger seat of Frederick Deering's Land Rover. When the pickup exploded, he shielded his eyes from the bright glow and jumped out of his skin when some smoking debris landed with a loud thump on Frederick's hood.

"Told you we weren't far enough away," Albert Hardy said from the driver's seat.

Logan pointed out of the window at the rocks. "Any farther back and they'd have seen us. We don't want to take any chances. They may take shots at us. Plus, we want them racing down here, hoping it wasn't Lemuel's vehicle in flames."

The elderly shopkeeper nodded forward at the burning pickup. "They're in for a disappointment."

"Thanks for helping us, Albert. Without you, we wouldn't have had any way of driving Lemuel here."

"Not much breath left in these old bones, son. Might as well offer it to a worthy cause."

"It'll work. Frank seems like a man who gets things done."

"Maybe. He's definitely like an itch smack bang in the center of your back. Anyway, we need to get this hunk of metal turned around; we're about to go on the ride of our lives."

* * *

Griffin hit the dash. "Stop!" He jumped from the breaking pickup and, shielding his eyes from the bright glare of the flames, strode toward the wreckage. The fire was hungry and rapidly consuming the vehicle, but he could discern the dark shape of someone in the passenger seat. *"Lemuel?"* He jogged toward the fireball and felt an intense heat burning his skin. *"Lemuel!"* He chanced another step and reared back in agony.

Arms locked around his waist and yanked him backward.

"It's too late, Griffin."

He turned to look at Angelita, the broad woman who had grabbed him. He put his hands on his head and allowed himself only a couple seconds of grief before dropping his arms. He turned toward the wreckage and stared at the vehicle behind. *Frederick.*

The vehicle began to drive away.

He turned back to Angelita. "Get after him. Bring him back here."

"Yes, Griffin," Angelita said and ran to the first pickup.

"Alive! It is me, and only me, who gets to skin him!"

She held her hand in the air to signal she'd heard him.

"Walker ..." Griffin pointed to one of his older men, with an abundance of white hair, both facially and on his head. "You go too."

"Yes, Griffin," Walker said.

As he watched Angelita steer the pickup around his son's fiery grave and begin its chase down the hillside, Griffin gritted his teeth. He wanted to be in that pickup. He wanted to be there when they finally caught up to that worthless man who had started the rot in the Nucleus. He desperately wanted to carve the man into pieces as he begged for mercy. But that joy would have to wait, because one thing was clear here.

Crystal clear.

This had been a diversion. Someone had done this to draw his attention from the Nucleus.

He turned to his five remaining companions. "We need to get back to the focus. As quickly as we can."

* * *

Frederick had claimed it would take at least an hour to wade through the trees and undergrowth that peppered the side of the hill, so Jake had instructed Logan to wait at least this long before springing the surprise. After thirty minutes, the two men reached a break in the trees.

Jake gazed at the summit, checked his watch, and shook his head in despair. "We need to speed up."

"There are traps everywhere."

"You know the route."

"Roughly! I know the system they use, but I still have to keep a close eye on where I stand."

"If anything happens to Celestia, you'll be the first to die. Maybe that will put a spring in your step?"

It did.

Fifty minutes into their journey, the ground leveled out, and Jake noticed wooden huts in the distance. He fought the impulse to bypass Frederick and accelerate to close the gap. When the pastor turned back with a pale face and said, "It gets worse. Traps are everywhere around here," he realized he'd been wise to suppress that urge.

"How the hell do these people hunt?" Jake asked.

"Carefully."

Jake looked down as he followed Frederick and saw large bear traps scattered everywhere. He shuddered at the thought of those yawning metal jaws snapping shut on his leg. He checked his watch again and whispered in Frederick's ear, "We have ten minutes."

"Okay," Frederick hissed.

Jake had to admit Frederick's ability to weave a path through such an obstacle-ridden space was impressive, but the man remained a leech who had sucked on the blood of others to satisfy his needs, so he offered no praise.

Ahead, Jake heard a loud commotion in the Nucleus. It was hard to decipher exactly what was being screamed and shouted.

"What's happening?"

"Griffin started his reign by burning people alive. Did you think it would get any better?"

"Well, surely he needs people to build a community?"

"He would kill them all and start it again with just himself if that's what it took."

Jake grunted. "You two are alike."

"Nothing alike. I am rational. Griffin is anything but."

Before Jake could call out Frederick's nonsense, the pickup exploded in the distance.

Despite it being expected, Frederick startled, and Jake was forced to steady him, for fear he might stumble into a trap.

"I hope your plan works," Frederick said. "This place was already on fire, but you just turned it into a furnace."

"Shut up. Where's the dwelling?"

Frederick pointed to the left. "We are weaving toward it. The traps break away on our left in a few yards, and we can pick a better route. If we continue the way we are going, we'll just stroll straight into the focus, the main residential area. Not a good idea."

"So, get weaving, then."

Frederick did.

For about another five minutes, Frederick inched his way left with Jake close behind. The metal teeth reached upward at them from all angles. The commotion in the focus had ended, and silence wound its way toward them through the trees. Jake hoped Griffin and his soldiers would be journeying toward the source of the explosion.

"Can you see it?" Frederick asked. Where the trees ended, several dozen yards ahead, was a large wooden hut. "The heart of the Nucleus—"

A loud snapping sound reverberated, and the pastor wailed and toppled.

Jake wrapped his hand around the man's mouth to stifle his scream, but this caused him to lose his balance too. They went down together.

On the ground, Jake spied Frederick's leg and grimaced. The remains of his ankle bone were keeping the teeth from closing. If Jake stayed here, stifling the injured man's scream, he would be a sitting duck if anyone came to investigate the commotion. If he tried to drag Frederick to safety, he risked his own life by stumbling on another of the bear trap. And for what reason? He knew where the dwelling was now. Celestia, if he found her, would be able to find the path down.

He put Frederick in a headlock and broke his neck.

17

WHEN SHERIFF GORDON Kane was requested at his front desk, he threw down his divorce papers and rose to his feet.

Twenty-five years of marriage, countless affairs, which he'd forgiven her for, and now, on the cusp of his twilight years, his pension and his plans for a holiday home were on the rocks. She'd suck him dry, and she'd be off with her lovers, her *countless* lovers, enjoying a retirement on him.

He looked at his *I love New York* mug, which he'd attempted, poorly, to glue back together. It was him that had been the mug. And now, inevitably, it was him that had been smashed. He grabbed the mug and, as he left the room, dropped it into the bin.

Scott and his twin brother, Brad, were the only other deputies on duty with him today. He found them alongside the desk sergeant, who'd called through for him. Two other visitors occupied the waiting room: Albert and the truck driver who had been sitting with Frank Yorke the other night in The Crown.

He addressed his officers. "Why are they here?"

"Something's wrong," Brad said. Apart from the ponytail, Brad, Scott's identical twin, was a mirror image in every way, down to his hot-headed temper.

"It's time to make a choice, Gordon," Albert said.

He tutted and shook his head. "That's *Sheriff*, Albert."

"I'm sorry, Sheriff. Old habits die hard."

Gordon smiled while looking at his officers rather than the visitors. "It's been a long time since we were on the playground, old man."

"It's been a long time since we were friends."

Gordon sneered at Albert. "That was your choice. Yours. Not mine."

Albert narrowed his eyes. "You made decisions I couldn't stand by and watch."

"What? Like keep this town safe? Peaceful?"

"Funny thing is, Sheriff, it's never seemed that way to me."

"You had opportunities to be part of it. You opted out—"

"Sorry to interrupt, boss, but they're outside."

"Who are?" Gordon asked Scott.

"The Nucleus."

Gordon drew back, confused, shook his head, and snorted. "Aw, come on—"

"Boss," Scott said, "they're outside. Two of them."

"Why?" Gordon narrowed his eyes.

"These two"—Scott pointed at Albert and the truck driver—"wound them up somehow."

"Like I said, Sheriff, you have a choice to make," Albert said.

Gordon looked from one face to the next. He was already full of adrenaline from the divorce papers, but this unfolding situation now had him in a real spin. "What bullshit is this?" He turned to the entrance and went outside.

You got to be shitting me. He didn't know the names of the two people at the bottom of the steps, but he recognized them alright, skulking around Brady Crossing for supplies. They *were* Nucleus.

And both carried rifles.

The white-haired man nodded a greeting, while the woman with a shaved head made a show of cracking her rifle to check if it was loaded.

Shit. Gordon turned and went into the station. He closed the door behind him. "Jesus," he said to Albert. "What the hell is happening here?"

With his hand still clutching the handle of the door while his entire body grew cold, Gordon listened to the story of how Merithew had fallen to Griffin. He also heard how Frederick and Frank Yorke had gone into the hills to get Celestia.

"This is fucking madness!"

"Agreed." Albert nodded. "However, Frank has chosen to do what's right."

"He will die up there, you simpletons!"

The truck driver smiled. "You don't know Frank all that well."

"I know him alright. I know *all* of you. You are all fucking insane. Do you not understand who they are? *What* they are?"

"Of course." Albert stepped forward and put a hand on Gordon's shoulder. "But it's too late now. The wolves are at your door."

Gordon brushed off Albert's hand. "Why, though? What do they want?"

"They want to know why Logan and myself delivered Lemuel's corpse to Griffin."

"Did you kill him?"

"No," Logan said. "That was Frederick."

"So, go and tell them that!"

"Why? It won't matter," Albert said. "They won't leave without us, and when we're up there, we aren't coming back. So everything is on your shoulders now, Gordon. Are you going to send us to our deaths?"

"You talk nonsense, Albert." Gordon turned and walked out again.

The woman was still looking down at her rifle. "Are they ready?"

Gordon steadied himself against the handrail at the top of the steps. "You're looking for Frederick. These men are not important to you."

The man shrugged. "They delivered something to us on our lands, so they are now obligated to return to answer questions about that delivery."

"They didn't kill Lemuel," Gordon said. "That will have to be enough for you."

The two visitors from the Nucleus stared long and hard at Gordon. They then smiled at each other.

"Sheriff, you understand the way things are," the man said. "Please send them down. There is nothing to be concerned about. If they're innocent, they'll not be harmed."

"If I let you take them up there"—he nodded into the hills—"we'll never see them again."

"You have a minute, Sheriff. Remember, we know you, and you know us. It's a relationship worth preserving, don't you think?"

Gordon went back in, put his hands on his desk, and stared down. He shook his head from side to side. "Fuck ... fuck ... *fuck*!" He turned back to face Scott and Brad. "What do you think?"

They shrugged at each other.

"Come on, boys! You are always so goddamned outspoken. When I actually need an opinion, where the hell is it?"

They both looked away.

"Give me your gun, Scott."

Scott, trembling, unholstered his service weapon and handed it to the sheriff.

Gordon tutted. "Been years since I've needed to use one of these ... *years,* darn it!" He felt Albert's hand on his shoulder again. Gordon brushed it off. "Don't patronize me, Albert. How is this right? I'm about to destroy the foundations of this community."

"It won't take much," Albert said. "This community is built on quicksand."

"Fuck this," Gordon said, checking the gun was loaded. "Who needs reelection anyway? I'm too old for this bullshit. Plus, my wife wants a divorce!"

"Sorry to hear that, Sheriff," Albert said.

"Don't be. She's a bitch. Well, I guess if I start a war, I can hide in a trailer somewhere with some old crow." He opened the door, looked down at the two soldiers from the Nucleus, sighed, shook his head, and gripped the handrail again. He eyed the burning in the distance. "The Nucleus on fire?"

"Lemuel's vehicle. The other fire is the church."

"Jesus." Gordon laughed. "I can't believe the pastor gave you a church! Of all the things!"

"The pastor will pay," the man said.

"I don't doubt it."

"Now, we want what we came for," the woman said.

"Well, thing is, you may be undergoing great change in the Nucleus, and I dig that. That's your prerogative. The place could do with a revamp, I'm sure. However, down here, in Brady Crossing, Mossbark, we're undergoing changes of our own."

"What're you talking about?" the woman asked, taking a step up the stairs.

"I'm saying things are different now. We're not doing what you say. So, you can leave, because they're not coming out."

The woman looked at the man, snorted, and started up the steps proper. "You are not what you think you are, Sheriff!"

The sheriff aimed the gun at the woman coming toward him. "I'm asking you to turn around, drive back up the hill, and ...."

"And what, Sheriff?" The woman's eyes narrowed.

"And go fuck yourselves."

The woman paused, considered, then started quicker up the steps. She hadn't even lifted her own rifle. She did not fear his gun. God, his weak reputation really preceded him!

Gordon said, "We're really going to do this, then?"

The woman, two steps from him, looked up and smiled. "Do what? Start a war? Shoot, or move out of my way!"

Gordon shook his head.

"Do you know how many of us live in the hills, you pathetic man?"

"If what Albert has just said is to be believed, you are struggling for people. That's why you welcomed the pastor in and began some breeding program. I think after Griffin has had his way, numbers will be even further down."

"Have you ever killed anyone?" She began to raise her rifle.

The sheriff shot her in the head, and she fell backward down the steps, wiping out the man at the bottom.

"There's a first time for everything."

At that point, Brad flanked him, wielding his weapon also. They waited for the white-haired man from the Nucleus to wiggle free of the dead woman.

He stood and surveyed the body of his companion. His gaze moved to the rifle he'd dropped when he'd fallen.

Feeling more alive than he'd felt in as long as he could remember, Gordon asked, "What's it going to be, intruder?"

The man held up his hands. "I'll go."

"No, you won't," the sheriff said and smiled. "You're under arrest."

Fuck the Nucleus, he thought. *And fuck my wife.*

18

WHILE BABYSITTING THE maligned children of the Nucleus, Thaxton heard the wail from the old woods.

"What's that?" Sullivan asked.

"Someone's just stepped on a trap."

"Shit," Sullivan said.

Are you surprised? Merithew had been the glue keeping this place together. And, sure enough, merely hours after his demise, the world was already burning around them.

Thaxton tasted bile when he thought of his role in this new burning world. As a medicine man who understood the human body, he'd been forced to drag his old friend's corpse from the dwelling and dismember him. Of course, he'd worked slowly and meticulously, showing Merithew the same respect he'd afforded him in life. Due to the shit hitting the fan, he'd not had chance to dispose of him yet. He planned to take him to the patch of ground where his own parents were buried, and there, he would give him a respectful send off. On the quiet, of course, because he now belonged to Griffin's regime. He couldn't fight the order of things. The Nucleus and the preservation of its beating heart surmounted everything. The elders had voted for change. He would honor that. And if Griffin asked him to shoot these so-called half-breeds when he returned, with tears in his eyes and shame in his soul, he would have to comply.

"I'll stay," Thaxton said, "and watch the children. You go."

Sullivan nodded and turned. What Sullivan lacked in mental capacity, he made up for in loyalty and compassion. He too would follow orders, despite the gentleness of his heart.

What a sorry situation this is, Thaxton thought, refocusing on all those innocent children. *What a sorry situation indeed.*

* * *

Jake didn't expect to get to the next tree with his leg intact, but with Celestia in danger, he let the wave of adrenaline take him. He skipped around several bear traps and installed himself behind an old oak. He held the rifle vertically against his chest so if anyone did come to investigate Frederick's wail, the muzzle wouldn't be poking from behind the tree.

"Anyone there?" a man's voice called.

Jake chewed his lip and tightened his grip on his rifle.

"You! Sit up, or I'll shoot!" He'd spotted Frederick.

You think that if he was alive or conscious, he'd be lying still with his ankle being mangled by your barbaric trap?

"Now!"

Clearly, you do.

Jake heard the crunching of undergrowth as the man

took his investigation further into the forest. Realizing his palms were sweating, he loosened his grip on the rifle, slightly, but kept his body tense, ready to spring.

"Pastor Deering?" More crunching. "Pastor, is that you?"

Jake heard a slap. "Pastor?"

Another slap.

Jake shook his head. *He isn't waking up, dummy.* He held his breath. He didn't wish to flip around this tree and shoot this man. Discharging his rifle would undoubtably bring more men like this. This man *needed* to think Frederick had come alone, that the shock of having his foot almost cleaved off had stopped his heart. Let him report that to his men. Hopefully, they were too preoccupied with other matters to retrieve the body.

Jake felt something on his foot, and he looked down. A cold stone of fear dropped in his stomach.

A rat.

He sucked in his lips to prevent himself from gasping.

The disgusting, long-tailed rodent scurried back and forth around his foot and over the toe cap of his boot and would pause intermittently to sniff at his ankles.

He kicked out.

The rat rolled backward and then scurried away.

"You're dead, ain't you, Pastor?" the man said.

Jesus, finally! Now go!

The rat returned, boldly mounting Jake's left boot to continue its investigation.

Didn't I make myself clear enough?

Jake kicked again.

The rat spun through the air and landed on a patch of leaves, twisting and squirming with its repulsive little legs thrashing at the air.

"Anyone else there?" the man said.

Shit! Now look what you've done, you little bastard!

The rat righted itself and turned to face him.

You really are one stubborn, grotesque thing.

The rat stood on its hindlegs, sniffed the air, and bared its jagged teeth.

Jake could hear the man crunching around in the undergrowth behind the tree.

Now I'll have to deal with both of you—

The rat charged. It mounted Jake's boot, but not for his ankle this time. It scurried up his leg instead. The claws penetrated the denim of his jeans and scratched his legs. Before Jake knew it, the rodent was clinging to the denim around his groin. He tried to brush it away with his rifle, but the little beast was wily and swerved his attempts.

"*Is there someone there?*" The voice was directly behind the tree.

He was fucked now. If he shot at him, he would draw more unwelcomed faces, and, with him dead beside Frederick, Celestia would be left to the mercy of Griffin and the Nucleus.

The rat clung to the front of his jacket.

What the hell are you trying to do? Again, he tried to hit it away. This time, he caught the rat, but its grip held. He saw the muzzle of a rifle on his right, so Jake darted around the lefthand side of the tree, quickly raising his rifle so he could place his own muzzle to the back of the man's head. "Drop the rifle. Now." He kept his voice low.

The man dropped his rifle, while Jake felt the rat move again.

He gulped when he felt it squirming around his neck, the hair bristling against his Adam's apple and the long tail clipping the underneath of the chin. Jake took his hand from the rifle's trigger and seized the rat.

The beast writhed as he yanked it free from his neck.

He drew his hand back to throw it, but the rat squirmed free.

It scurried down his arm, then the length of the rifle, and onto the back of the man's head.

Yelling, the man tried to grab the animal scavenging around in his hair.

Shit. Jake's cover was well and truly broken.

Jake watched the rat evade the man's hands. It lunged forward and sank its teeth into one of his fingers. The man yanked his hand away, and Jake expected the rat to go with it. It didn't. It stayed there with a chunk of flesh in its teeth.

What the hell? Jake backed away.

Overwhelmed as he was with panic, the man's hands came again, desperate to get the rat off his head. He started to spin and stagger away, rubbing at his hair, as if he were cleaning it rather than trying to stop a feral creature burrowing—

Snap!

With his foot in a trap and his hands still in his hair, the man fell backward.

Snap!

The man took some shallow ragged breaths, twitched for a few seconds, then went still.

Jake stepped over him and glanced down. He quickly looked away. But it was too late. He would never unsee that image. The jaws of the trap had pinned the rat to the side of his head, crushed his skull and burst his eyes.

* * *

Knowing his cover was broken and that if he didn't move fast, he would become the third body in this forest, Jake threw caution to the wind. He hurdled three traps and chanced the undergrowth that lined the edge of the forest. As he crunched through it, he kept expecting to hear that horrendous snapping sound again. He thought of Frederick's foot hanging on by threads of muscle and bone.

He was so desperate to clear the forest that he misjudged his speed and collided into the side of the dwelling with a thud. Recovering, he staggered around to the front.

He didn't know whether it was the invincibility he felt from surviving that ordeal in the forest or just his desperation to reach Celestia, but he thrust open the door with little caution.

The stench of death flowed from the dwelling, and his bravado was suddenly replaced with the cold, hard realization he may just be too late.

19

FOR THE FIRST time in his life, Thaxton welcomed the sight of the malevolent Griffin. Barely a minute had passed since Thaxton had heard more yelling from the forest. This time, he feared it'd been Sullivan. Thaxton wasn't scared, but he knew chasing off alone into a battle with an unknown enemy was a poor option, especially following Griffin's explicit instructions to guard the children.

Thaxton knew Griffin as a cold man. He behaved cruelly without a flicker of remorse and met any challenge, no matter how dangerous, without a quiver of nerves. How peculiar then, Thaxton thought, that Griffin's eyes were currently darting erratically, and his facial muscles were twitching.

However, he didn't have the time or the courage to ask Griffin what had shattered his icy, arrogant veneer. "Griffin, I think we may be under attack."

"*Where?*"

Thaxton pointed toward the forest by the dwelling.

"Two screams. One, I think was Sullivan, who was investigating the first."

Griffin's eyes continued to dart, but he remained rooted to the spot.

Here was a man who, throughout his existence, had wielded an ax at the merest sniff of a threat. He supposed it was more statesmanlike to consider options before acting, but Thaxton didn't buy this as the reason Griffin was stalling.

"It was a distraction," Griffin said.

"Sorry?" Thaxton said.

"The explosion. They killed my son."

"I'm sorry, Griffin."

"Come with me to the forest." Griffin turned to his five remaining soldiers. "The rest of you, watch the half-breeds, and if anybody moves from their homes, shoot them. Someone within the Nucleus may be working against us. How else could these intruders find a way through our defenses?"

* * *

The dwelling looked like it had been home to a massacre. A trail of blood led from the entrance to a covered rectangular structure at the back of the room. Jake surveyed the room and saw an upright skeleton in a display case and a dead woman on the bed. "My god ..."

"How Frank? How can it be you?" Celestia eyes filled with tears.

"I couldn't leave town without discussing my top ten black-and-white movies."

Celestia smiled despite her tears. "I'm too young to know anything about black-and-white movies."

The Rotten Core

"And you call yourself a connoisseur?"

Jake looked at the dead woman again and flinched. He almost asked Celestia who this victim was but stopped himself. Time would be against them.

He fell to his knees beside her chair and saw her ankles were bound with several ropes to the chair legs. Her wrists were also tied behind the back of the chair. He pulled a penknife from his pocket, flipped it, and began to work at the ropes on her right ankle.

She continued to weep.

Jake dreaded to think what she had endured.

"Lemuel," she said. "If he comes back—"

"Lemuel's dead."

She sighed; he imagined it was from relief.

He managed to get through one rope on her right ankle. "Is it loose enough?"

She tried to wriggle it. "No."

"Don't worry. Let me go again." He started on another rope around the right ankle.

"Did you kill Lemuel?"

"Unfortunately, I don't have that badge of honor. You'll have to thank someone else for that. I'm sorry, you know, if he did anything before I got here."

"He didn't get the chance." She nodded at the woman on the bed. "With me, anyway." She lowered her head.

"He did that?"

"Yes."

Jake used the sudden rush of anger to saw harder at the rope. He broke through. "Try again."

She wriggled her foot and slipped it free of the third rope.

He started on the first of three ropes on her left ankle,

which required him to lower farther onto the floor. His heart thrashed in his chest.

"They killed my father too," Celestia said.

"I'm sorry."

"In front of me."

"They'll pay, Celestia. I promise you that. Those who did this to you *will* pay." He paused to wipe sweat from his brow and went at the rope again.

"It's okay, Frank. He deserved to die."

"He loved you."

"He was bad."

"A lot of things are bad about this place, and you are most certainly better out than in. Try again."

She tried. "No, too tight!"

He went at the next rope. "Okay, let's address the elephant in the room."

"Elephant?"

"That plastic container full of bones over there."

"Hamlin's bones. Son of our founder, Althea. I told you all about it the day by the mine."

Jake laid on his side in a position he believed would get him the best run on the rope. Sweat ran down his brow and into his eyes. He rubbed at it with the back of his hand. "You didn't tell me they kept the poor boy on display." He finally sliced through the rope. "Wriggle."

She freed her second ankle. "Yes!"

He started on the knot binding her wrists behind the chair. "So, was that boy really eaten?"

"Yes."

"Jesus. I thought you were embellishing the other day."

"I wasn't."

"I know that now. I just met one of those little fuckers outside."

"There's a covered cage over there. It's full of them."

He grimaced as he spied where the beasts were kept. He recalled the chunk of that man's finger in the dead rat's mouth outside. "Who in their right mind would want to breed rats like that?"

"My father. Our people have always done this. Ever since Hamlin—ever since the monsters took him—and *we*, the Nucleus, began."

"I'm surprised no one rethought the family tradition at some point. I just saw one in action outside—nothing cute about those creatures."

"I think some may have escaped when ..." Her tears started to come again.

Merithew? He looked at the blood trail leading from the cage. *Jesus, Celestia, did you have to watch that?* "We can process all of this later ... together ... when we're safe."

He was already going at the rope and was just gaining good traction when he heard deep voices outside of the dwelling. *Fuck ...*

"They're here," Celestia hissed. "Hide, Frank. Please, they'll kill you. They'll *fucking* kill you."

Jake slipped the penknife into her right hand and tucked the serrated edge under the rope he'd already started working on. "You need to keep going."

The voices drew nearer. He watched her slowly work the blade on the rope. It would take some time, but it was all they had. He rose, swooped for the rifle, and pinned himself to the wall beside the door.

It swung inward and stopped against him.

He held the handle so it kept him hidden. Hopefully, the person who'd opened it was too preoccupied to notice its failure to swing back at him.

"Griffin," Celestia said. "You were right. What my father did was wrong. I will—"

"*Shh.*"

"I don't—"

"I said shush, *dammit!*"

Jake held his breath. The bastard knew he'd been infiltrated and was listening. Jake had the rifle pressed upright against his chest while he maintained his grip on the doorhandle. He listened to the killer take a second step into the dwelling. Jake pressed himself hard against the wall.

If Griffin detected him, Jake was in serious trouble, because he couldn't maneuver this weapon quickly enough in the space he was crammed into.

Jake took some breaths as slowly and quietly as possible. To be honest, the sound of his thrashing heart worried him more.

"Nothing here, Thaxton," Griffin said.

Jake released the handle to allow Griffin to close the door.

It stayed open.

Assuming Griffin and Thaxton must have left it open in their haste to find the intruder in the trees, Jake gently pushed it, and the door began to slowly arc around. He waited until Celestia's face was revealed.

She wore a mask of terror.

The door continued its trajectory, revealing the rifle against Celestia's temple, before completing its journey to reveal a tall, muscular man with long red hair and a look of wildness in his eyes which suggested things were about to get a lot worse.

"I could smell you, you prick." Griffin narrowed his eyes. "You're the one who spoke to Merithew that day about her." He looked at Celestia and back at Jake. "Are you two fucking?"

Jake narrowed his eyes. "She's a child."

"So? Is it true, then?"

"We're friends," Celestia said.

"Now, isn't that nice?" Griffin said. "Not too close, I hope, because that friendship has just run its course."

Jake took a deep breath. "Listen, I don't know who you are. I don't even care what your endgame is. I came for my friend. We can walk away, and you can continue doing whatever it is you're doing here."

"Whatever it is I am doing here?" Griffin smiled.

Jake noticed the look of concentration on Celestia's face as she worked the rope on her wrist.

"Thaxton?" Griffin said.

Thaxton slipped in through the open door and stood beside Griffin.

"The man wants to know what I do here."

"You're our leader."

"Yes." Griffin pushed the muzzle of his rifle against Celestia's head.

She winced.

"Stop!" Jake tasted bile in his mouth. "Please."

"Do you know what this bitch's father did to our land?" Griffin asked.

"Some of it," Jake said

"And?"

He looked away from Celestia. "It sickened me."

"And who do you think has to clean up the whole sorry, fucking mess?"

"As I said. We don't want to stand in your way."

Griffin chewed his bottom lip for a moment, regarding Jake. "You really are a cowboy, aren't you? You managed to get into the Nucleus. No one has ever managed to do that. Tell me, does anything faze you?"

"More than you know. The horrors that have taken place here faze me deeply, but this girl hasn't harmed anyone, so I ask that you release her. Start afresh, don't take this onto your conscience."

"Conscience?"

Jake nodded.

"Do you want to hear what I have lined up for *my* conscience?"

"I just want to take Celestia and—"

"Children. I have lined up children—all the bastards from Merithew's nasty little regime."

Jake felt nausea in the pit of his stomach. "No—"

"*Yes.* I'm cleaning up Merithew's mess."

"Killing children?" Jake felt the nausea quickly become a burning sensation in his stomach. "You cannot—"

"I can."

Jake ached to strike, but he willed himself back. Celestia's life would be the cost of his impulses. Instead, he glared at Thaxton. "Do you *all* support ... *this*?"

"The Nucleus *always* supports its leader," Griffin said.

"I'm asking you, Thaxton. Do you support this?"

Thaxton looked down.

"Thaxton?" Griffin said. "Tell the man."

"It is the way," Thaxton said. "Our leader knows best."

Jake tightened the grip on the rifle still pinned against his chest. "Is one of your own children about to die, Thaxton?"

Thaxton shook his head.

"Hardly surprising," Jake said, trying to stem the anger boiling inside him. He looked at Celestia. Her facial expression told him that she was still busy trying to escape. He had to keep them talking, just long enough for her to free herself, bury the penknife in this monster's leg, and buy him a second to ready his rifle.

Griffin said, "I forget your name."

"Frank."

"Frank. Here's a question for you." He clucked his tongue and sized up Jake for a moment. "Did you kill my son? Lemuel?"

"That wasn't me."

"Positive?"

"Positive."

"So, it wasn't you who left him burning by Netow's bend? I mean, it does coincide with your visit."

"The burning truck was my idea, yes, but I assure you he was already dead when it was set alight. His death wasn't because of me. He attacked me at Frederick's house and—"

"So, he died fighting you?"

"Frederick hit him around the back of his head."

"Frederick ... I've just seen his body."

"He stood on a trap leading me here."

"A trap designed to maim rather than kill?"

Jake shrugged. "Heart attack?"

"Did you kill him to hide the truth that you executed my son?"

Jake shook his head. "That's not my style."

"And Sullivan, my soldier, outside ... what happened to him?"

"A rat attacked him. Then he fell on a trap."

"People just seem to keep dying around you, Frank."

Hopefully, Jake thought, staring at Griffin.

Griffin looked at Thaxton. "Keep your rifle on Celestia. If she moves, kill her." He looked back at her. "I'd prefer you to live, acorn."

"Fuck you. Don't you use that name," Celestia said.

"And yet you've spent most of your life being called that." He smiled. "How will you ever come to terms with what he really was?"

"You're no better. You're worse."

"You will live, acorn, and you will give me another son. We have lost enough of our people today because of your father, and so you will go some way to making amends for his devastation."

Jake stared at Celestia. Was she almost through that rope yet?

Griffin turned the rifle on Jake and stepped forward.

Behind him, Thaxton raised his own rifle to restore the threat on Celestia's life.

Jake felt his insides sinking; he'd gotten here too late. This could only end one way.

Keeping the gun trained on Jake's chest, Griffin said, "You've heard. She can live. My gift, on the condition that you do not fight what comes next."

"Gift! To live as your slave! Offer declined," Celestia said.

"What kind of man are you, anyway?" Jake asked.

Griffin shrugged. "Pragmatic. Don't worry yourself, Frank. She will get over herself, and then she will live like a queen. Throw down the rifle."

Jake didn't move.

"Do not tempt me. I can accept Celestia's passing. Thaxton, our guest has one more chance, and one only. Throw down the rifle, Frank."

Jake narrowed his eyes, kneeled, placed the rifle on the ground, and stood.

Griffin prodded him in the chest with the muzzle of his rifle. "Now, keep walking backward ... that's it ..."

Jake kept his gaze on Celestia as he did so. He could see in her creased brow that she was still struggling in her escape. At least her ankles were free. If only Thaxton didn't have that rifle on her, she could stand and run now. Through the forest, she would know the route. She could be free.

He bumped into the plastic case. "The boy behind me, Hamlin? His mother, Althea? How would they feel about what you are about to do to their descendants? *Their children?*"

"Truth is, Frank, I don't know. I can only hope they are accepting of it."

"Accepting of what? A community full of ruthless child killers?"

"How would you know what Althea envisaged?"

"Most don't possess a nature like yours, Griffin."

"The most you speak of are not from the Nucleus. You're not one of us, Frank. At least not in life. In death, what remains of you will go on to feed our lands." Griffin forced Jake left toward the covered cage. "Althea envisaged a community that could preserve itself, no matter the cost. It is my duty to preserve it, and to do so, the costs, I'm afraid, are high."

Jake heard the rats scurrying about in the cage behind him.

"Now turn around and go to your knees," Griffin said.

Jake recalled the feel of the rat against his chest, his neck, his chin ... "I'd rather not."

"It wasn't a request."

"I'd rather you just killed me."

"I'm trying to."

"With your rifle, you prick."

"Turn around now, on your knees, or you will watch Celestia die before I kill you anyway."

He started to turn, then paused over the memory of the rat biting deep into the man's finger. "I will not play these goddamn games—"

"On. Your. Knees."

Jake showed the palms of his hands and started to turn. He felt the rifle press into his shoulder.

"*Knees!*"

"Okay!" Jake lowered himself to his knees. As he neared the wild creatures, the sounds of their writhing and squeaking intensified. "What kind of monster are you?"

"You burned my dead son in front of me." He snatched away the blanket to reveal countless rodents squirming beneath him. "Now, I've had quite enough of your face. Open that cage and put it in."

"I *can't!*"

"Let me help you." Griffin leaned over him and flipped back the top of the cage.

The furry mass of bodies scurried and gathered around the center.

Jake thought of his son, and he thought of Piper—two people he loved dearly, two people he would never see again. He turned his head to look at Griffin's other captive. "I'm sorry, Celestia!"

He felt Griffin's hand on the back of his head forcing his face into the cage.

Those hairy faces that hadn't already turned up did so now. Their noses twitched, and their sharp, jagged teeth glowed in the light from the bright bulb overhead.

He gritted his teeth to prepare for what was coming, desperately trying to keep his mind on his son and Piper,

The Rotten Core

but the beasts were already on their hindlegs now, and he was losing focus on what truly mattered to him.

He knew this must happen for Celestia to live, but fear made him desperate, so he tried to force his head back out of the cage.

Griffin was a strong man. His struggle was in vain.

The first rat jumped, and the pain began.

20

OUTSIDE BY THE smoldering church, Griffin's five soldiers exchanged uneasy glances as the half-breeds huddled and wept.

To one of Griffin's most trusted soldiers and mother of two, Ethlyn, they simply looked like children—scared, innocent children. However, she cherished the Nucleus and its many ways with all of her being. So she admonished her four companions for their unease. "*Focus!*" she hissed. "Griffin will return soon, and his word will be the way."

The soldiers nodded.

They wouldn't question her. A mere word from her to Griffin would bring their lives into forfeit. They knew this.

"This is *not* the way, Ethlyn, and you know it," someone said, stepping up behind her.

Ethlyn turned with her rifle. "Corrie, you have been confined to your home."

Corrie had blood down her front and on her cheeks. She threw her knife on the ground. "It isn't much of a home any longer. The husband I have killed has just bled out on

The Rotten Core

our rug. My son is crying over his corpse. And my daughter is at the end of a rifle."

"She is *not* your daughter, Corrie."

"She has suckled from me, Ethlyn. She is as much my daughter as your girls are yours."

Ethlyn shook her head, but she heard the truth in her words. The words filled her with both doubt and fear, but the man who was soon to return from the forest scared her more. "We will follow the way."

Corrie stepped toward her.

"I will have to shoot if you come closer, Corrie."

"Then, shoot," Corrie said, taking another step. "If it really is the way, shoot. My husband is dead, my son has been driven mad by these ways, and you are about to execute a baby, so shoot. I'd rather be out than in."

Ethlyn gulped. She readied the rifle. She was within a couple yards. "Corrie, please. I will help you, after, I promise. Marston is a good boy. Don't make me—"

Edlon stepped forward and pushed down the muzzle of Ethlyn's rifle. "Enough, Ethlyn. This is not who we are."

Ethlyn glared at Edlon and threw her rifle to the ground. She put her arms around Corrie as she staggered right into her. "I'm sorry, Corrie—"

A loud male scream sounded from the dwelling.

After Frank started screaming, Celestia cut through the ropes and watched her father's closest friend, Thaxton. He'd brought her gifts as a child and had swung her around by the arms when she was merely a toddler. Disposing of her father's corpse was one thing, but would his fear of Griffin really drive him to shoot a girl he'd adored?

She'd no choice but to put this to the test.

She stood, showing him the penknife she'd cut herself free with. *Please*, she mouthed.

A tear ran down his face.

Frank screamed louder.

She flinched, expecting to hear Thaxton's gun discharge and feel an intense pain as a bullet tore through her insides.

This didn't happen.

Instead, he nodded at her and turned away.

She turned and charged for Griffin's back with the penknife raised.

* * *

Clutching the cage in agony, Jake desperately tried to pull his head away, with one rat hanging from his right earlobe and another from his left cheek. He stopped screaming to draw breath and heard a yell of pain behind him. He yanked back with all his might, landed on his ass, and dragged the cage up and over.

Jake seized the writhing, furry body on his cheek and tore it free, ripping his flesh and worsening the pain. After throwing the beast across the room, he reached up to find that the other rat had already gone. Unfortunately, so had his earlobe.

Before him, a furry wave rushed from the upturned cage.

Jake scurried backward on all fours, past the redheaded leader of the Nucleus.

Griffin was writhing, face down, trying desperately to reach around his body to the knife in his upper back, but it had been buried centrally, and he couldn't get his hand to it.

The blood that had already been thick on the dwelling floor had transferred onto the injured man's face.

Jake wasn't the only one who'd noticed this.

The thick wave of rats broke over Griffin.

Jake squinted when natural light invaded the dwelling. He looked around to see Thaxton and Celestia at the door.

"Frank, come on!" Celestia shouted loudly to be heard over Griffin's screams. "*Now!*"

He turned back and saw he was too late to follow Celestia out the door. Most of the rats had opted to stay and feast on Griffin, but many had broken off to head in his direction. The furry wave wasn't as swollen as it had been seconds before, but there were enough vermin there to drown him.

Jake closed his eyes.

When the pain didn't come, he opened his eyes to see the hairy mass had taken a sharp right before reaching him. It didn't make sense. He watched the rats reach up and grip the blanket hanging close to the floor. Then, en masse, they scurried up the material.

Of course. The dead girl. That poor, dead girl.

Before the rats had covered her completely, Jake looked away in disgust and pounced to his feet. As he charged for the exit, he chanced one last look at the writhing furry mass of bodies covering Griffin on the ground. He noticed a large rat rise on its hindlegs and watch him. Jake paused at the doorway to give it the finger.

The rat regarded Jake a moment longer, sniffed the air, then burrowed into Griffin's face through his cheek.

Jake closed the dwelling door behind him, collapsed to his knees, and vomited.

* * *

At first, Jake felt too sick to communicate properly. However, once the dwelling had been turned into a raging inferno, courtesy of Thaxton and several other members of the Nucleus, Jake welcomed a return of clarity.

Celestia, who'd sat beside him the entire time on the grass, had an arm around the small of his back and rested her head on his shoulder.

He held a cotton shirt, which one of the residents here had given him, over his damaged ear. It stung and bled heavily, and the thought of his lobe in the guts of one of those rats turned his stomach yet again.

At least said rat was now burning alive.

He allowed his damaged cheek, which was also insanely painful, to bleed freely.

"It's over, Frank," Celestia said.

"That's not my name."

"Really?" She drew her head from his shoulder.

He turned his head to face her. "It's Jake, but that's between you and me only."

She considered this for a moment, and then said, "Of course. Pleased to meet you, Jake."

The corners of his lips started to turn up, but his damaged cheek didn't appreciate this, so he halted the smile, wincing.

"No need to talk, Jake."

At least his pain would stop her pursuing the reason he'd lied to her—for now, at any rate. He nodded.

"I do need to go and speak to my people," Celestia said.

"Yes …" He winced again. "Tell them you're out of here."

Celestia smiled. "Thank you for coming for me, Jake."

"Don't." Jake turned his head from side to side. "I'm just glad you're safe."

The Rotten Core

Celestia kissed him on the forehead and stood.

After Celestia had left him, Jake watched the fire for a time and was glad when the dwelling roof finally crash in. Griffin, the rats, and a shrine made from the corpse of some poor long-dead boy were all gone forever.

He thought of that girl. That *innocent* girl.

Someone's daughter.

He heard Celestia's voice and turned to see her talking to her people up ahead.

Was this all of them? There couldn't be more than forty. The Nucleus was smaller and more fragile than they'd wanted the world to believe.

AFTER ...

GORDON THREW THE last of Mrs. Kane's belongings onto his doorstep, closed the front door, and turned the key in the new lock he'd just fitted. *Good riddance.*

When his soon-to-be ex-wife cruised up later in her new boyfriend's expensive car for her things, she would get no reply from the doorbell, nor would she be able to get access to the house.

He wouldn't give her the satisfaction of gloating. He could almost imagine the loathsome comments: *"You just need to get on with your life, Gordon. Find happiness like I have ... someone who truly completes you."*

Easier said than done, Mrs. Kane, after you've made me sell the house, taken half my meager lifesavings, and sunk your teeth into my salary while you bronze yourself on a Caribbean Island alongside your property developer.

"It's my fault though," Gordon said, demolishing a tumbler of whiskey. "All my fault." The writing had been on *this* wall for many years—most of their married life, in fact. "But you just had to maintain the status quo, didn't you, Gordon?" He poured himself another glass. "Keep the motherfucking peace."

He threw back another glass and remembered the woman's head he'd burst with a rifle on the steps to his department. He slammed down the glass and went through to his office. He approached his wall containing the web of images he'd started to spin this morning.

He touched a picture of Lemuel; underneath was written, ALTON BANK'S KILLER and DECEASED. He moved his finger across a thread to a picture of Pastor Frederick Deering: LEMUEL'S KILLER. MISSING. Then, a picture of Merithew: DECEASED. A picture of Griffin: NEW LEADER? He traced his finger over many other members of the Nucleus, including those connected to them. The truck driver, Logan, for example, was there. As was Albert Hardy.

He looked at the ariel photographs of the Nucleus. He'd had Scott and his twin brother, Brad, fly a drone over there. A risk, yes. It could have been spotted. But what the hell?

"It's time to get real," Gordon said.

He ran his finger over the pictures until it settled on Celestia's beautiful young face. Then his trembling finger traced a piece of thread down ... and down ... until it was pinned against Frank Yorke's face.

"Yeah." Gordon smiled. "Fuck peace."

Jake stayed at Celestia's place while his face healed. She was busy with her people but still found the time to keep him company and feed him well. "Fresh food hunted from the forest."

"As long as it's not rat."

She hadn't laughed.

"I'm sorry, bad taste."

"No, the tradition is dead and buried. I don't hold any fondness for the memory. I'm just devastated over what the beasts did to you."

"Don't worry. I was always ugly anyway."

Over those days, it became clear, quickly, that Celestia had no intention of leaving the Nucleus. She never said as such, but he could just tell by the way she spoke regularly and fondly of her people.

"Corrie will reach out to Mossbark for learning resources to refurbish the school."

Jake nodded and smiled. "Education is everything."

"Yes. And Thaxton and Ethlyn are building new windmills so we can increase the energy. Edlon had a great idea for a community center to try to heal the fractures the crisis caused. It will be a while before some of my people are on talking terms again."

Daily, Celestia brought him these updates of the wonderful changes taking place in the Nucleus, until it really did become the only focus of conversation, and Jake began to long for their frivolous exchanges regarding classic movies. Interestingly, she never asked him why he'd lied about his name, so, in return, he hadn't pressed her on her intentions for the future.

One afternoon, while he was finishing some rabbit stew, Celestia entered, pale and shaken up.

He sat back in the chair. "What's happened?"

"Thaxton saw a drone overhead."

Jake nodded. He wasn't surprised. The Nucleus had been penetrated now. Logan and Albert had already visited Jake in the immediate aftermath and had told him about the confrontation at the station between Sheriff

Kane and the two soldiers from the Nucleus. The Nucleus had been rendered vulnerable. The place was on borrowed time.

He'd warned Albert and Logan not to reveal the true numbers who inhabited the Nucleus, because that really would be the final nail in the coffin. *"Not yet,"* Jake had pleaded. *"Allow Celestia time to decide what she is doing first. There are children here too. We don't want another Waco on our hands."*

"They're watching us, aren't they?" Celestia said.

"Yes. They will become bolder by the day too. I think it's time for you to move on, Celestia."

"Where to?"

"Come with me."

Celestia looked stunned. "Why?"

"Nothing like that! Surely, you know this by now! You're special to me, but not in that way."

"Like a daughter?"

"Special, Celestia. We really don't have to overthink it."

She stared at the table, clearly in thought. Eventually, she said, "I can't leave my people."

"Celestia ..." Jake leaned forward. "You were desperate to leave when I met you."

"That was different. Things were very wrong back then."

"There are still a lot of things wrong with this set up."

"You would think that, but it's—"

"No," Jake said. "There is. You all live out here, alone —*vulnerable*. It's a cult, Celestia. Nothing more."

"I wouldn't expect you to think anything else. Why would you? But the people here are good people, and that's what really matters."

"I don't doubt it. But the place remains vulnerable to

conflict and tragedy. That will never change if you live on the fringes of society with your own ways, your own laws."

"Maybe," she said, sitting. "But they have asked me to lead, and I have accepted."

Jake stood, turned, and paced the kitchen. Eventually, he faced her. "I really wish you hadn't done that."

"I know. But if not me, who else?"

"There are others—"

"I am the direct descendant of Althea."

"Griffin wasn't a direct descendant?"

"No. And look how that almost ended. We owe you a debt for what you did, but we need to move on. I know how it should be."

"Celestia, it's not my place to stop you, but this decision —*your* decision—will break me."

"You know I don't have a choice. I won't let this place crumble."

Jake shook his head. "But it will. You are strong and wonderful, but it will. I'm certain. Even if you stay. The Nucleus will be torn down."

"Maybe not. Maybe I have a secret weapon."

"And what's that?"

She smiled.

It took him a moment to realize what she was insinuating. He grunted. "I think that power has gone to your head already."

"We all want you to stay. You saved their children. There are people out there who would die for you."

"That, in itself, sounds like a burden I don't want."

Celestia rose and approached him. "But it's one you have."

He scowled. He could feel himself losing his temper.

"Look. I don't know who you think I am, but that really isn't me."

She took hold of Jake's arm. "I think it *is* you."

Jake shook his head. "You don't know me. You don't know the real me."

"I *know* you care. You care about others more than yourself. I know you *need* to help. What would happen if you just stopped?"

"I wish I knew. I've been trying for god knows how long."

"Stay, Jake. Stay, and help us."

"Even if I stayed, I won't be a match for what is coming."

She hugged him. "Whatever you do, I will always love you for everything you did for me. For us."

"I can't stay." Jake hugged her back. "I'm sorry, Celestia."

"Don't be sorry. A man like you doesn't deserve to spend his entire life being sorry."

* * *

SALISBURY, ENGLAND

DETECTIVE CHIEF INSPECTOR Michael Yorke was fortunate to have Emma Gardner beside him. The sight before him made the world spin and his legs buckle. His trusty detective inspector took his weight and helped him to the garden wall of the house directly opposite the Pettman residence.

The road was occupied with the fire service and ambulances. The paramedics were assembled before their vehicles, ready to spring—although for what, Yorke had no idea.

The gas explosion had left Jake's former residence a blackened, crumbling shell.

Yorke took long, deep breaths to fight off the panic attack.

"No one is coming out of that," Yorke said.

Gardner didn't reply. She either didn't want to admit he was right or was simply too emotional to speak.

Yorke waited on that garden wall as time slowly ground on. It was in complete contrast to the panicky rapid movements of those around him: firemen, paramedics, other police officers, and rubberneckers.

He had control of his balance and breathing now, but he still couldn't find it in himself to lift himself from the wall to start to investigate.

"Jake ..." Yorke said.

"He's not even in the country," Gardner said.

"Obviously," Yorke said, gulping more air. "That's not what I mean. He needs to *know* what's happened."

"We don't know anything ourselves yet."

Yorke stood and saw Gardner's trembling face and the sadness in her eyes, but she was holding it together. *Impossibly. Somehow. For him.* And here he was, shouting at her, but he couldn't help himself. "We know enough. Someone blew up his ... his house!"

"It was a gas explosion. It could have been an accident."

"It was Article SE."

"It's too soon to make those assumptions."

"Sooner rather than later, Emma, is the best time to face up to the truth."

"Not when your, sorry, our judgment is so clouded."

"It was Article SE. They've gotten sick of waiting for him. They moved on his family."

Gardner flinched. She would know he was right. Their entire day-to-day life revolved around investigating coincidences that turned out to be anything but.

"Let's hope for the best," Gardner said. "Just for a moment longer. Let's hope that Sheila and Frank weren't in there."

Yorke sat beside Gardner. He noticed she was crying now, so he put his arm around her shoulder and pulled her in close. "Okay, let's wait a moment longer."

I've failed you, Jake, Yorke thought. *I promised to keep them safe, and I failed you.*

He rubbed his eyes, realizing he was crying too.

Someone burst from the smouldering house with someone over their shoulder. They were shouting.

Yorke and Gardner rose to their feet.

Gardner said, "Did she just say—"

"Yes," Yorke said. "I think she did."

The paramedics ran up the path toward the distraught firefighter.

"I'm sorry, Jake," Yorke said. "I'm *so* sorry."

YOUR FREE DCI YORKE QUICK READ

To receive your FREE and EXCLUSIVE DCI Michael Yorke quick read, *A Lesson in Crime*, scan the QR code.

Scan the QR to READ NOW!

CONTINUE JAKE PETTMAN'S JOURNEY WITH ROCK AND A HARD PLACE.

A violent community raging against extinction. An emboldened daughter rising from the ashes of a tyrant. A burned-out sheriff searching for meaning through murder.

And Jake Pettman, trapped in the middle.

Following the collapse of the Nucleus, Jake vows to stay and protect Celestia while she rebuilds. When the drones overhead indicate that Sheriff Gordon Kane and the people of Mossbark are plotting to rise against the weakened community, Jake demands that Celestia strengthen the Nucleus's defenses.

But Celestia is a new leader with a new vision, and instead decides to open her lands to the world beyond. And all the fire and fury that burns within it.

Leaving Jake with a choice to make: let the Nucleus die, or get himself killed trying to save it.

Whatever he chooses, he can be sure of one thing:

Every choice has deadly consequences.

Scan the QR to READ NOW!

Also by Wes Markin
ONE LAST PRAYER

"An explosive and visceral debut with the most terrifying of killers. Wes Markin is a new name to watch out for in crime fiction, and I can't wait to see more of Detective Yorke." – *Bestselling Crime Author Stephen Booth*

The disappearance of a young boy. An investigation paved with depravity and death. Can DCI Michael Yorke survive with his body and soul intact?

With Yorke's small town in the grip of a destructive snowstorm, the relentless detective uncovers a missing boy's connection to a deranged family whose history is steeped in violence. But when all seems lost, Yorke refuses to give in, and journeys deep into the heart of this sinister family for the truth.

And what he discovers there will tear his world apart.

The Rays are here. It's time to start praying.

The shocking and exhilarating new crime thriller will have you turning the pages late into the night.

"**A pool of blood, an abduction, swirling blizzards, a haunting mystery, yes, Wes Markin's One Last Prayer for the Rays has all the makings of an absorbing thriller. I recommend that you give it a go.**" – *Alan Gibbons, Bestselling Author*

One Last Prayer is a shocking and compulsive crime thriller.

Scan the QR to READ NOW!

JOIN DCI EMMA GARDNER AS SHE RELOCATES TO KNARESBOROUGH, HARROGATE IN THE NORTH YORKSHIRE MURDERS ...

Still grieving from the tragic death of her colleague, DCI Emma Gardner continues to blame herself and is struggling to focus. So, when she is seconded to the wilds of Yorkshire, Emma hopes she'll be able to get her mind back on the job, doing what she does best - putting killers behind bars.

But when she is immediately thrown into another violent murder, Emma has no time to rest. Desperate to get answers and find the killer, Emma needs all the help she can. But her new partner, DI Paul Riddick, has demons and issues of his own.

And when this new murder reveals links to an old case Riddick was involved with, Emma fears that history might be about to repeat itself…

Don't miss the brand-new gripping crime series by bestselling British crime author Wes Markin!

* * *

What people are saying about Wes Markin...

'Cracking start to an exciting new series. Twist and turns, thrills and kills. I loved it.'

Bestselling author **Ross Greenwood**

'Markin stuns with his latest offering... Mind-bendingly dark and deep, you know it's not for the faint hearted from page one. Intricate plotting, devious twists and excellent characterisation take this tale to a whole new level. Any serious crime fan will love it!'

Bestselling author **Owen Mullen**

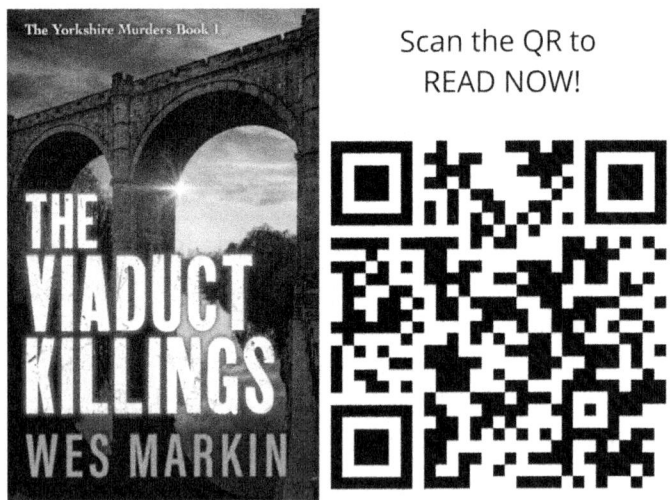

Scan the QR to READ NOW!

Acknowledgments

So, what was originally meant to be a trilogy has grown to four books and is now on the way to six! I had my plans, but the characters had other ideas.

Thanks again to the most supportive group in the world. Without them, little of what you just read would be possible.

My wife, Jo; my children, Hugo and Beatrice; and my entire supportive family. Then, in no particular order: Donna Wilbor, Jenny Cook, Katherine Middleton, Karen Ashman, Dee Groocock, Keith Fitzgerald, Claire Cornforth, Carly Markin, Paul Lautman, Holly Sutton, Brian Peone, all of my ARC readers, and those fantastic bloggers who always get behind me – Shell, Susan, Caroline, Jason and Donna. Thank you to Cherie Foxley for the atmospheric cover.

I hope you all join me in June when Jake Pettman has a choice to make. Does he stay in the Nucleus? Or, does he leave Celestia to an unknown fate?

Stay in touch

To keep up to date with new publications, tours, and promotions, or if you would like the opportunity to view pre-release novels, please contact me:

Website: www.wesmarkinauthor.com

- facebook.com/WesMarkinAuthor
- instagram.com/wesmarkinauthor
- twitter.com/markinwes
- amazon.com/Wes-Markin/e/B07MJP4FXP

Review

If you enjoyed reading **The Rotten Core**, please take a few moments to leave a review on Amazon, Goodreads or BookBub .

Printed in Great Britain
by Amazon